Praise for *Sweet Thing*

"Sassy and sweet, *Sweet Thing* melts in your mouth and goes straight to your heart!"

—*New York Times* bestselling author Katy Evans

"5 stars!!!! This is what I've been craving, waiting for . . . This is one of my absolute favorites this year, and just one of my plain old favorites altogether. . . . It gave me that feeling again. The feeling I got from back in my earlier 'indie' reading days, connecting to books that would soon become my favorites of all time. . . It had all that heart, all of that emotion, all of that wit, that charm, the supporting characters, all of that angsty and intensity, all of the hero's absolute sweetness. . . . This book has pulled me out of my reading slump and has invigorated me."

—Maryse's Book Blog (*****)

"I have a new book boyfriend and his name is Will Ryan. I'm in love. Oh, and did I mention he was a bit of a rock star? *Sweet Thing* was a sweet, heartbreaking and romantic story that kept me up reading all night!"

—Aestas Book Blog

"This is 5 HUGE stars—a soul-searing, beautifully written book that now owns a piece of my heart."

—Shh Moms Reading Book Blog

Sweet Thing

A Novel

RENÉE CARLINO

ATRIA PAPERBACK
New York • London • Toronto • Sydney • New Delhi

ATRIA PABERBACK

A Division of Simon & Schuster, Inc.
1230 Avenue of the Americas
New York, NY 10020

Permission to reprint lyrics: "Ask," by Hal Leonard Corp. and Alfred Music Publishing; "A Satisfied Mind" by Hal Leonard Corp. and Fort Knox Music; "Pictures of You" by Hal Leonard Corp.; "Sweet Thing" and "Gloria" by Alfred Music Publishing; "Girl from North Country" by Special Rider Music.

First Atria Paperback edition January 2014

ATRIA PAPERBACK and colophon are trademarks of Simon & Schuster, Inc.

For information about special discounts for bulk purchases, please contact Simon & Schuster Special Sales at 1-866-506-1949 or business@simonandschuster.com.

The Simon & Schuster Speakers Bureau can bring authors to your live event. For more information or to book an event contact the Simon & Schuster Speakers Bureau at 1-866-248-3049 or visit our website at www.simonspeakers.com.

Cover design © Zoe Norvell
Cover photographs © Ferran Cubedo

Manufactured in the United States of America

10 9 8 7 6 5 4 3

Library of Congress Cataloging-in-Publication Data is available.

ISBN 978-1-4767-6393-4
ISBN 978-1-4767-6394-1 (ebook)

Sweet Thing

Prologue

Lauren

Airports are the great human distribution factories, and people-watching here can provide a writer with infinite possibilities. Every second there is a new, brief snapshot of humanity; it's an endless stream of fodder. In fact, next to me in the security line at this very moment is a Tibetan monk, standing perfectly still and wearing his patience like a mask; a mother discreetly nursing her baby; and a marine, looking sharp and prideful in his best dress blues. I wonder where they are headed today and for the rest of their lives. I wonder if I can discover something unique and worth writing about by simply observing them in line. As I watch, I think about the imagery I will create, the picture I want to paint. I imagine colorful words dancing across the page. My hand twitches from the desire to jot down the details pooling in my head.

"Do you need a hand?"

I'm jolted out of my trance and realize my kids are bouncing around, the security agent is barking, I'm holding up the line, and we're all still wearing our shoes. *Shit.*

The face belonging to that voice looks to be that of a woman in her midtwenties; her long dark hair is pulled back into a flawless ponytail. She's dressed in what I would call monochromatic collegiate wear; basically she looks like a Gap

1

ad, and she's holding a little gray bin with her shoes and belongings nestled perfectly inside it. The dark eyebrows that frame her big, round, hazel eyes are arched, waiting for my response.

"Yes! Please! Will you grab his shoes?" I point to my three-year-old son. "Would you mind carrying him up there for me?"

"No problem."

On the other side of the metal detectors I study the girl while we put shoes on the boys.

"What's your name, kid?" She has a fairylike voice, but her choice of words is anything but.

"Cash."

"Cool name," she says and appears to truly mean it. "I'm Mia—nice to meet you."

"I'm Hayden!" shouted my four-year-old.

"I like your name, too."

I stand up and introduce myself. "Hi, Mia, I'm Lauren. Thanks for your help. Corralling kids at an airport can be crazy."

I inspect her appearance and feel unusually drawn to her. She's thin, fit, her skin vibrant and her face calm. I see something in her that resembles the me of ten years ago. She's so put together, just like I was at that age; it's those few years right before the real world gives you a swift kick in the ass. I thought about cutting my head open and spilling the contents into hers so she could skip over the impending crap I knew she would soon face. The problem with that idea is that wisdom is not the same as information; it's something entirely different. It's often mistaken for good advice, but wisdom cannot be imparted to someone. Wisdom can only be earned; it's a by-product of experience, not necessarily knowledge, otherwise I would be stalking Oprah right now, begging for a transfusion.

Maybe your early twenties are about wearing daisy dukes, withdrawing from a zillion college courses, changing your major five times, one-night stands, alcohol poisoning, having sex with your neighbor while his girlfriend watches, dating a distant cousin, cocaine, bad credit, or bad eye shadow. Either way, by twenty-five most of us start thinking about other things. The big questions: What do you want to do with the rest of your life? Who will you marry if you marry at all? What career will you choose? Do you want children? It seemed like everything I knew at twenty-five morphed into everything I didn't know by twenty-six, when I was suddenly hit with the realization that many of the decisions we make in our twenties are permanent.

Those decisions seem easy for some and, sure, you could say those people are just the shallow puddles we trudge through, but I would argue that those people are lucky because right now as I watch this girl—the past me—looking serenely self-possessed, I know that she is standing on a great precipice. I can tell by looking at her that she is the still water you only ever skip rocks over. The world as she knows it is about to be turned upside down, and if she doesn't learn to swim, her own depth will drown her. I feel a strong desire to whisper "surrender," but I don't. Like everyone in this airport, she is headed somewhere, possibly the first stop on that brutal journey of self-discovery. Like the rest of us, she will have to learn the hard way that we are not always in control. Sometimes it takes the love of others to show us who we really are.

Navigating an airport with two small children is no easy task, and before I get on that plane, I'll wonder if I packed enough snacks, if the DVD player is charged enough, or if I'll have enough energy to rock my thirty-pound toddler in the space between the smelly lavatory and flight attendants' station. As I chase my kids around, trying to squeeze Benadryl into their tiny mouths, I wonder if the decisions I made in my twenties were right for me. Will my marriage endure the test of time? Am I a good mother, wife, writer, neighbor, dog owner? Then I remember the journey that brought me to those decisions, and that memory gives me great solace, because the memory is a reminder of who I am among all the chaos that is life.

Before I head to my gate, I look over at Mia and wonder what she thinks of me, all frazzled and disheveled with food stains on my clothes. I wonder if she knows that sometimes we figure things out, and then life changes and we have to figure it all out again. I'm sure she'll learn that soon enough, and I'm sure she'll have her own story to tell. . . .

TRACK 1: Fledglings

Mia

The airport security agent was losing his patience. "Ma'am, I said you need to remove your shoes and place them into the bins." She wasn't intentionally ignoring him; she was preoccupied—well, more like staring into space. If we were graded on how efficiently we removed our belongings in order to place them in those little gray bins, I would have gotten an A-plus. The woman in front of me, however, was failing miserably. Her two children were running around, screaming like banshees, while she appeared to be daydreaming.

I tapped her shoulder lightly but she didn't respond. Finally I cleared my throat and said, "Do you need a hand?" I figured I might as well since I wouldn't be going anywhere until she did.

She mouthed the word *shit*, then said, "Yes! Please! Will you grab his shoes?" She pointed to a little blond, blue-eyed cherub. "Would you mind carrying him up there for me?"

"No problem."

I walked up to the little boy, who immediately quieted. I gave him a big smile, then yanked his shoes off and threw them into the bin moving swiftly down the conveyor belt. "Ready, kid?" He nodded and I picked him up and carried him toward the metal detector. The warmth of his little arms around my neck radiated through me. I smiled at him, crossed my eyes, and made a silly face. His giggle sounded like music. I pried his clinging legs and arms from around me to set him down.

We ushered the little boys through the metal detector and then proceeded to collect our things on the other side. I followed her over to the benches to help put shoes back on the boys. "What's your name, kid?"

"Cash," he said shyly in his small, squishy voice.

"Cool name." In fact, it was my favorite. "I'm Mia. Nice to meet you."

"I'm Hayden!" shouted his dark-haired brother. They were almost identical in height, but Hayden had dark hair and dark eyes.

"I like your name, too," I said, smiling.

His mom stood up and introduced herself. "Hi, Mia, I'm Lauren. Thanks for your help. Corralling kids at an airport can be crazy." She let out a long breath.

I noticed that we resembled each other. Same straight, dark hair, fair skin, and hazel eyes. It was eerie. She could have been my sister, or maybe she was me in ten years? There was something different about her, though. Her eyes were sunken and hollow, and she looked exhausted. In that moment I wondered if I would ever be a mother, or if I even wanted to be. I thought maybe if I found the perfect husband—stable, wealthy, business-minded—it could be a possibility, but definitely not in the near future. I decided if I did have children, I would surely have my shit straighter than this lady.

For being all of twenty-five, I was admittedly a bit of a control freak. I actually used to embrace that facet of my personality. I thought being an independent woman who was in control and made decisions with her head and not her heart was evolved. Making the right choices equaled guaranteed success in my mind. Of course, I didn't know then that my definition of success would change so drastically.

My eyes scrolled down the monitor, searching for flight 25, DTW in Detroit to New York City's JFK. Failing to remember what gate the clerk had mentioned, I cursed myself. I was nothing if not punctual. Okay, 35B. I walked briskly, passing Lauren and her two kids as she chased them around outside the duty-free. Flying must suck for her. For a brief moment, I hoped we weren't on the same flight and then I immediately felt guilty for the thought. I decided I'd offer to help if she ended up on my flight, seated anywhere near me, though I'd much rather sleep.

I love flying. It's an escape for me. There's nowhere to be; it's like surrendering to fate. Fate was always such a hard concept for me to understand, but I bought into it when necessary, like on a plane or the subway. When I fly, I allow myself to believe in fate simply because it's too tedious to worry about whether or not the pilot is pouring whiskey in his coffee. I let everything go when I fly, just like when I play the piano. It's the closest I get to religion; it's the closest I get to faith.

I'd have no one to answer to for a couple of hours and I was looking forward to it. I promised myself I wouldn't think about anything. I wouldn't worry about what I would do with my father's apartment, his belongings, the café, or pretty much anything else my father owned in New York. I would just get out there and continue living his life until I could figure out what to do with my own.

When my father had passed away suddenly a month before from a heart attack, I'd been devastated. Although I'd grown up in Ann Arbor, essentially raised by my mother, Liz, and stepfather, David, whom I referred to as Dad, I was still very close to my biological father, Alan Kelly. I'd spent summers in New

York, helping out with his café, hanging with the then-bizarre East Village crowd. My father was the only child of Irish immigrants. His parents had given him every last penny to open Ave. A Café in the East Village in 1977, renamed Kelly's Café in '82, and then finally renamed again to simply Kell's in '89. In the '70s it was the ultimate hangout for any troubadour and *trobairitz* alike. It was, and remains, a place with a liberal and artistic vibe, something my father practically exuded directly from his pores. It would be bittersweet to be back there.

I made it to my gate on time. There was no sign of Lauren. I breathed a sigh of relief and then directed a brief request to the universe asking that it seat a tired, antisocial traveler next to me. I boarded and found my seat quickly. I threw my bag in the overhead bin, sat down, and began my preflight ritual: super fuzzy socks on, earbuds in, Damien Rice on the iPod, travel pillow around the neck. I was ready. The window seat remained empty as the last few passengers came on board. I had a ridiculous grin on my face, prematurely thanking the universe for leaving the seat empty until I glanced up and saw a guy headed toward me. I have to admit, he was gorgeous, but as soon as I saw the guitar case, my stomach turned sour.

Oh no, please, world, do not let this egoist, wannabe, probably smelly musician sit next to me.

As he approached, he blurted out, "Hey!" Pausing, he looked right into my eyes and said, "Do you want the window seat? It's all yours if you do."

"Huh? Uh, no thanks." *What the hell is this guy doing?*

"I'm a terrible flier," he said, hesitating. "Please, I need to be in the aisle, I'm sorry, do you mind? I'm Will, by the way."

Moving to the window seat, I mumbled, "Yeah, fine, you can sit there. I'm Mia." I stuck my hand up in a motionless wave, intentionally avoiding a handshake.

Don't get me wrong, I love music; I live for it. I'm classically trained on the piano and I can hold my own on almost any instrument. Growing up in Ann Arbor, it seemed like every kid played the piano or the freakin' cello, but I had a knack for music in general, much of which I owed to my father. During the summers in New York, he exposed me to world music, rock and roll, blues, jazz, you name it, then I would go home and work on Rachmaninoff's Opus 23 all winter long. Playing the piano the way I was taught, combined with the loose methods my father encouraged during those summers, always created this blend of discipline and revolution in my style. I tried to embrace the blend, but sometimes it felt like a conflict.

I believe my mother was drawn to my father's love of music, his free spirit and beatnik ways, although she would never admit that. She referred to what she had with him as one wild week for a very naive nineteen-year-old. It was the summer of 1982 and she had been in Cape Cod on a family vacation when she and a couple of friends decided to take a day trip to New York. One day turned into five, and my mother returned to Cape Cod knocked up. My father owned it from the beginning, but my grandparents wouldn't allow their teenage daughter to move to New York, unmarried and pregnant. As I got older, I wondered why my father hadn't followed my mother to Ann Arbor. I knew he wanted to take responsibility for me and I knew he cared for my mother, but I don't think he was ever a one-woman kind of man. His lifestyle was so far removed from anything that resembled traditional domesticity.

After I was born, we lived with my grandparents while my mother attended the University of Michigan, eventually acquiring a law degree. That's where she met David, and they've been inseparable ever since, even practicing law at the same firm. I think my stepdad provided my mother with the sense of stability that my father couldn't, or wouldn't. I admired David for that. He treated me like his own, and even though I sometimes disagreed with him, especially as a teenager, I always felt loved by him.

In the beginning my father would come visit me for long weekends here and there until I was old enough to travel to New York for the summers. He and David had an enormous amount of respect for each other, even though they couldn't have been more different. What they had in common was an unconditional love for my mother and me. After my father became aware of the fact that I called David "Dad," he simply said, "He is your dad, luv, just like me, but to keep it straight, why don't you call me Pops?" And so I did.

My mother's group of androgynous, pseudointellectual friends would have referred to me as the ultimate indiscretion if it weren't for the fact that I was gifted musically, valedictorian of my class in high school, and now an Ivy League graduate. Choosing a business major over the arts at Brown was a surprise to everyone, but I yearned for a more organic experience when it came to music. I didn't want to spend one more minute trudging through a Bach piece while being hypnotized by the metronome. I wanted a degree I could use and I wanted music to be my hobby. I was still wondering how I was going to use that degree. . . .

I had shut the window screen, my eyes, and brain off to the world when I was jolted by the weight of my own bag being tossed onto the seat next to me. My eyes darted open and up to Will, who was forcefully rearranging everything in the overhead bin.

"Sorry, baby, I've got to make room for her," he said, grabbing his guitar and hoisting it up.

I rolled my eyes at the thought of him personifying his

guitar. He grabbed my bag, shoved it in the bin, and collapsed into his seat. I shot him a slightly annoyed look. "Why didn't you request an aisle seat?" I asked.

"Well, you see, sweetheart, I like to be right behind the emergency exit. I'll hop over this seat in front of me, jump out the door, and be down that super slide in a split second," he said with a self-satisfied smile.

"Then why not request the exit aisle?"

"I am not the person for that job, trust me."

"Damn, chivalry *is* dead. It doesn't matter anyway; our lives are in the hands of these hopefully sober pilots and this nine-hundred-thousand-pound hunk of metal, so . . . "

"Can we stop talking about this? I don't think you understand." He pulled a rosary out of his pocket and proceeded to drape it around his neck.

"Something tells me you have no idea what that's for," I said, giggling. "Are you Catholic?" He was desperately trying to peel a tiny price tag off one of the beads. "Oh my god, you bought that in the airport gift store, didn't you?"

Putting his finger to his mouth, he said, "Shhh! Woman, please!" He looked around as if he would be found out. "Of course I'm Catholic."

A light chuckle escaped me. "Well, God would know, so wearing that around your neck instead of chanting your Hail Marys is probably pissing the big guy off, and that's not good for any of us."

He let out a nervous laugh and then whispered, "Hey, little firecracker, you like taunting me, don't you?" Waiting for my response, he looked directly into my eyes and smiled cutely.

I suddenly felt bashful and shook my head nervously. "Sorry."

Still smiling, he squinted slightly and then winked before looking away and pulling a stack of pamphlets out of the seat-back pocket.

While he reviewed the safety information flyer, we began taxiing toward the runway. I noticed a few things in that moment. One, Will was universally attractive. Even though he dressed a little edgier and had slightly imperfect teeth, he could have easily been a print model. He stood a tad over six feet and was thin with muscular arms, maybe from years of playing guitar. He had brown, disheveled hair and dark eyes, a chiseled jaw, high cheekbones, and great lips. As he read, he mouthed the words, the way a child reads silently.

Two, he didn't smell bad at all—as a matter fact, he smelled heavenly. A mixture of body wash, sandalwood, and just a hint of cigarette smoke, which would normally repulse me but for some reason it suited him. He wore black pinstriped slacks that hung on his thin hips, a silver-studded belt with a wallet chain, and a red T-shirt that said "Booyah!" above a silk-screened picture of Hillary and Bill Clinton playing ping-pong. I didn't get it.

Three, he was genuinely scared to fly and it was apparent that he would be white-knuckling it the entire way. I made the decision to try to calm his nerves by being friendly and chatting him up.

The pilot came on and announced we were cleared for takeoff. "Jesus Christ! Did he sound drunk to you?" Will blurted.

"Not at all. Relax, buddy, everything will be fine, and you should probably tone down the Jesus Christs, at least while you're still wearing that thing." I pointed to the rosary around his neck. He looked down at the beads like they were about to perform a circus act.

Nervously he said, "Hey, hey, can you open that screen? I need to see us get off the ground." I obliged as he peered over me and out the window.

"You're funny, Will. You want to sit in the aisle seat, yet here you are, leaning over me to look out the window."

Ignoring my comment, he took a deep breath in through his nose, tilted his head to the side, and with a half smile whispered, "You smell good, like rain." I was totally caught off guard by his proximity; a delicious chill ran through me.

"What kind of guitar do you have?" I asked abruptly, attempting to change the subject.

"Um, an electric guitar?" The answer was like a question.

"No, I know that. What kind?"

"Oh, it's a Fender." He squinted his eyes and smiled. He seemed somewhat charmed and probably grateful that we were talking about guitars while the plane was barreling full speed down the runway. He gripped the armrest, still not totally at ease.

"Is it a Telecaster, Stratocaster . . . ?"

"As a matter of fact, it's a blond Tele. I also have a Gibson acoustic and a vintage Harmony at home."

"I love the old Harmony guitars. On my fifth birthday my father gave me his H78. It was the first guitar he bought with his own money. He ordered it from a Sears catalog in 1970."

His eyes shot open with surprise. "That's awesome. Your father must be a cool guy."

"He just passed away a month ago."

"Shit . . . I'm so sorry," he said with genuine sympathy.

"It's okay, but I'd rather not talk about it right now. Let's talk about guitars," I said, realizing it would be for both our benefits.

When we hit cruising altitude, he relaxed a little and began describing the magical pickups on the Harmony and the modifications he'd made to the Telecaster. He clearly knew what he was talking about, and I found his enthusiasm sweet.

We continued into an easy conversation about our favorite musicians. We agreed on everything from Led Zeppelin to Bette Midler. We talked about Miles Davis, Joni Mitchell, Debussy, the Niazi Brothers, and Edith Piaf. It was the most intense and diverse musical conversation I'd ever had. We talked nonstop for the entire length of the flight.

I told him about my musical background and also how I was going to live in my father's apartment with my yellow Lab, Jackson, and run my father's café, and maybe teach piano lessons on the side. He told me how he was working as a bartender in a swanky boutique hotel lounge in SoHo. He said at the moment he was literally living in a storage closet in Chinatown until he could afford an apartment. He was playing guitar in a band that he wasn't too excited about. Between practice and his job and the few gigs they played a month, he was never home.

I thought about the spare bedroom in my dad's apartment for a second and then pushed the idea out of mind when I reminded myself that Will was a complete stranger. Even though I found his neuroses more endearing than scary, I figured inviting a struggling musician to live with me was not the best idea.

As the plane started to descend, Will gripped the armrest. "Mia, we're going down. I need to know everything about you right now! How old are you, what's your last name, what street do you live on? If we make it out of this, I think we should jam together, you know, musically or whatever."

He was being adorable. My body tingled with warmth from his gaze. I shifted nervously before answering, "My last name is Kelly, I'll be at my father's café most days—Kell's on Avenue A. Come and have a coffee with me sometime and we'll talk music. Oh, and I'm twenty-five."

When we were safely on the ground, he smiled sweetly and said in a low voice, "We both have double first names. I'm Will Ryan, twenty-nine. I live at twenty-two Mott Street in the storage closet. I work at the Montosh. I'm O negative, you know, the universal one, and I play in a band called The Ivans. Oh, and I love coffee. It was nice to meet you, Mia."

"It was nice to meet you, too." I genuinely meant it.

"We made it," he said, pointing out the window as we taxied to the gate. "You know they say people who have stared death in the face are bonded for life?"

I laughed. "You're cute, Will."

"I was going for irresistible," he said with a brazen smirk. He handed me my bag and let me go in front of him. His warm breath on my neck caused me to shiver and stumble in the aisle. He chuckled. "You're cute." When another passenger jetted out of his seat, bumping me, Will blurted out, "Hey! Watch it, buddy!" I turned around to see his sexy smile. His lips flattened, he narrowed his eyes, and then whispered, "See, baby, chivalry isn't dead."

When I stepped out into the crisp March, New York air, I sensed him walking behind me, but I didn't turn around. Luckily there wasn't a cab line, so I got one right away, hopped in, shut the door, and shouted, "Alphabet City, Manhattan!" As we pulled away from the curb, I glanced over at Will. He was blowing a lungful of smoke into the air with curiosity in his eyes, like he was listening to God. His gaze met mine and with an exaggerated wave he mouthed the words, *Good-bye, Mia.* I thought I caught the words "sweet thing" falling from his lips just as he left my view.

As the cab wove in and out of traffic, I couldn't get my mind off him. The entire flight I didn't think once about my future, my father's apartment, or the café, and I don't think Will worried much about the possibility of crashing. We kind of hit it off; in fact, we did hit it off. He had this silly—to the point of being honest—quality about him. When I thought about our conversation, I remembered how he called Pete, the lead singer of The Ivans, the world's biggest douche bag. It was clear to me that Will was in a band for the love of music and not for fame or sex; I was sure he didn't need any help in that department. I knew there was something about him that drew me in, but I convinced myself at that moment that Will was not boyfriend material—not in my book, anyway. I thought maybe we could be friends; after all, I didn't have many in my new city.

The last time I had been in New York was for my father's funeral one month before. I knew I had my work cut out for me, which gave me a rush of anxiety. I needed to sort through Pops's things and make room for my own. As I made my way through the door leading to the stairwell, I stopped at the mail slot and slipped my key in but could barely turn it from the amount of mail jammed in the tiny box. I managed to shove the massive pile under my arm and carry the rest of my things up the stairs to the landing. I set my bags down and searched for the right key. I tried five keys before finally unlocking the door. It occurred to me that the giant key ring was one of a handful of discoveries I would make about my father.

The first thing I noticed when I entered the apartment was that it was very clean. Someone had been there, probably one of the two regular women in my father's life. Either Martha, who was like a sister to him—she also ran Kell's—or Sheil, who was his on-and-off girlfriend. Both women had been in Pops's life for decades and both were like family. They were going to be lifelines in the months to come as I ventured through my father's belongings and his story.

After tossing out a large amount of junk mail, I sifted through a few financial statements and bills before I got to a letter from the probate lawyer. I leaned over the kitchen counter, closed my eyes, and inhaled deeply before opening it. My father's scent was still somehow wafting through the still air in the apartment, as if the residual effects of living were reminding me that at least his spirit was alive. My eyes welled and my heart ached over his loss. I committed his smell to memory, a mixture of espresso, petula oil, and hand-rolled clove cigarettes that had imbued every article of clothing he owned with a combination of earthy spice and sweetness. I smiled slightly at his somewhat painful memory and then addressed the task at hand.

In the days following my father's heart attack, my mother and David had put their lives on hold to follow me to New York to make arrangements. That week was a foggy memory, filled with shock and pain, but the ease, grace, and familiarity that my mother displayed through it all was inspiring and intriguing to me. I wasn't sure if it was born out of her love for me and desire to help when she knew I was hurting, or if it was a deeper love for my father that I hadn't known she felt. As disjointed as my family seemed growing up, in Pops's death we were all brought together. Isn't that how it always is? It was like my mother and Martha were sisters who shared an untold story, each one falling perfectly into a rhythm in the apartment and at Kell's.

The day before the funeral, we'd worked in the café and I had watched my mother navigate the espresso machine with a certain know-how. "Were you a barista in another life?" I had said to her.

"It's not rocket science, honey." She had a natural-born acumen in almost everything she attempted to do. It was a trait I admired, and one I wasn't sure I had inherited.

My mother and Martha had arranged the funeral while David had taken care of all the legal aspects of my father's estate. I knew I had to make some decisions but I wasn't ready at the time, so I had decided to go back to Ann Arbor after the funeral, wrap up my life, and then move to New York for a few months until I could decide what to do. Moving to New York had never been part of my plan before Pops died, but that's where I found myself now.

Everything regarding his estate was cut and dry. I was the one and only recipient of his assets. However, I knew there would be items that Pops would want Sheil and Martha to have, and I was sure he would have requests regarding Kell's. When I opened the letter, I knew from the tone and formality that it was something Pops had dictated to his lawyer and then signed. He wanted to be official. Everything financial had already been dealt with in another section of his will. I knew the letter I was about to read would address his personal belongings, along with his hopes and dreams for Kell's. I skimmed through the logistical pieces in the beginning, obviously added by the lawyer, until I got to the specifics. I braced myself.

Sheil Haryana and Martha Jones shall have access to my apartment to gather their personal belongings, as well as any music, letters, or photographs that pertain to them.

Several moments passed as I studied the sparse document. I ran my index finger under each word, slowly searching for a hidden message, but there was nothing more. *It's all up to me. He left it all up to me.* I was shocked by the weight of that news; he'd trusted me with everything he had spent his whole life building. The realization made me miss him even more.

The buzzer rang, startling me out of my daze. I went to the speaker. "Yes?'

"It's Martha." I buzzed her in immediately and could hear her bounding up the steps with my four-legged friend. I opened the door and fell to the floor as Jackson pounced on me with the full weight of his front legs.

"I missed you, buddy!" He licked my face and shifted from paw to paw as I scratched behind his ears. I stood up and sank into Martha's embrace. "Thank you for taking care of him, and Kell's."

"Oh, my Mia Pia! It's so good to see you, sweetheart." She pushed my shoulders back to study my face. Looking right into my eyes, she said, "We have some work to do, don't we."

That was the understatement of the century.

TRACK 2: Hello, I Like You

Sorting through a box of pictures, Martha pulled one out and held it up. "Do you remember this, Mia Pia?" I scanned the black-and-white photo as the memory came flooding back. We were at the Memphis Zoo, all of us. I was about six, sitting on top of my father's shoulders. On one side of us stood my mother and David, and on the other side stood Martha and her husband, Jimmy. We were all smiling exuberantly at the camera except for my mother; she was looking at my father and me. Her smile was different; it wasn't excited—it was warm and full of love.

Martha, Jimmy, and Pops had been on a road trip all over the United States. My mother and David had decided we would meet them in Memphis. Just moments after we took the picture, it began raining. Instead of calling it a day, my father pointed and shouted, "To the butterflies!" Showered by the warm rain, he skipped toward the exhibit with me bouncing above his six-foot-four frame. I held on to his ruddy brown locks while he hummed "Rocky Road to Dublin." I remember feeling safe, loved, and exactly where I should be. Inside the screened enclosure, he pointed to a chrysalis and explained metamorphosis to me.

"Pops, will I have a metamorphosis?"

"Of course, luv. We are ever changing, always learning, always evolving."

"So I'll be a beautiful butterfly one day?"

He smiled and chuckled. "You're a beautiful butterfly now. It's the change that happens in here that matters." He pointed to my heart.

Before handing the picture back, I stared at it for several moments, absorbing everyone's youthfulness. Martha's hair had gone completely silver since that time and her eyes, still wildly expressive, had dulled from a stunning blue to a cloudy gray and were now framed with heavy lines. She rarely wore makeup; instead, she maintained her classic hippie vibe, always in colorful shirts and long, flowy skirts or faded jeans. I handed the picture back while she continued sifting through the box. When she reached for it, she glanced up and noticed my puffy eyes. She began taping up the box hurriedly.

"Hang on to all of this for yourself, sweetie, and go through it when you're ready."

I carried the box to the hall closet and shoved it onto the top shelf for another time.

Sheil and Martha came to the apartment several times in the days after I arrived in New York. They gathered items that were meaningful to them while we all worked to make the place seem more like mine.

Sheil remained quiet in her grief. Her silence was perceived as indifference to some, but I knew better. She had traveled here from India twenty years ago as part of a music troupe. Once she met my father, there was no looking back. An accomplished sitar player, Sheil had become very successful, working with the World Music Institute. Her transcending beauty and passion when she plays has made her a sought-after musician for many different kinds of acts looking to add that Eastern sound.

Even though I never saw her cry outwardly, I knew she was in a lot of pain over the loss of my father. She had found him in the apartment just moments after his heart attack. At his funeral she'd played a very long and sorrowful piece of music, but her face remained completely stoic. When I hugged her afterward, I realized the front of her sari was drenched. Tears had poured from her eyes without any change in her facial expression. It's a sign of pure pain and pure surrender when your soul cries without any fight from your body, and that's how I knew she was deeply affected.

Pops's funeral was more like a tribute. A large crowd had gathered in the garden next to St. Brigid's Church, where several musicians played songs and patrons of the café spoke about his generosity and character. That day had been uncharacteristically warm for February in New York. I remember how I marveled, through tears, at the shards of light piercing through the trees, flooding the space with warmth and energy. It was a beautiful way to say good-bye to his body and a reminder that his spirit would remain. It was exactly what he would have wanted, something more like a peaceful memorial concert outdoors as opposed to a sad wake at Kell's. In my father's will he'd requested to be cremated but had left no instructions regarding his remains. In my heart I promised that I would do something with his ashes. I would find a way to give his spontaneous, loving spirit one last hurrah.

Sheil lived in the apartment directly above Kell's. My apartment was one building down and situated above Sam's Italian Restaurant. Sam's does not serve any coffee; they send all their customers to Kell's, claiming we have the best cappuccinos. In return, we let them use a small storage space in our back office. It's been a worthwhile relationship.

"Martha, I'm going to work seven days a week until we get the books straight," I said one morning before we opened the café.

"You most certainly will not—you'll burn out."

"I don't know if we're making money or losing money and I'm not going to hire someone until we figure out the finances."

"I can tell you without looking at the books that we're doing just fine," she said, glancing toward the door where several patrons had begun to gather. "Anyway, your father kept meticulous records. If it says we're in the black, then we are." She was right about that: my father was a good businessman and record keeper.

The café was like a museum. One wall of the long narrow space was exposed brick, completely unmarred. The opposite wall had beige wainscoting that met solid, navy-blue paint and was almost entirely covered by black-and-white photographs. The photographs varied between pictures of famous patrons, musical performances that had taken place in the café, my father's friends or employees over the years, and quite a few of me. It seemed there was at least one from every stage of my life. The counter, refrigerator case, and register were old but still gleaming, and the espresso machine, as loud and cranky as it was, sparkled in the light of the low-hanging fixtures.

Above the counter was a chalkboard with my father's simple handwriting of the beverage names and descriptions. The only spots that visibly had been erased over the many years were the prices. I briefly pondered the cost of the very first cappuccino served at that counter. Perhaps a nickel. Times had certainly changed, the prices had changed, and more pictures had been added to the wall, but other than that the café remained the same. The floors were old, worn, distressed wood but they were cherished like the tables and chairs and the bar that stretched across the front window. I'd spent many summer nights with my father cleaning and oiling the wood. The scent of citrus oil and espresso always mingled heavily in the tight space.

Pops had taken great care to preserve the quality and character of the café. I remember one day as I was cleaning between the wooden slats of a chair, he came over and put his hand on my shoulder. I looked up into his caramel-colored irises. He smiled all the way to his eyes. "Remember to leave your pride inside, luv, but make sure you keep it alive," he said. The hand-rolled clove peeking from the side of his mouth always emphasized his husky, accented voice.

I wanted to feel that pride in the café while humbly working to maintain its quality, as my father had taught me, and even though I didn't know what the future held for me and Kell's, I wouldn't disgrace his memory by letting his life's work fall apart. I chose to work either an opening or closing shift seven days a week while Martha and Sheil alternated days. Jenny, who was the only other employee, would fill in the gaps so that there would be two people working most of the time. Jenny had worked at Kell's for a few years. She was two years older than me, and every time I visited New York, she and I would fall back into an easy friendship.

It was at least a month before I settled into the routine at the café. I started to recognize the regulars. Joe and his brother Paddy spent several mornings a week at their usual table in the corner. I would often find myself standing close by, shamelessly eavesdropping on their hilarious conversations. The familiarity of the fading Irish accents filled my heart with warmth.

"Somebody requested that type of music? That junk? That shit?" Paddy said to Joe in disbelief one Tuesday morning.

"I believe they did, Paddy."

"And she played it? Is she stupid?"

"For tirty-tree years I've been going to that dance hall, Paddy, and she has been there every single Sunday playing the same music until last week. Somebody must have requested it. She's not stupid—she doesn't understand."

"Does she know English?"

"She does."

"Well, then, how do you explain it?"

"She doesn't understand the two—how if you have nice music, people will dance and come back, but if you play that crap, people will leave."

"Give her another illustration, Joe, to help her understand. Maybe you can tell her that if the food is terrible, people won't eat it."

"I actually enjoy the food. I love broccoli, and I like stew," Joe said matter-of-factly.

Paddy looked at Joe with a puzzled but interested look. "Do you like spaghetti and meatballs?"

"Of course I do, but they only serve Irish fare there, Paddy. I thought you knew that."

Jenny danced through the jingling café door, waving a flyer around like a crazy person, momentarily distracting me from Paddy and Joe.

"Looky looky, a cute boy came in last night and asked to put this up, but I'm keeping it for myself." It was a very simple flyer advertising three bands playing that Friday night at a nearby bar called The Depot. I didn't recognize the first two but tensed up when I saw The Ivans at the bottom. Guess they weren't exactly headliners. "You wanna go with me?" Jenny said, wearing a stupid grin.

"What did the guy look like?"

"Hot."

"Did he ask for me?"

"No, why would he ask for you?"

"Well, I met this guy on a plane, and um . . . never mind.

Yes, I'll go with you, but we'll have to rearrange the schedule so I can go early since it looks like they'll be playing first."

"Who will be playing first?"

"Well, I mean, I just want to see all three bands."

"Oh, okay, yeah sure, whatever. You're the boss."

"Hey, Jenny, just one thing. Did the guy have any tattoos?"

"Oh, yes. He had a big, thick angel wing on his forearm . . . very sexy. I couldn't stop staring," she said, wiggling her eyebrows.

It was Will.

Friday snuck up on me. I wrapped everything up at the café and had a few minutes to run to my apartment and change before Jenny met me on the street. I decided on some black skinny jeans, flats, a black tank top, and a little gray blazer. I've always been the monochromatic type, never really wearing many colors or patterns. I brushed out my long dark hair, put on a little mascara and lip gloss, said, "Be good" to Jackson, then headed for the door and down to the street where Jenny was waiting.

"You look amazing, Mia."

"Really? You are too kind, girl. Anyway, look at you—you look great!" She did. Jenny was much more dressed up than I. She wore a silk shirt, shimmery skirt, bomber jacket, and chunky heels. Jenny is the polar opposite of me. She's curvy with blond hair and light eyes.

When we arrived at The Depot, there were a few scattered people in attendance. We made our way to the bar, where Jenny ordered a beer and I asked for my usual going-out drink: vodka soda with a splash of cranberry. The bar was filling up, and The Ivans began taking the stage. There was a sprinkle of applause.

"That's the guy!" Jenny belted out.

I nodded, acknowledging her. She was gawking at him as he tuned his guitar with his back to the audience. It annoyed me that she was a girl who swooned over musicians. I liked Jenny, so I was going to overlook it. After all, I knew Will could get my temperature up, too, but I wasn't there for his attention. I simply wanted to see if he had any talent. The way he talked on the plane made me think that he was at least a decent guitarist. I don't know why it mattered or why I cared, but I did.

The drummer and bassist had also taken the stage, but there was no sign of the lead singer yet. Will was wearing black jeans and a plain gray T-shirt; I think we sort of matched. He was wearing black classic Adidas sneakers with a piece of duct tape over the toe of his left shoe.

The band began building up a beat. Will played a soulful and haunting guitar riff while the bassist plucked an equally haunting line. The drums came in low and patient. I was mesmerized. Their sound was dynamic and original. Will was in deep concentration and still slightly turned toward the drummer in the back. It was clear that this was some sort of long intro. I watched as he studied the guitar and slightly manipulated the neck to change the sound. There was a bluesiness to his style, but it was definitely faster and harder. Pete, the lead singer, sauntered out on stage shirtless.

"Yuck!" I gasped. Jenny shot me a look of agreement. I expected him to walk up to the microphone and begin belting out something beautiful to match the music the band was making, but that was wishful thinking.

"Check, Check, one . . . two . . . three!" Pete shouted into the microphone. The band stopped abruptly. Will was expressionless as he turned toward the audience.

The drummer smacked the drums one last time, threw his arms up in the air, looked right at Pete's back, and loudly whispered, "Fucker!" Pete turned around and flipped him off.

"Can I get some more reverb?" Pete directed to someone

offstage. It was clear the band was jamming and the audience was enjoying it, but he didn't give a shit. He was the typical front-man egomaniac. When the band started to play and he began singing, I was mortified. There was so much reverb on his vocals it sounded like we were in a train depot and someone was calling out arrivals and departures over a speaker system.

"What a waste!" I said to Jenny.

"Yeah, the band seems really good but the singer is so full of himself and he sucks." Pete was dancing all over the stage like a fool. Will and the other musicians just kept their heads down over their instruments. When there was a guitar or drum solo, Pete would stand at his microphone and shout "uh-huhs" and "yeahs" like a total numbskull. Onstage, Will was not at all the playful guy I had met on the plane. He kept his head down, his eyes were in the shadows, and he never looked out into the crowd. I might have guessed that Pete's antics embarrassed Will, but I didn't think he flustered easily.

As soon as The Ivans finished their set, I turned to Jenny. "You ready?"

"Really? Don't you want to see the other bands?"

"This was fun. It's just, I have to get up super early."

"No worries, girl, the guitarist is delicious, but I think I'm over my groupie days."

I hesitated for just a minute to see if Will would look in my direction, but he didn't. He was lugging a giant amplifier backstage. I even counted to ten in my head, but he never looked up.

We dashed out of the bar and headed toward the subway. Back at my apartment we had some wine. I played a few fun songs on the piano for Jenny. That was the bonus of living above a restaurant, no one really complained about the noise. My father had an old upright piano that I loved. It was nothing like the baby grand my mother and David had bought me on my sixth birthday. My father's piano had history and texture and a character to the sound. Jenny sang along to the songs she knew. We had a great time. She told me I was an amazing musician and I told her she was a great friend and that I was glad my father had hired her. Jenny stayed that night in the guest room and we managed to be asleep by ten.

The next morning, I got up at six a.m., took Jackson for a run, and then made some flyers to find a roommate. I realized with Jenny over that I could use the company and Jackson could, too. He was thirteen. He had grown up with me in Ann Arbor, where he'd been the constant recipient of my stepdad's attention, especially during my first two years in college when I couldn't take him with me. Jackson had grown used to having a lot of space and daily walks. It would be nice to have another person help with that responsibility. I didn't need the money, so I could be very picky about whom I chose to rent the room to. As I left for the café, Jenny was just getting up.

"Hey, I'm going to Kell's. I'll see you later. Help yourself to whatever and stay as long as you want."

"Thanks, girl!" Jenny yelled back as I headed out the door.

I approached Kell's armed with flyers. Right as I got to the door, I noticed Will. He was sitting at the wooden bar that faced out the front window. He was in the seat farthest from the door, chewing on a little plastic straw and staring out to the street, all broody. He removed the straw, and from where I stood, I could see his mouth move ever so slightly. I approached him unnoticed, bent down toward his ear, and whispered, "You talkin' to God?"

He jumped up, arms stretched out to offer a hug. "Mia! You know I'm not religious. How are you?"

My mind went straight to a visual of Will kissing the rosary crucifix around his neck on the plane that day back in March and I laughed softly. I went in for the hug. He wrapped his arms around my shoulders and I think I felt him kiss the top of my head. We barely knew each other, but it didn't seem like that.

"I'm really good," I said.

"I saw you last night at The Depot with Coffee Girl and then you were gone. What's up with that?"

"You saw me?" I wondered why he hadn't acknowledged me.

He laughed. "Did you notice we were dressed almost exactly the same? You were like my little twin." I squinted at him but didn't respond. We stood there gazing at each other for several moments and then he poked my arm with his index finger and said, "You looked great." An image of me grabbing his finger and sucking on it shot through my mind. *Good Lord!* "So what did you think of the band?" he asked.

"The band is amazing, but Pete is a total goober and he's a terrible singer on top of it."

"I know, right? We should have known when he wanted to name the band For Pete's Sake."

I laughed loudly at the idea. "No, but seriously, you guys are good. You owe it to yourselves to find a decent singer."

"Pete put the band together, that's the thing. We can't kick him out of his own band. It's just for practice, anyway. At least for me. I'm always looking out for new possibilities. What's that?" He pointed to my flyers.

"Oh. I'm looking for a roommate."

"Perfect, I'll take it!" He was wearing a giant grin.

"No offense, Will, but we barely know each other and I was kind of hoping to find another girl to rent to. I mean, you know, you could be like an ax murderer or something." I smirked.

"Didn't you see the movie *Single White Female*? Have you really thought this through?" He was deadpan, but I knew he was being silly.

"You have a point, buddy. I'll think about it. In the meantime, can I get you a coffee or something?"

"No thanks, I have somewhere to be. Rain check?"

"Will, you can come back anytime during business hours and someone will serve you a coffee."

He half-smiled, then squinted his eyes and said, "But I want to have a coffee with you."

It was astonishing what Will could do to me with a sexy smirk and few trivial words. My legs were trembling and then, as if I had no control over my mouth, I said, "The room is yours if you want it. Rent is four hundred dollars; you can move in now. It's the apartment above Sam's. But I have to tell you, if we're going to live together, then we have to keep it strictly friends. Got it?"

He cupped my face with both hands and I felt the callused pads of his fingers on my cheeks. I flushed all the way down to my toes and then my knees buckled. I grabbed his waist as he planted a hard, ridiculous, closed-mouth kiss on my lips. Then he said, "Baby, that's a great idea!"

"Will!" I shouted at him.

Still holding my face, he cocked his head to the side. "What? This is how I am with my friends." Just then Jenny walked in the door. Will immediately stalked over to her, grabbed her face, and planted the same kiss on her, then sighed. "Hey, baby." He sped out the door, turned around, and looked at me through the glass. With his arms held out to his sides, he said, "See? I told you. I'll be at your place at noon tomorrow." Then he was gone.

Stunned, I turned toward Jenny, who was equally shocked.

"What the fuck was that?"

"That's my new roommate."

She chuckled. "Right on."

What had I done? Friends, we were going to be friends, I told myself. That's it. But it didn't seem like Will made rules like that for his life. He reminded me of my father, and that scared me.

I turned and began studying the many photos on the wall at Kell's.

There were pictures of my father with Bob Dylan, Allen Ginsberg, Andy Warhol, The Clash, Willie Nelson, and Patti Smith, to name a few. I thought about the future of the café. Although the East Village was now a much safer place for a young, single girl to live, I missed the culture that used to exist. Kell's had been the hangout, but times had changed. We still had our group of die-hard regulars along with the people sent to us from Sam's who wanted to sit and enjoy an after-dinner creation, but the mornings were brutally slow for a coffeehouse. Most cafés had been reduced to a get-your-coffee-fast joint, where you popped in for your morning latte served up in a paper cup. My father refused to conform to that standard. No coffee was "to go" in our café. Still, back in the day, there was the seediness of the punk rock era in the East Village. The freedom and creativity were rampant, which drew people to gather in places like Kell's. Gone were those days. I wasn't entirely sure I would have fit in anyway.

Whenever I had to make a decision, I would hear my mother's voice of reason. I knew we were not the same, my mother and I, I was sure of it. After all, I was my father's daughter, too. But sometimes I felt her path made more sense. The safety and predictability of her thought-out plans was appealing to me. She was sensible; she made decisions with her head. Yet even though my mother was the more grounded parent, growing up I continued to heed my father's words; his passion was contagious. The last time I'd spoken with Pops, he'd reminded me to give love and get it in return and to quit fixating on my future. It wasn't your typical father-daughter talk, but, then, it never was with him.

My stepdad David's advice, on the other hand, was mostly logical and usually in the form of a written exercise. If I had a hard decision to make, he would say something like "Draft me a list of pros and cons, Princess." My mother would always be standing right behind him, nodding in full agreement. Before I left for Europe, he insisted that I create a detailed itinerary complete with train schedules and weather forecasts. It was a bit over the top, but it came in handy.

Pops's only words before I left for Europe were "Have a blast, luv, and stay away from the opium in the red-light district."

In the more recent years at the end of every phone call we shared, Pops would address me by my real name and quote Arthur Rubenstein. "Remember, Mia, 'Love life and life will love you back.'" He was the eternal lover and optimist; he took it seriously and he wanted me to do the same. I imagine that he and Will would have hit it off.

When the café phone rang, I darted behind the counter. Martha grabbed the receiver and in a singsong voice answered, "It's a beautiful morning at Kell's. . . . Oh hi, Liz, how are you?" I listened intently as Martha spoke to my mother. I kept my back to her, looking out onto the café, but I was hanging on every word. "Oh yes, dear, Mia is adjusting quite well. . . . Really?"

I turned around, shot my hands out, and mouthed, *What?* to Martha. She shrugged her shoulders and continued listening. "I'm not sure, Liz. Mia is right here, though, if you'd like to talk to her." I frantically shook my head back and forth, signaling a firm no. She held the receiver out to me and arched her eyebrows. I took it from her hand but stood there transfixed before putting it to my ear. After Martha disappeared into the café kitchen, I looked over at Jenny, who was slowly catching on. She darted to the espresso machine and flipped the old monster on.

"Oh, hey, Mom!" I yelled. "It's really busy here and I don't know if I'll be able to hear you over the espresso machine, but I'm fine, everything is great! I'll call you later!"

"Okay, honey, I just wanted you to know I'm coming out next week. Just me. I miss you!"

"Okay, I love you."

"Love you, too, be safe!"

Jenny turned the machine off while I stared blankly at her. She knew I didn't want my mom knowing that I'd invited Will to live with me. "Mia, you're an adult and Will seems like a nice guy. I mean, I'm sure there were coed dorms at Brown. What did your mom think of that?"

"No, Jenny, it's the tattooed, starving artist, musician types that my mother disapproves of."

"Well, she liked Pops enough, 'cause here you are." She smiled.

She had a good point. Could my mother really preach to me about this? Will would simply be my roommate—I wasn't sleeping with him and he wasn't twelve years my senior like my father was to her. She had been a wild child compared to me.

After I'd graduated from college, I'd traveled through Europe for a year with my three roommates from Brown. My grandparents had funded the entire trip. They'd told me to get everything out of my system because they expected me to come back and be a grown-up. In Europe I went to every museum possible, spent a lot of time watching live music and even more time chugging wine.

Still, I was the only one of the girls who didn't have a different guy in her bed every night. I had plenty of offers—European guys don't hold back. I remember once in Barcelona I met this beautiful Basque man, suitably named Romeo. We hit it off immediately and the attraction was strong. I kindly turned down the offer to go back to his place that night because I planned to get up early the following morning. My plan was to take the three-hour train to Madrid. I was dying to get back to the Reina Sofia Museum so that I could stare at Picasso's *Guernica* a little longer. I thought since Romeo and I were obviously into each other, I would invite him to come along to Madrid with me. He admitted he had never been to the Reina Sofia. I thought what Basque man would not want to see this amazing work of art that has so much historical significance to his people? He wasn't intrigued; he turned me down and continued his quest to find a woman to bed that night.

The next day, I stood in front of the giant *Guernica,* wondering what Picasso had been thinking, when it occurred to me that it was more about what he was feeling, how he projected that into his art, that inspired me. And so it began, my secret and suppressed obsession with the sensitive, tortured artist soul. An obsession I was still fighting tooth and nail, and one I wouldn't admit to anyone, even myself.

I spent the two years after Europe living with my mom and David in Ann Arbor, trying to figure out what to do with my life. I was always so scared that I might make bad decisions. I dated no one because the guys I was attracted to didn't seem suitable for the future I envisioned. I gave piano lessons to kids, studied for the GRE, and researched colleges for grad school. When my father died, the decision to move to New York was made for me. Still, I was determined to stay focused on success. I would only pursue sensible relationships while I worked on getting Kell's back to its glory, and I would continue working toward a bigger career in business. I knew art and music would always play a role in my life, but I refused to fall into the bottomless and crowded vat of starving artists.

The bells on the door to the café jingled as Mr. Suitable walked in. He was well-built, on the stocky side, and definitely shorter than Will, but in great shape. He was wearing perfectly tailored gray suit pants, a white dress shirt, no tie, top button open and the shirtsleeves rolled up on his thick forearms. He was varsity-quarterback handsome. He had pale blue eyes, dark blond hair, and thin lips, with a hint of baby face. He looked like the guys I was used to seeing on the campus at Brown, very upright and all business. I think I was noticeably gawking at him because he had a crooked, cocky grin on his face. If I could have moved, I probably would have looked over to find Jenny in the same condition. A moment later I saw a little mini-me walk in behind him.

Damn! He's got kids. Does that mean he's married?

"Hi, welcome to Kell's. What can I get you?"

He squinted his eyes and quickly glanced down my body and back up, then fixed his gaze on the chalkboard above me. I felt a flush creep up my cheeks at his once-over. "I'll have a cappuccino, and for this guy . . . Hmm, what is Little Luv's Cocoa?" he asked while patting his cute son on the head.

"It's just hot cocoa," I said shyly.

Jenny chimed in, "With a giant homemade marshmallow in it. It's divine and it's named after her." She jabbed her thumb toward me and my face flushed again.

"Your name is Little Luv?"

Cocky bastard. Handsome, cocky bastard.

"Yes . . . I mean no. My father used to call me luv." He nodded and smiled and then looked me up and down again. I felt like he was undressing me with his eyes, and I found myself starting to enjoy it.

"Okay, he'll have the cocoa."

"Little Luv's Cocoa," Jenny corrected. I elbowed her.

"Sorry, yes, Little Luv's Cocoa," he said without taking his eyes off me.

"You got it. That'll be six forty." As I reached to grab the ten-dollar bill out of his hand, he held onto it for a second too long, forcing me to tug at it. I smiled and gave him his change. "Have a seat; I'll bring your coffee out to you."

I glanced over at Jenny, whose eyes were as round as quarters. As the man walked away, she stuck her tongue out at his back in a vulgar, licking gesture. I burst into wild laughter and then stopped abruptly when he glanced back at us.

I didn't want him to think we were laughing at him, so when I took his coffee to him, I said, "I'm sorry about that. It's just my friend thinks you're really good-looking." I saw Jenny glaring at me out of the corner of my eye.

"What do you think?" he asked.

I must have been beet red; my plan backfired. *Shit, shit.* "Um, well, I guess I would have to agree."

"Um, well, I guess I'll take that as a compliment, then."

I smiled shyly and scurried away. Before the man left, he stopped at the bulletin board and read over my advertisement for kids' piano lessons.

When he tore off a little phone number tab, I said, "That's me," and pointed my finger right at my boob like an idiot.

"Okay?" He hesitated. "I'll call you?" It was a question. I shook my head up and down frantically.

He smiled and chuckled and then, just like that, he was gone. "He wasn't wearing a wedding band!" Jenny sighed with happiness. I didn't respond.

TRACK 3: Ask Me

The following day at exactly 12:01 the door buzzer sounded. *Punctual, I like it.* I skipped over to the speaker. "Yes?"

"Hey, it's Will." I buzzed him in. He was up the stairs in a second and rapped a silly little beat on the door.

I opened it wide. "Hey, come on in."

"Hi, roomie."

He stepped in, then stood there transfixed for a minute before looking around. I observed his every move. He walked through the living room and kitchen, which was one big loft-style room. The kitchen had a breakfast bar and two big windows facing out to the street. The other side of the room was floor-to-ceiling bookshelves full of records, CDs, and books. "Ah, Mia, this place is great. Are those your dad's old records?"

"Yeah." I felt a twinge of sadness about Pops. Will set his bag down next to the coffee table that sat between two identical beige sofas that faced each other. The upright piano was against a little section of wall just as you entered the hallway.

"I love this piano," Will said as he ran his fingers over the keys. He was like a kid in a candy shop. My father had black-and-white photos everywhere. Will paused at a picture of my father and me from a few years back. He turned to face me, his eyes narrowed into the listening-to-God look. Then he smiled and said, "You're beautiful." I realized how handsome and expressive Will's face was close up. The way he spoke to me made me believe that he could never tell a lie.

"Thank you," I said softly and then moved to change the subject. "I'll show you the room." He walked behind me down the hall toward his new room. I was unreasonably nervous, like I had just asked him to take me to bed. I showed him the large bathroom that we would be sharing. He seemed happy and said it was literally the size of the storage closet he had just moved from. The two bedrooms at the end of the hall were identical, one on the left and one on the right. I was in my father's room on the right, which had a window out to a courtyard in the back of the building. The room on the left had windows that faced out to the street. It also had a little platform and fire escape, which I figured Will could smoke on since there would be no smoking inside the apartment. I pointed to the closed door of my room. "That's my room." I hoped he got the message that it was off limits. "And here's yours."

I let him walk in front of me and then I stood in the doorway and watched him as he looked around. On the wall was a poster of a long-haired Eddie Vedder singing onstage back in the grunge days. He was shirtless and sweaty, his eyes closed as he gripped the microphone.

Pointing to the poster, Will smirked. "Not your father's, I take it?"

"This used to be my room during the summers."

In his best girly voice he said, "It's like he's singing right into my soul."

"Shut up!" I said sheepishly. "Take it down—do whatever you want." I pointed to the window. "You can smoke out there."

"I quit."

"Good for you," I said sincerely. The room had a bed with a blue bedspread and a dresser in the corner. I had taken everything else out.

"This is perfect," he said, smiling widely.

"So we have to figure out some kind of rules for privacy and all that."

"Well, you work days and I work nights, so I'm sure it will be fine." He stared at me and then continued, "What did you mean, like a sock on the door type of thing?"

"No, no. You're right, it will be fine. Anyway, we can just figure it out as we go."

"Sounds like a plan, roomie." Then he winked.

"Okay, so where's the rest of your stuff?"

"That's it," he said, pointing to the big duffel bag he'd brought in. "Oh, and my guitars and a little practice amp that Dustin, our drummer, is bringing over in his van. He'll be here in a bit."

"I just realized I know nothing about you. Do you have a family? Where are you from?" The idea that I'd just invited a relative stranger, who owned nothing, to live in my apartment gave me a stomachache, but the weird thing was that I felt like I had known Will forever.

"I'm from Detroit. My entire family still lives there. My mom works in a bakery at a grocery store and my dad is a retired electrician. I have twelve brothers and sisters."

"Really? I'm an only child. I can't imagine having a huge family like that—it must have been awesome."

Relaxing his stance, he leaned his tattooed forearm onto the dresser and crossed his feet. Jackson came over and sat next to him. Will unconsciously began petting Jackson's head. It made my heart warm. "Actually, I don't have twelve brothers and sisters. I have one brother and eleven sisters." He paused. "My brother, Ray, is the oldest and I'm the youngest, with eleven girls in between. I swear my parents just wanted to give Ray a brother, so they kept having more babies. By the time I was born, Ray was sixteen and didn't give a shit. On top of it, they all have *R* names except me. It's a fucking joke."

"You're kidding? Name 'em," I demanded.

In a super-fast voice, Will recited, "Raymond, Reina, Rachelle, Raelin, Riley, Rianna, Reese, Regan, Remy, Regina, Ranielle, Rebecca, and then me, Will."

"Surely they could have figured out another *R* name?"

"Well, my brother was named after my dad, so my mom felt like I should be named after someone too, being the only other boy and all. So I was named after my grandfather . . . Wilbur Ryan."

"Oh my god!" I burst into laughter. "Your name is Wil-bur?"

"Hey, woman, that's my poppy's name, too."

Still giggling, I said, "I'm sorry, I just expected William."

"Yeah, it's okay. Everyone does." He smiled and winked at me again.

The winks were making me blush. "So what's your family like?"

"I love 'em—they're great. Most of them are married with kids. I have so many nieces and nephews I don't even know all their names. When I go back home, I just call them by some physical trait like Freckles, Dimples, Small Fry, things like that. They love me. My family doesn't get the music thing, though. They always thought I was a little weird. Instead of G.I. Joe figures, I wanted records. I'm totally self-taught and I can pretty much play anything. During the holidays, I bust out a bunch of cheery holiday songs that my family can sing along to. They tell me things like, 'You're so fun, Will, with your guitar music,' but to them it's not a serious thing." The buzzer rang. "That's probably Dustin."

We both walked to the speaker. I pushed the button and said, "Hello?"

"Dude, get down here, I'm double-parked."

"Dude?"

"Oh. Sorry, dude, can you tell Will to get down here?"

"Sure."

I looked up at Will, who shrugged. "He's from California." As though that explained everything. "Come on." He motioned toward the door. "You should meet them."

When we got out to the street, I saw Will take a pack of cigarettes out of his pocket, tap the bottom, and grab one out with his teeth. "I thought you quit?"

"I did." He tossed the pack to one of the guys leaning against the van, then took the unlit cigarette from his mouth and tucked it behind his ear.

He pointed to his ear. "That one's for looks." He turned toward the van. "Hey, guys, this is Mia, my roomie. Mia, this is Dustin and Nate."

Dustin had long, brown hair and a skinny, wiry build like a typical drummer. Nate was taller and thicker with a shaved head. Both guys smiled politely at me as we shook hands. "I saw you guys play at The Depot the other night. You were so good, but you have to get rid of Pete."

"Yeah, no kidding," Dustin said.

Nate chimed in, "You wanna be our singer, Mia?"

I knew he was joking, but I answered him anyway. "I'm too shy."

"She can play piano for us, though," Will said.

"Well, I'd have to think about that," I said, glaring at Will. I had never even thought about playing music live or with a band. Growing up, I played at more than a few stuffy recitals, and in high school I had some fun playing in cafés around town in Ann Arbor, but that was as far as I ever planned to take my music career. The thought of playing in New York City among the overwhelming talent seemed more terrifying than thrilling.

Will grabbed the guitars and small amp from the back of the van. He handed me the acoustic. Heading back into the building, he shot the guys a look and yelled, "See you Saturday."

I waved. "Nice meeting you," I said, then followed Will back toward the stairs.

They both shouted, "Bye, Mia!" in silly voices.

When we got back up to the apartment, I opened the case I was carrying and admired the black Gibson acoustic guitar inside.

"My dad's guitars are away in cases. I have two stands if you want to use them."

"I would love that, Mia. Thanks." He went into his room and began getting settled. I brought the stands in. "Perfect." He took them from my hands.

"You can play in the living room whenever you want."

"Really?"

"Yeah, definitely, except for when I'm giving lessons."

"Of course," he said. He glanced at his watch. "Oh shit, I've got to be at work early tonight so I'm gonna get going in a minute. Thanks for everything."

"No problem," I said and headed down the hallway to the kitchen. I put The Smiths on the stereo and began cutting up some veggies for a salad.

I heard Will singing to the song as he came down the hallway. He imitated Morrissey's voice perfectly, accent and all. It was uncanny.

"*So if there's something you'd like to try . . . if there's some-thing you'd like to try . . .* " I turned to face him; he raised his eyebrows, looked right at me, and sang, "*Ask me, I won't say no, how could I?*"

Then he shot me his sexy smile. My knees buckled. My god, would I ever get used to it?

He winked and said, "Bye, roomie. Come and have a drink if you want."

He was dressed in gray jeans and a black short-sleeved dress shirt. He normally looked so edgy, so rock and roll, but with the collar he looked quite dapper. He must have also run his hands through his hair with a bit of gel because it was out of his face for once. It was definitely his hot bartender look.

"Bye, buddy," I whispered as he went bolting out the door. I hadn't slept with anyone in two years. Frankly, it was un-natural. The way I reacted to Will made me think that I really needed to give up the saint act, but I wasn't into one-night stands. The last boyfriend I'd had was back in college. His name was Bryan York and he was in the music department at Brown. Go figure. Except Bryan was the nerdy type of music guy. He played the tuba and wanted to be a marching-band director. He was beyond nice, but a little strange. It was my senior year and I lived off campus by then. Students occupied most of the apartment building I lived in, so it still had the dorm feel.

A few months after Bryan and I had started dating, every-one in the building noticed that he would do random drive-bys. I guess he was checking to see if my car was there, even though he never confronted me about anything and didn't have a possessive bone in his body. At any rate, he was driving by rather regularly, so he quickly earned the nickname Spyin' Bryan. It became such a well-known nickname that people would refer to him as Spyin' Bryan right to his face, and he would just go with it. Poor drip. I knew it wouldn't last. We broke up but remained friends. That was my last boyfriend.

The last time I had sex was New Year's in Portugal two years ago. It was with some guy I met in the plaza at midnight when everybody was throwing champagne bottles into a giant pile. The crowd was wild and I was feeling festive, or drunk, and someone told me that the Portuguese make great lovers. I wouldn't know; I don't remember a thing about it except that I'm fairly certain I wore a blue wig through the whole escapade. The next morning I woke up in a strange apartment, still wearing the blue wig. There he was, lying on his side, elbow propped under his head. He was staring down at me, smiling and inhaling my hangover dragon breath. He didn't speak a word of English. We tried to communicate awkwardly for ten minutes until I got dressed, stood at the door, blew him a kiss, and took off. I swore to myself I would never perform the walk of shame again.

I had to get out of the heady mind space I was in. I looked out the window and it was still light out, so I decided to take Jackson for a run. I stopped into Kell's afterward. Thursday nights were fairly busy because of a little poetry group that met there. The group is made up of older folks from the good old days and a few college kids who like to do slam poetry. I tied Jackson up outside, got him a bowl of water, and then went in behind the counter to make myself some tea. "Hi, Martha. Why are you still here?"

"I'm wrapping up. Jenny is running late. Oh, Mia, a man came in with a little boy. He asked if you were here and then asked about piano lessons for the boy."

"Huh." I wondered why he hadn't just called the number in the first place. Then Jenny came dancing through the door with a huge smile on her face. "Why are you so happy?"

"It's poetry night. I love watching these college boys slam," she said as she raised her eyebrows up and down.

I turned toward Martha. "You can go. Thanks for everything."

"Of course, Mia Pia. See you tomorrow," she said as she gave me a big squeeze.

Martha left and I realized I had never returned my mom's phone call from the day before. "I better get home, Jenny. I need to talk to my mom."

"Don't tell her about Will unless you're prepared for a lecture."

"Yeah, you're right." I kissed her on each cheek and said, "Ciao, bella." I thought about it as I left the café. My mother would find out about Will soon enough. As I made my way up the stairs to my apartment, I could hear my phone ringing. I ran in and jumped for the receiver. Out of breath, I managed a labored "Hi."

A man's voice came on. "Um, hi. I'm sorry, am I interrupting something?"

"No, I just ran up my stairs."

"Oh, this is Robert Thompson. I was in Kell's the other day and picked up a number for piano lessons. Is this Mia?"

"Yeah. Do you have a child you'd like to put in piano lessons?"

"Yes, I think we kind of met. I was in there with my son and you helped me at the counter?"

It was Mr. Suitable.

"How's it going?"

"It . . . " He paused. "It's going well, thank you. How about yourself?"

"Great. When would you like to bring . . . ?" I waited.

"Jacob."

"When would you like to bring Jacob over?"

"Whenever you're available." His tone was slightly curt.

"How about Saturday around six?"

"Perfect," he said.

"I live above Sam's restaurant, down the block from Kell's. Just hit the button for two when you get here and I'll buzz you in."

"Okay, we'll see you Saturday, Mia."

He didn't ask me how much the lessons were or how long they lasted. I wondered how safe it was to give piano lessons in New York City. I would have to arrange something where I let Sheil or the ladies at Kell's know when I was going to start a lesson. That's what I would do. My phone rang again.

"Hello?"

"Hi, sweetheart. I was worried about you."

"Sorry, Mom, I got busy. Aren't you coming out this week?"

"I can't for at least a few more weeks." There was a long pause. "Okay?"

"Yes, of course," I said in a low voice.

"I've been slammed at work. Everything okay, Mia? You sound distracted. How are you holding up?"

Suddenly my feelings shifted from being worried about what my mom would think of Will, to being disappointed that she wouldn't be coming sooner, to feeling alone and missing my father.

"I'm fine. I miss him." My voice cracked.

"I know." She took a deep breath. "Aw, Mia, I'm so sorry I can't be there sooner. Just know that he's with you, sweetheart, coursing through every single one of your veins." She whispered the last part, sounding pained.

I hovered over the piano and tapped a continuous beat on the middle-C key while I pondered her comment.

"I suppose he is," I said as one tiny tear traveled down my cheek.

We said our good-byes. That night, with Jackson at my side, I cried myself to sleep thinking about my father. I woke up hours later and reached for the glass of water on my nightstand. I glanced at the clock; it was three thirty a.m. There was no light coming from Will's room, but I could hear him sleepily strumming his guitar. The healing sound sent me drifting into a much more contented sleep.

The next morning I got ready quickly. As I headed toward the hall, I glanced into Will's room. He was shirtless and sound asleep on his side, facing the window. His tattooed arm was up over his head, his bicep almost covering his eyes. He looked peaceful and warm, and it gave me the sudden urge to strip down and crawl under the covers with him. I shook my head to clear the thought, then motioned for Jackson to go lie down. He walked in and sniffed around, and Will reached his arm back, petted the dog's head, then patted the bed, calling him up. Jackson jumped up and curled into a ball against him. I took a mental photo and then tiptoed down the hallway and out the door.

It was a slow day at Kell's. At five, I went to the market and got all my favorites: wine, cheese, strawberries, and chocolate. I was going to play some music and indulge, alone. When I walked in, Will stood up abruptly from the couch and reached out to grab my bags.

"Let me help."

"When do you go to work?" I asked while handing over the groceries.

"I don't work Fridays, in case we have gigs, and there was nothing tonight."

"Oh. No barhopping with the boys?"

"I work in a bar, Mia, and I play in bars. It's kind of nice to be home at night once in a while." He paused and asked without a trace of sarcasm, "Is that okay?"

"Yeah, of course. So you'll probably want to have some quiet time and hit the hay, then?"

"Actually, I thought maybe we could have that coffee. You know, just as friends."

"I have wine," I said.

"Even better."

I started to cut up the strawberries and cheese and spread our feast out on a platter along with the chocolate, some almonds, and a few crackers.

"Yum, that's the best," Will said, eyeballing the plate.

"Yeah, it's great with wine."

"It's great with anything; it would be great with tequila."

"I don't know about that."

"No, seriously, I'll show you." He disappeared to his bedroom then came strolling down the hallway with a big smile and a bottle of Patrón.

I took in Will's appearance. He was wearing baggy, faded blue cargo shorts low on his hips along with his usual belt and a plain white V-neck T-shirt. He had just a tiny sprinkle of chest hair. Barefoot and unshaven, he looked hot.

He found glasses in the first cabinet he opened. He poured us each a shot, grabbed a piece of cheese off the platter, and popped it into his mouth. He swallowed, held his glass up, winked at me, then shot it back.

"That's perfect! Now your turn."

I grabbed a piece of cheese, ate it, and then drank the tequila, slower than recommended, I'm sure. "Gross! That was disgusting. Your theory sucks, Will."

"I know, I just thought we needed an icebreaker."

I rolled my eyes at him and he playfully elbowed me.

I opened the bottle of red wine and poured us each a glass. Will put a Muddy Waters record on from my father's collection. I stood in the kitchen while he sat at the bar on the other side of the counter.

"I would've never been able to find a room for this price, especially where I could play my guitar. I just wanted to say thanks again. I really appreciate this."

"You're welcome. It's nice to have the company and I think Jackson will appreciate it, too. By the way, I wanted to ask if you can take him out when you're around if I'm not here?"

"Of course. I'd be happy to. I love dogs. I always wanted one growing up, but my parents didn't need another mouth to feed, you know?"

"Yeah, no kidding."

We continued chatting for a while. I went off to my room to change into sweats and my favorite old, faded Clash T-shirt. When I came back out, he smiled at me and said, "You're cute. This is gonna be like a slumber party, huh?"

I rolled my eyes. "Not exactly."

We polished off the wine and I reached for another bottle. I wondered if it was a good idea, but we seemed to be getting along really well and we were keeping it clean, so I figured why not. During the song "I'm Your Hoochie Coochie Man," Will pulled a harmonica out of his pocket and played along perfectly to the music. I felt inspired and a little tipsy, so I went over to the piano and played some slow boogie-woogie blues along to the song. He walked up next to me like he was going to sit, so I stood and turned the piano bench perpendicular, allowing him to sit behind me. It's too hard to play when someone is seated right next to me at the piano. We sat back to back. When the song ended, I started right into a medley of famous blues songs while he accompanied me with the harmonica. We continued drinking the second bottle of wine on the couch.

He sat down next to me with his acoustic guitar and said, "This is a song called 'Little Mia.'" Then he smiled really big. As soon as he started playing, I knew it was the song "Little Martha" by The Allman Brothers.

I laughed. "You're a cheater." He winked at me, but I was quickly distracted by his playing. I looked down at the angel wing tattoo as he plucked the guitar strings. I could see the muscles in his forearm moving; his strong and accurate fingers played the song perfectly. He watched me intently the entire time while I thought about other uses for his skilled hands.

When he finished the song, my chest was tight and I felt that familiar ache I got in his presence. "Play something for me," he said.

"I think I'm too drunk."

"That's the best time."

"Okay." I stumbled over to the piano and sat down at the edge of the still-perpendicular bench. I couldn't even see straight as I started fumbling over the keys. The melody for the Tori Amos song "Icicle" started to form and I leaned forward to concentrate. I played the haunting parts haphazardly and loud. I got completely lost in the moment and began mumbling something from the song about feeling the words. I was feeling it, that's for sure. I was feeling it right on the edge of the piano bench until I realized Will was gawking. He looked completely stupefied and then he smiled really big. I felt my face flush and my heart race.

I immediately stopped playing and in a very determined voice I said, "I'm going to bed. Good night, Will."

"Good night," he murmured breathlessly.

As I stood up, I tripped over my own lame feet and fell smack on my face in the hallway. "Ow! Fuck!" He was at my side in a second, hoisting me up. When I stood, I noticed he had a curious look in his eyes. He grabbed my chin with his index finger and thumb and tilted my head up.

"You okay, baby?" he said with a crooked, cocky smirk. *Oh, that sexy smile.* I couldn't even respond. I just stared up at him, mouth slightly open. He closed his eyes and leaned in to kiss me, but instead his face met the palm of my hand.

"Jesus Christ, Mia, I was just gonna kiss you."

"No, Will, this is what I mean. We have to keep it just friends."

Then it happened. I said something I wished I could take back as soon as it came out of my mouth. "You're not even my type!" He looked shattered and dumbfounded. I stalked off to my room feeling nauseous, embarrassed, but, more than anything, scared that I had hurt him for no good reason.

TRACK 4: Cheers, Baby

The next morning I was awakened by Jenny plopping down forcefully onto my bed. I covered my face with the blanket, shielding my eyes from the light. "Mia, it reeks of alcohol in here."

"Yes, I had a few drinks last night," I said, moaning.

"Is that why Will tried to kiss you?"

"What?" I shot out of bed, then collapsed right back onto it from the sudden head rush.

"How'd you know that? How'd you get in here?"

"Will buzzed me in and then he left. He left you a note on the counter."

"Where'd he go?" I scrunched my eyebrows.

"I don't know, but he looks dashing in a suit."

"Will has a suit?" I directed the question back at myself. "I need to see this note." I rushed toward the kitchen. I was feeling my stupidity from the night before. Not only did I hurt physically, but I was also suffering from a major moral hangover. I shouldn't have been so mean to Will. I could have told him how I desperately wanted to lick his arms while he played the guitar, or how tempting his mouth was during our moment in the hallway. I could have told him how I felt and then explained that I wanted to keep it simple and that's why we couldn't sleep together. Instead, I was a jerk.

Will's note was on a coffee filter, printed in perfect block letters.

HEY, ROOMIE,
SORRY I TRIED TO KISS YOU LAST NIGHT,
YOU WERE JUST SO DAMN CUTE. IT WON'T
HAPPEN AGAIN. I HAD FUN, THOUGH. LOVED
YOUR SHOW... WINK.

I was relieved but strangely disappointed that he was relatively unfazed by my rejection. Visions of Will traipsing random, faceless women back to his room ran through my mind. I dry heaved, but I knew if we were going to be strictly friends, then I would have to accept him bringing women home. My mind wandered to where debonair Will in his suit might have gone that morning. Jenny came in and snapped me out of it.

"Geez, what kind of show did you put on?" she asked, looking over my shoulder at the note.

"It was nothing. I just played a few songs for him."

"Why don't you like Will?"

"Jenny, I like Will fine, but I don't want to date an almost thirty-year-old, struggling musician who rents a room from me for four hundred dollars a month."

"Oh, so that's what this is about? He doesn't make enough money for you. Hmm, you don't really seem like the type to care about that, but I guess you do." She smiled sarcastically at me.

"Jenny, I'm just like everyone else. I want to meet a man who is a team player. Not someone who is swept up in his feelings and art. Besides, I don't even think Will likes me; he's just a guy in a band who will sleep with anyone."

She studied me with a tolerant expression, then said, "Whatever you say, Mia. I'm going down to Kell's." Heading for the door, she glanced up at a picture of my father, stalked over to it, and kissed it. "See ya, Pops."

I knew Pops loved Jenny because he had talked so highly of her. I felt like she was sort of my father's parting gift to me. She was a good friend, a straight shooter. She didn't kiss my ass because I was her boss. I would need that honesty to make it through my time here.

Later, I popped into Kell's. It was another slow day for the café, so I took a seat and nursed my hangover with some herbal tea. I spent the whole afternoon staring out the window, people-watching and eavesdropping on Paddy and Joe.

"Have you been takin' your pills, Paddy?"

"I have, Joe."

"And have you had your levels checked again?"

"I have."

"Jesus Christ, Paddy, are you goin' to make me ask you a hundred questions?"

"Don't worry about me. I'm eighty-seven years young, can still move like the Lord of the Dance, and I haven't smoked in twenty-five years. I'm fine."

"I think you need to diversify your activities, is all I'm sayin'. You know I've been doing that yoga stuff with Beverly over at the senior center?"

There was a long pause. I turned to read Paddy's expression. He looked thoroughly disappointed. "But we're Catholic, Joe."

Suppressing laughter, I stood up, turned toward the two brothers and smiled. Joe grinned from ear to ear and then, loud enough for me to hear, said to Paddy, "Isn't Alan's girl a beauty?"

"That she is, brother."

I mouthed a thank-you to my father's old friends and then waved to Martha and Jenny before heading home. Robert and

Jacob would be arriving shortly for the lesson, so I threw on a sweater, jeans, and some Converse. I cleaned the apartment a bit before sitting on the couch to wait. I noticed Will must have been home because he'd set the mail on the counter. I was surprised I hadn't seen him walk by Kell's. I hoped he wasn't avoiding me.

When the buzzer rang, I immediately hit the button to open the door. I ran over to the phone and dialed Sheil.

"Hello?"

"Sheil, I have people coming up for a lesson; I just wanted to let someone know."

"Okay, darling. Do you want me to come down there?"

"No, but if I don't call you in an hour, send the troops. Love ya." I hung up and ran to the door. I opened it before Robert had a chance to knock.

"Hi, Jacob, I'm Mia," I said to the little guy. "Come on in."

"It's a pleasure to meet you, Mia." Jacob was way too mature for a preschooler.

"Hi, Mia."

I looked up at Robert. He was wearing a sincere smile. "Okay, let's get started. Come on over to the piano, Jacob, and have a seat. Robert, can I offer you something to drink?"

Robert was standing between the two couches. He was looking down, examining the coffee-table books. He didn't answer me for a whole twenty seconds and then his head shot up as though he'd just realized that I'd asked him a question.

"Oh, no thank you, I'm fine," he said as he pushed the books around on the table. Apparently nothing jumped out at him because he sat down and began scrolling around on his phone.

"*A Photographer's Life*, the Annie Leibovitz one, is really good. You know her? She's done a lot of work for *Vanity Fair*."

He shook his head. "I'm fine, thanks."

There were so many interesting options on the table that I was really surprised nothing sparked Robert's interest. Along with the Annie Leibovitz book, there was *Cecil Beaton: The New York Years* and a book called *Def Jam Recordings: The First 25 Years of the Last Great Record Label*. On top of the three books, there was the latest issue of *The New Yorker* along with a copy of *Guitar* magazine that Will had left. I shrugged, then turned around to stand behind Jacob at the piano.

"Okay, little man, let's get started." I showed him a couple of fun exercises to build dexterity in his fingers. He liked making the steady sounds, even if it wasn't in the form of a song yet. He swung his feet under the bench and laughed as he pounded on the keys. He told me his mom really wanted him to learn to play. I said his mom was a smart cookie and that I'd teach him everything I knew. Just then Robert stood up and walked over beside me.

"Why don't you play something, Mia? You know, so Jacob can hear a finished product." The words "a finished product" struck me as odd, but I proceeded to sit down next to Jacob, who didn't move from the center of the bench. I shimmied a bit, trying to get enough space to reach the pedals comfortably. Robert was clearly more interested in watching me play than hearing me play because he stood directly over me. With Jacob right next to me and Robert hovering, I decided on an easy piece since I probably wouldn't be able to play well anyway. Just as I began playing Erik Satie's Gymnopédie No.1, Robert spoke up. "Watch what she's doing, Jacob." Jacob looked like he was frantically trying to remember every move my fingers made.

In a low voice I said, "Jacob, close your eyes and just . . . listen." Jacob closed his eyes while I played the slow-moving song with resolute attention. Even though Gymnopédie No. 1 is an easy piece consisting mainly of a one-note melody and very little rhythmic complication, it has always evoked great emotion in me. I hoped it would for my audience as well. Jacob and Robert remained quiet while I continued. Once I finished, they both clapped, Jacob a little more enthusiastically than Robert.

I coached Jacob while he made several futile attempts at re-creating the song I had played. "Jacob, I want you to practice the exercises I showed you earlier. When your fingers are strong enough, you can play just like me, okay?"

He nodded and then looked up at his father. "You'll learn, kiddo, just do as she tells you."

I could almost feel the expectations little Jacob had riding on his four-year-old shoulders. It was reminiscent of how I'd felt at that age. My lessons in Ann Arbor were rigorous. The joy and reprieve came when I was in New York playing alongside my father. I felt the desire to give Jacob that experience, so I began playing the most enthusiastic version of "Chopsticks" I knew how and Jacob joined right in until we were making a beautiful but terrible noise. Robert shot me a slightly disapproving look.

We kept pounding on the keys for another few minutes until I finally gave in. "I think that's it for today." I stood up from the bench and headed toward the door. Jacob scurried out onto the landing and Robert turned toward me and smiled.

"The learning has to be fun or he won't want to continue," I said kindly.

Robert smiled. "It was really good, Mia. I think Jacob will enjoy this. Dana, his mom, is going to be thrilled."

"So this wasn't your idea?"

"Well, I have Jacob every other weekend and his mom has been urging me to get him into some kind of activity. I suggested tennis but she thought piano would be better for him. I think maybe she's right." I sensed a double meaning from his expression. "Did you study music in college?" he asked.

"No, I took lessons growing up and I guess I just stuck with it," I said. He nodded his head and smiled kindly. I knew the next part would get him. "I actually have a business degree from Brown."

He came to life. "You're kidding me? I did my undergrad at Brown."

I wouldn't say I was shocked, but the fact that we had the same alma mater was something of a coincidence.

We continued talking about college and then Robert called Jacob back into the apartment so we could talk some more. We realized we weren't at Brown together because Robert was eight years older than me. He'd been divorced for two years and was living in an apartment on the Upper West Side, but his ex and Jacob lived in Greenwich Village, which explained why he was down in my neck of the woods the day we met in the café. He told me how Jacob loves the playground at Tompkins Square Park and how he'd been popping into Kell's for a couple of years.

I basically told him my life story in a matter of minutes. He said he remembered meeting my dad once and that he was sorry for my loss. You could have knocked me over with a feather when Robert told me he was a vice president at J.P. Morgan. He was getting better by the minute. I thought he must be the most successful thirty-three-year-old I knew. Then the conversation shifted.

"Mia, I'm really impressed that you're taking over your dad's business and I think it's cool that you have this little hobby." He pointed to the piano. "I feel a lot better about Jacob taking lessons now."

I knew what he meant and I can't say I totally disagreed. He didn't want Jacob messing around with something that would take him nowhere, but the way he said "little hobby" just irked me. I thought about telling Robert that I loved music and it was a huge part of my life, but instead I just nodded my head and smiled. I couldn't believe he would think a child taking piano lessons could possibly be a bad thing. I decided to overlook his little blunder and focus on the fact that he was a good-looking, successful guy with hopes and dreams for his son.

When Jacob started getting antsy, Robert said they'd better go. I reached out to shake his hand. He took my hand in his and held it up. For a second, it looked like he was inspecting my fingernails or debating what to do next. Then he looked right into my eyes and gently kissed my knuckles. He lingered there long enough that when he released my hand, I felt the air touch a hint of moisture left from his lips.

"Maybe we can grab a bite sometime?"

"I would love that," I said in a low voice, somewhat shocked by the gesture.

"I'll call you." Just as he reached the stairs, he turned around. "Oh, I almost forgot, how much do I owe you?"

"Just dinner."

He nodded. "I'll make it worth it," he said and then jogged down the stairs.

When I closed the door, I leaned against it and exhaled audibly. I thought about the events that had just transpired. I felt giddy and excited over the prospect of going on a date with Robert, but I couldn't help but wonder why his marriage had failed.

The next two days flew by. I saw Will once on Monday as we passed each other on the stairs. "What up?"

"Yo!" I said as I high-fived him. I heard him chuckle behind me as he headed out to the street.

On Tuesday, I spotted a new bottle of my spring-rain body wash on the counter with a note next to it.

HEY ROOMIE,
I NOTICED YOU WERE GETTING LOW. WINK.

My heart skipped a beat. I couldn't tell if Will was flirting or if he was being friendly or if it was all the same to him, but I knew I liked it either way.

When I got home on Tuesday, he was sitting on the couch with his head back, eyes closed, listening to music and looking beautiful. "How was your day?" he said, his eyes still closed.

"Pretty good." I loved the fact that there was always music playing in our apartment. Either it was a new playlist on the iPod, a record or CD on the stereo, or one of us jamming away on an instrument. "This is great. Who is this?" I asked.

"It's Bon Iver; the album is amazing. He recorded the whole thing in a little cabin in the Wisconsin woods," he said, finally opening his eyes and looking at me.

"I can tell. The resonance seems totally organic."

Will's head shot back. "That's exactly what I thought."

I sat down on the couch next to him. He reached down and scooped up my feet at the ankles, then brought my legs over his lap, turning my body in the process. I was still sitting up awkwardly.

"Lay your head back; let's listen," he said, and I knew his intentions were pure. I put my head back on a throw pillow and closed my eyes. His hands rested on my lower legs, positioned across his thighs. During certain songs, he would gently drum the beat on my shins. Every time he did it, I couldn't help but smile and peek up at him. His eyes remained closed; he was totally in the moment, in the music . . . I loved it.

We listened to the whole CD like that. Eyes closed, not saying a word. When it started to play over again, we both opened our eyes. Will looked down at me with a tiny smile touching one side of his mouth. He had peace in his eyes, or maybe it was desire.

"What's the name of the album?" I asked.

"*For Emma, Forever Ago*," he said.

Lucky girl.

"Hey, where'd you take off to Saturday morning? Jenny said you were in a suit?" I didn't want to bring up anything that might lead into a discussion of my little gaffe on Friday, but I was dying to know about suited-up Will.

He smirked and laughed lightly. "Oh yeah, the suit. We all have matching suits. The guys from the band and I do weddings sometimes. Minus Pete of course—we just do instrumental stuff, you know? Saturday was crazy; we played for like seven hours and then partied with the bridesmaids until the maid of honor passed out and tossed her cookies all over Dustin's lap."

"Oh." I felt a touch of irritation at the possible meaning of "partied with the bridesmaids."

Will got up. "I'll show you a picture."

Great, I hope he doesn't think I want to see some picture of a bunch of blitzed girls wearing taffeta, or, worse, blitzed girls wearing nothing.

I stood up and walked toward the kitchen table where he was scrolling through his phone. When I approached, he held the phone out, showing me the screen. It was a photo of the three guys with their suits on and instruments in hand. Will had the black Gibson, Nate a stand-up bass, and Dustin a set

of bongos. They all looked serenely self-possessed and professional; I was quite impressed. They were seated in a half circle
next to a rustic gazebo. I could see other instruments in the
photo. Leaning against Will's chair was a ukulele and, next to
Dustin, a steel drum. I hoped I would get to see the guys play
at a wedding someday.

"I had no idea, Will. This is so cool."

He grinned sheepishly. "It's just for extra money and we
get to play all types of music—it's pretty fun."

As I walked over to sit next to him at the table, I stubbed
my toe. Searing pain shot through me. "Fuck!" I hopped on
one foot. Will stood up and pulled my chair out so I could sit.
He sat back down and, without saying a word, grabbed my
bare foot and put pressure on all five toes, relieving the pain.
He was analyzing my expression. I had my bottom lip tucked
entirely into my mouth using my top teeth.

He smiled. "You okay, baby?" I shook my head yes. "Is
'fuck' your favorite swear word?" It occurred to me that I
cursed like a sailor around Will and I had no idea why. I paused
at the thought and then figured, why stop now?

"No, definitely not." I took a breath. The pain had sub-
sided but Will was still holding my foot in his lap. He started
giving me a foot massage; it felt divine. "There are at least five
swear words I like better than fuck. My favorites are compound
words like apeshit, craphat or batshit, but above all, my numero
uno, all-time favorite swear word is assclown, without a doubt.
Asshat runs a close second. I must say, very few things give me
greater pleasure than calling someone an assclown when they
really fit the bill. I love it more than puppies and baby seals."

Will laughed hysterically. He calmed down and shook his
head back and forth. Still smirking, he said, "Mia, you are
such an enigma." I think I felt the same about Will.

Moments later he got up to get ready. He left around seven to go to work at the bar. Our little hangout session was a success. No drinking, no slips, just getting to know each other as friends. I didn't mention Robert to Will; I figured that was my business.

I didn't see Will at all on Wednesday, but I heard him. When the café slowed down, I walked over to Sam's to pick up our weekly order of cannolis. Denise, the owner, has been making the delectable pastries since 1979, and we'd been stocking them in the cooler at Kell's ever since. Sam's was quiet except for the muffled guitar sound coming through the ceiling. Will was playing something. I couldn't put my finger on the tune, but it made me smile and it made Wednesday a good day.

TRACK 5: Religion

The next morning, I sat at the breakfast bar to paint my nails, or attempt to, anyway. Will came into the kitchen for a cup of coffee. He was wearing black jeans and a plain black T-shirt. His wallet chain jingled as he moved about the kitchen. Black on black on a man made my fingers tingle. Black on black on Will did more. I focused on my nails.

"Good morning, roomie. Aren't you usually at Kell's by now?"

Staring down, I answered, "I'm going in late. It's poetry night and Jenny wants me to meet some guy she's into. I guess he does slam poetry or something."

"Yeah, Tyler, he's my guy."

"You know him?"

"He's my best friend. He's awesome. You know he's like eight feet tall, right?"

Will had a way of speaking where even though his exaggerations were obvious, it seemed as if he truly believed what he was saying. It was as though Will's perception really was reality. He probably barely knew Tyler, and Tyler was probably six-five. "Where have I been?"

He eyed me speculatively. "I don't know. Here, let me do that." He took the polish out of my hand, and I made no argument. As he painted my nails quickly, he hummed a mindless tune. There wasn't a single smudge or streak. Once again, Will proved he had extremely competent hands.

"Impressive, Will," I said, admiring his work.

"Eleven sisters, remember?" He leaned across the bar, pushed on the front of my nose with his index finger, and said, "Boop. Gotta go, sweet thing."

He grabbed his guitar and headed out the door, humming away. I sat at the bar until my heart slowed down to a reasonable pace.

Later that day at Kell's, Jenny told me everything about Tyler. I knew they had been dating for a couple of weeks and she was already head over heels, but our shifts hadn't been overlapping enough for me to get all the details. Jenny said Tyler wrote website content for a living. I laughed when she described it as prolific writing. She scowled at me and said, "Yeah, I know he's not exactly Faulkner, okay, but he does write poetry and that's some romantic shit." In the short time I had known Jenny, it was obvious to me that even though she could be goofy and fun loving, she knew exactly who she was and took herself seriously. It was a quality that underlied her confidence, and one I admired and envied.

Jenny had been at Kell's for so long because my dad paid her well. Pops barely made any money from the café. In fact, there were years in the recent past where Kell's actually lost money because Pops continued giving health benefits and raises to his employees. They were like family to him, and they were becoming my family, too. Because my father owned the buildings that housed Kell's, Sam's, and my and Sheil's apartments, he was able to keep the café afloat and live pretty comfortably on the rental income. He didn't care if Kell's made money; he was just determined to keep it open because it meant so much to so many people. Jenny saw that loyalty in my father and she continued working for him, and now me. The income at Kell's was enough to live on for her, and the schedule gave her the freedom to pursue other projects. She designed websites, mostly for people she knew with small businesses, and she coached a little kid's soccer team on the weekends. I knew Jenny and Martha were in it for the long haul with me, which motivated me to start making decisions.

I was making up my mind about what to do, but there were still questions. I knew I would keep the café open, stay in my father's apartment for now, and teach piano lessons. But then what? I wanted more. I wondered if I could finally put that business degree to use. I thought maybe I would get to know Robert and he could help me. I made a short list of things I would need to do, starting with reading *The Wall Street Journal* and ending with buying a suit, none of which were accomplished in any reasonable amount of time.

The big life questions ran through my mind on a continuous loop at times. It seemed like the only reprieve I felt from my stresses was when I was with Will.

Just before the poetry group arrived, I got a phone call from my mom saying she had booked a flight for Thursday of the following week.

The café door jingled and in walked Will, wearing a cheeky grin. He was followed by a thin, extremely tall man who looked like he stood at least seven feet tall. Not eight, though. Will introduced me to Tyler. During my conversation with Will that morning, he'd only mentioned that he knew Tyler, but Will hadn't said he would be at Kell's that night. I wondered if he showed because he knew I would be there. Then again, maybe Tyler really was his best friend.

Tyler was overly formal and polite to me; he mentioned how much Jenny loved her job, and I realized that Tyler saw me as Jenny's boss. I thought it was sweet that he was trying to impress me. Jenny came out from the back and went straight into Tyler's insanely long arms. They seemed really happy.

Everyone sat down and Will asked for a vanilla latte. He tried to pay me, but I wouldn't take it. I made his coffee with care and I even made a little heart design in the foam, the only design I knew how to make. Still, I worried what he would think. When I brought Will his coffee, he looked at the heart for a long second and then gave me a simple thank-you and took a sip. I didn't want to confuse him or send the wrong message, but he was so sweet to me, I felt like I should be the same to him. Even though he could get my blood pumping with a simple look or smile, I figured the only way to have him in my life for a long time would be through friendship. Like Martha and Pops.

Tyler and Jenny kept up the PDA throughout the night. When Tyler got up to do his slam, Jenny whistled really loudly and over-the-top, soccer-coach loud. I didn't fully understand Tyler's poem—I think it was about New York and love in the big city. We all clapped wildly for him. With a shy smile he walked over to Jenny and buried his face in her neck. I looked over at Will from time to time. He was making friends with everyone in the café. The word "gregarious" came to mind when I saw him from a distance, telling stories so animatedly. At one point several patrons began urging him to get up and do some inspired poetry off the cuff. I heard him repeating, "In time, my people, in time."

For some reason I found Will's arrogance charming. That quality in a man never appealed to me, but I think because I'd witnessed Will's vulnerability on the plane and in the hallway that night, the arrogance just seemed cute. After everyone left, Jenny and I discussed Tyler's poem and her relationship with him. It was obvious by the way Jenny spoke that she and Tyler were on the fast track. After seeing them interact that night, it made perfect sense to me.

I went home to Jackson and an otherwise empty apartment. As I dozed off, I wondered where Will was. The thought gave me a gloomy feeling. I told myself that Will was simply my roommate, he owed me nothing aside from rent, and I shouldn't be keeping tabs on him. Then my mind wandered to Robert. Why hadn't he called?

Friday morning, I snatched the Bon Iver CD from the living room to play it in my room. Walking down the hall, I noticed Will's door was cracked a smidgen, the same way it had been the night before, and I figured he hadn't come home. I sprawled out on my bed wearing nothing but a T-shirt and underwear. Propping my hands behind my head, I closed my eyes and imagined the CD I was listening to was called *For Mia, Forever Ago*. I reveled in the feeling of being alone in my apartment and I let my mind wander to the fantasy. I opened my eyes for a second and was startled when I saw Will standing in the doorway, shirtless. His eyes, full of curiosity, met mine. I didn't attempt to cover up. I just remained expressionless. He glanced up and down my body and then I saw his mouth curl up into a tiny, sexy smile.

"Hi, Will. Whatcha doin', buddy?" I was trying hard to keep it light.

He slowly drank me in again before responding. "Just praying," he whispered and then walked out. I flew out of bed and threw on some sweats. It bummed me out that I didn't get more time to ogle Will standing in my doorway shirtless, wearing nothing but a pair of jeans and that silver-studded belt. I thought maybe I could get another look, but when I reached the kitchen, he had thrown on a T-shirt.

"Nice sweats. How 'bout some French toast?"

"Sounds yummy."

While Will made breakfast, I perused my father's record collection, looking for something fun to play. I settled on *The Divine Miss M*. I slid the record out of the sleeve, placed it in the record player, and set the needle on the first track, "Do You Want to Dance." Once the song started, Will shot me a huge grin. I danced back toward the kitchen and poured myself a cup of coffee, whirling around behind him as he stood at the stove cooking. When he turned to me, I pointed at him and sang the chorus, asking him to dance in my best Bette Midler impression.

He grabbed my hand and twirled me around, then dipped me and made a tiger growling sound against my neck, mock-biting it. Will could dance and, if I remember correctly, someone told me once to stay away from a man who could dance. In that moment, I couldn't understand why anyone would say that. I giggled, pushed Will back toward the stove, and took a seat at the bar. He handed me a plate of French toast with maple syrup, blueberries, and bananas. At first bite, I literally almost cried. I looked at him, my voice deadpan. "This is the best fucking French toast I have ever had," I said as a tear of joy formed in my eye.

He smiled appreciatively and then chuckled at my dramatics. "It's my mama's recipe. The key is real French bread and a couple of secrets I can't share or I'd have to kill you."

We finished our breakfast. I cleaned up and thanked Will, then went back to my room to get ready for the day. As I headed toward the front door to leave, he shouted from his bedroom, "Bye, roomie! Hey, we're playing at the Raucous Room in Brooklyn tonight if you and Jenny want to come by."

"Maybe." I walked out the door shouting, "Later, Wilbur!" and then trotted down the stairs filled with excitement to hear Will play again.

Jenny worked the morning shift with me at Kell's. We were slammed so we didn't talk much. When the phone rang, Jenny grabbed it. "It's a beautiful morning at Kell's!" She looked over at me. "Sure, hold on a sec." She rolled her eyes and handed me the phone.

"Hello?"

"Hello, Mia. It's Robert."

"Oh hey, Robert. Don't you have my house number?"

"I seemed to have misplaced that. I hope it's okay that I called you here?"

Why does this guy keep losing my number? He took two little number tabs and he had already called me once. Not a very VP banker thing to do.

"Yeah, it's fine. How are you?"

"I'm great. So, since Jacob is with his mom this weekend, I thought we could get dinner tomorrow? I could pick you up at seven."

"Okay," I said, even though I couldn't tell if he was asking me or telling me.

When I hung up, I looked over at Jenny, who was eyeing me derisively.

"What?"

"Nothing. It's just, he waited until Friday to call you for a date on Saturday? I mean, the guy is good-looking and he has a great career but . . . I don't know. I think . . . " As she fumbled over her words, I stood there looking dejected. "I'm sorry, Mia. I don't want to ruin it for you."

"No, I appreciate your honesty, but I'm just having dinner with him, that's all." I moved to change the subject. "Hey, do you want to go see The Ivans at The Depot tonight?"

"I can't. Tyler is taking me out for a special dinner." She shrugged her shoulders, like she had no idea what that meant.

"No worries."

After work I decided to go see The Ivans on my own. I sat at the bar and made small talk with the female bartender while I sipped on my vodka-soda-cran. A crowd of scantily clad twenty-one-year-olds started forming in front of the stage just as the band began to play. The set they played was similar to the one I'd seen before, except they slipped in a new instrumental song about halfway through.

Pete introduced the song. "This is a song I'm working on. I'm still looking for that magic inspiration to write some lyrics—maybe one of you ladies can help me out?"

Several times we heard "woo-hoo" and "yeah, baby" from the group of bimbos at the front. I recognized the music right away; it was the song I heard through the ceiling at Sam's. The song was beautiful and evocative, even without lyrics. Will's solo wasn't the typical solo; it was slow, bluesy, and delicate. His adroit hands played it without hesitation. During that song, Will looked out to the audience for the first time. Within two seconds his eyes met mine.

After the show, he set his guitar down and walked through the crowd toward me. I saw him thanking people who were high-fiving and patting him on the back. When he reached the bar, he looked around before speaking. "Hey, thanks for coming. Are you alone?" I nodded my head. "How'd you get here?"

"Subway."

He narrowed his eyes. There was a long pause and then he looked back toward the stage and waved good-bye to the rest of the band. "Ready?" he said as he stuck his hand out for me to take.

"What? I can get home on my own. Don't you want to stay with the guys?"

He shook his head slightly. "No, I'm done and we're going to the same place. Might as well go together, right?" He was uncharacteristically serious.

"What about your guitar?"

"Dustin will get it."

"Okay." I took his hand. As he led me toward the door, I looked back at the stage and saw Nate, the bassist, watching us. A tiny smirk played on his face.

We walked toward the subway, still hand in hand. When I gently removed my hand from his, he turned around and smiled. His expression said *You're cute, but we're just holding hands.* Again, I reminded myself that I needed to keep things straight.

"You guys were good tonight, except Pete. He still sucks."

"Yeah, I can't believe that guy. The new song is *not* his. It's *so* not his."

"He's such . . . " At the same time we both snapped out, "An assclown!"

Will laughed and grabbed my hand, pulling me onto the subway train. It was crowded and there were no seats open, so we stood near the door. He held onto the bar above his head as he leaned over me. He might have been sweating all night, but he still had the yummy Will smell with just a hint of muskiness. It was arousing. We stood two inches apart, facing each other. I held onto the pole next to me with one hand and gripped Will's free arm with my other. The way Will stood over me, with his head dropped down slightly, made me feel protected. I could feel his breath on my neck.

"Mia," he said, just loud enough for me to hear. "At night . . . don't ride the subway alone, okay?" I nodded my head and then closed the two-inch gap.

Once inside the apartment, we both headed toward our rooms. We paused at the end of the hall and turned toward each other. With a wink Will said, "Night, roomie."

"Night, Will."

Saturday morning, Will was gone before I got up. I got dressed and grabbed Jackson's leash to take him out. Normally, the moment I touched the leash the eighty-pound dog would practically leap into my arms, but that morning he wouldn't budge from his doggy pillow. I tried to move him; he just sat there staring sadly at me. It was clear he wasn't feeling well. I thought about taking him to the vet, but he was thirteen and at that point his problems had more to do with his age than a specific illness, so I decided to make him comfortable and cook up some chicken and rice for him. By two p.m., Jackson was up and about, almost back to himself. By four he was ready for a run through the park. The little episode scared me, but it seemed to be over as quickly as it started.

Robert picked me up and we had dinner at a fancy French restaurant on the Upper East Side. It was unusually hot for May in New York, so I wore a gray pleated skirt and a white, sleeveless, button-down blouse. It was a tad naughty schoolgirl, but I wasn't going for that. I felt underdressed at dinner until Robert complimented my outfit. I decided to let my insecurities go. He was dressed in a gray suit with a white shirt and striped tie. It looked a little too business-professional for a date, but it was a nice suit and he looked handsome. We had a less than interesting conversation about hedge funds, most of which flew over my head. I swirled my soup around and Robert devoured steak frites and foie gras, which wasn't my thing, to say the least. He was a true gentleman with exemplary manners, and even though I wasn't hanging on his every word, I thought his enthusiasm about banking was cute.

Afterward, he hailed a cab and rode back to the East Village with me. When we reached my building, he told the cabbie to wait so he could walk me to the door. I asked him to come in. I figured Will was playing a wedding since he'd been gone all day. We entered the dark apartment, and I was relieved when Jackson came to greet us. Will was gone but he had obviously come home because there was a Wurlitzer 200A electric piano resting against the wall next to the front door. I spotted a note on the counter:

NATE WAS GETTING RID OF THE WURLY
AND I THOUGHT YOU COULD HAVE SOME FUN
WITH IT.

Robert saw me smile at Will's thoughtfulness. "What's that all about?"

"My roommate Will is a musician and he brought this electric piano home for me."

"Will?" I think he was surprised I had a male roommate.

"Yeah, Will. We're just friends," I said hurriedly.

I changed the subject to my life in Ann Arbor, which was much more Robert's speed. I let him follow me to my room so I could show him a picture of my mom.

"She's beautiful, like you," he said as he leaned in to kiss me. He wasn't a bad kisser—it just seemed like his tongue was really big. My head was not where it should have been. I was thinking about the logistics of the kiss instead of enjoying it. I pulled his body into mine as I leaned back on top of the short dresser and ran my hands up behind his head, letting my fingers move through his hair. The moment intensified as he unbuttoned the top three buttons of my blouse so my lacy bra peeked out. Our kiss went deeper, then his mouth went to the crook of my neck and I moaned appreciatively. He grabbed my leg behind my knee, hitching it up as he slowly ran his hand under my thigh to my bottom, lifting my skirt in the process. It felt good to have a man's hand on my ass.

"Knock, knock," Will said, standing in the open doorway. Robert and I abruptly stopped and took a step away from each other. I adjusted my skirt and looked down at my open shirt, deciding I would draw more attention to it if I tried to button it up. "Sorry to interrupt. Shall I close this door for you?" Will asked, expressionless. He looked directly at me when he spoke, never once glancing at Robert.

"No, no." I looked at Robert.

He looked back inquisitively. "Do you want me to go?"

I shrugged and gave him a look like *sorry, but yes.* "I'll call you about Jacob's lesson?"

He nodded. I turned away from him and came face-to-face with Will, who for some reason was still standing in my doorway. I mouthed *what?* and gave him a dirty look. His lips curled up into a ridiculous grin.

I shook my head and decided it needed to be done. "Will, this is Robert. Robert, meet Will, my roommate."

Will smiled genially and reached out to shake his hand. "Nice to meet you, man."

"Likewise." Robert eyed Will. By his look, I guessed he hadn't expected my live-in "just friend" to be so good-looking.

Will reached over and hugged me, then let his mouth brush my cheek. "Night, Mia," he whispered. I shivered. He put his hands on my shoulders and stared at my face for a second too long. His smile had faded. It was the first time I saw a hint of sadness in his eyes. His hands slid down my arms slowly and then he turned and shuffled almost aimlessly across the hall and into his room, closing the door without making even the smallest sound.

"Is he always that affectionate . . . and strange?" I heard Robert ask, but I was a million miles away, thinking about the pained look on Will's face. "Mia?"

"What? Oh yes, he's very affectionate."

"Is he really?"

"Yes . . . I mean . . . no. No, no, we're just friends," I said, trying to sound convincing even though I wasn't sure I believed the words myself.

After Robert left, I hoped that Will would come out of his room, but he didn't and I couldn't bring myself to knock on his door. I wanted to thank him for the Wurly and apologize for the awkward moment, but I didn't get to.

The next day was extremely hot. I worried about Jackson in the apartment. At noon, I decided to go check on him. He greeted me at the door and I was relieved again. I leaned against the counter in the kitchen to listen to the muffled voices and music coming from Will's room. I watched as a very petite woman came strolling down the hallway. She looked to be about fifty years old and she was either wearing a very short dress or she had no pants on. Her eyes were caked with a ton of dark makeup and she wore way too much silver jewelry. If it weren't for her inappropriate attire and slightly haggard appearance, I would have thought she was pretty. She made her way to the fridge and grabbed a beer.

"Hi, I'm Teeny." She smiled and stuck her hand out.

"I'm Mia. You're a friend of Will's, I take it?"

"Yeah, we're friends," she said seductively.

Bile began to rise in my throat. "Enjoy your beer, Teeny," I said before heading to my room. As I passed Will's room, I looked in. He was sitting on the windowsill with one leg inside and one leg out. He was smoking. He turned and looked at me impassively. I waited to see some sign on his face. It was hard to tell anything from his look, except maybe indifference, like *Can I help you,* or *What are you staring at?* Without a word, I went into my room and shut the door to collect myself. Moments later I heard Will and Teeny giggling and then I heard a little scream from Teeny. I decided to bolt out of there and head back to the café. I couldn't help but glance back through Will's open doorway as I passed. He was giving Teeny a piggyback ride, hopping around like a fucking asshat. Teeny was spinning an imaginary lasso like she was going to rope a calf. I dry heaved and then shot down the hallway and out the door.

Back at the café, Jenny had arrived. She, Martha, and Sheil were all huddled behind the counter, looking at Jenny's hand. Jenny spotted me walking toward her. "Oh my god, Tyler asked me to marry him!" she screamed ecstatically and jumped up and down.

"What? How long have you known him?" I blurted out, shocked and still pissed from the Will episode. Sheil gave me the stink eye.

"Can't you be happy for me, Mia?"

"I'm sorry," I said immediately and sincerely. "I'm having a bad day. I'm excited for you. I know you guys love each other." It was true; I just didn't understand how it was possible and how they were so sure of it.

We hugged and then Jenny asked me to be her maid of honor. I was surprised—Jenny and I hadn't known each other long, but I was honored nonetheless. As the four of us talked about planning a wedding and setting a date, my mind began to wander to the current state of my life. I couldn't help but fixate on the fact that Will was probably screwing a weird woman in our apartment.

It was quiet when I got home. I grabbed a beer, popped the top off, and began guzzling it. Will walked into the kitchen, shirtless. He stood right in front of me without a word. This time I looked directly at his chest and then slowly appraised every detail of his body. Motionless, he stared at me as I studied the large tattoo running down one side of his torso. It was a beautiful, abstract design that could have been a painting. He had another small tattoo, the words "Soul Captain" written in wispy script across his heart. I looked down at the angel wing on his forearm and decided it was the most intricate wing tattoo I had ever seen. He was wearing black jeans, the belt he always wore, and, I'm pretty sure, nothing underneath. I followed his happy trail down to his waist and let my gaze pause on his thin hips and low-slung jeans. I looked down a little farther, then lifted my head to the brazen expression on his face.

"That woman is old enough to be your mother," I said flatly.

"Keen observation." He reached around me to grab a beer from the refrigerator. "I love women, Mia, and I love my mother. Teeny and I are just friends."

"What does that have to do with anything? Bringing a sleazy woman you barely know back to the apartment to screw in the middle of the day is not very considerate of her or me or your mom, for that matter."

"Like I said, we're just friends and she's not sleazy. I've known her for a while—longer than you, in fact. She does a show in the theater next to the Montosh."

"She a stripper?" I spat out.

"Performance artist."

"Same. Thing!"

"No, it's not the same, and calm down. She went home and we were just goofing off earlier. It was a hundred degrees in here, so she took off her shorts."

"Yeah, right." I crossed my arms.

Will shook his head at me before leaving the kitchen. As he headed down the hallway he shouted back at me, "I didn't have sex with her, not that it's any of your business. I didn't even kiss her. We're just friends." This time when he said "we're just friends," I couldn't tell if he meant us or him and Teeny. Either way, I was wrong for criticizing him. He got in one last dig, "By the way, how's Banker Bob?" Then he slammed his door before I could respond.

I knew it wasn't fair to denigrate Will for having a friend over, especially when the night before I'd left the door open and basically dry humped the banker on my dresser.

TRACK 6: You Get That, Right?

Things were getting weird at the apartment, so I knew I had to lay low for a while. Will must have felt the same because I didn't see him for days. We finally caught each other on a Wednesday afternoon before he went to work. We played music together and he kept telling me to stop keeping time, to shut out the noise and just feel the changes. He played everything by ear without regard for technique. Music was about feeling to him; it was purely innate. When I played the way he showed me, the sound was fuller and rich with emotion. I was learning a lot from his instinctive interpretations of songs. Even though I was classically trained, he was much more talented, even with no training at all. It was like a divine gift, or it was his passion that had manifested into the gift. After every session with Will, I felt like I had purged all the negativity or stress I was feeling that day. As I sat, still tinkering on the piano, Will stopped next to me before heading out for work. He bent down, kissed the top of my head, and said, "You're so good and you don't even know it. Night, baby." The minute he closed the door, my eyes welled up . . . My father used to tell me the same thing.

My mom flew in the following day. She took a taxi to Kell's. I let her hold me in the café kitchen for what seemed like an hour. We'd missed each other. She looked the same with her light brown bob, not a hair out of place, and some variation of a business-casual pantsuit. She always dressed conservatively and mostly wore earth tones; she thought it softened her lawyer energy, but I thought it just made her look like the Republican that she wasn't.

That afternoon, around a small table in the back of the café, my mom and I sat with Sheil and Martha and reminisced about my father. We told stories, laughed, cried, and hugged each other over and over between cranking up the loud espresso machine and serving our short supply of customers. I gave my mother the key to my apartment and warned her about Will. I expected some kind of "inviting musicians to live with you is stupid" lecture, but it didn't happen. She just took the key and said she'd see me in a bit.

When I climbed the stairs to my apartment that night, I expected to find her curled up on the couch with a book. Instead, as I reached the landing, I heard the sweet sound of Will's guitar and another sound, unfamiliar to me. I walked in to find my mom at the Wurlitzer playing, "I Feel the Earth Move." She was singing horribly out of tune. Will nodded his head encouragingly as he accompanied her with some interesting funk guitar on the Telecaster. I spotted the notorious bottle of Patrón on top of the Wurly. He looked up at me and smiled sheepishly. I rolled my eyes at him.

"Okay, lovely ladies, that's it for me tonight," he said as he put his guitar in the case. "Liz, it was a pleasure to meet you. I see where your daughter gets her beauty." He kissed my mom's hand. Her giddy look made my eyes roll again.

"Oh, thank you, Will. It was so nice to meet you."

"Where are you headed to?" I asked.

"I have a gig tonight at nine." He paused before heading out the door then whispered back to me, "Night, Mia."

I thought it was strange that Will said *I* have a gig, not *we*.

I also couldn't help but feel like it hurt him to be around me, or maybe it just annoyed him.

"Mia, he's cute," my mom said, wiggling her eyebrows.

I scowled at her as if her comment was complete blasphemy. "He's a musician!"

There was a long pause. "So are you, sweetheart."

I had never had a serious conversation with my mom about men. She never lectured me on whom to date or live with. I'd made a strict set of rules for myself.

As I studied her silly, drunken expression, I recognized something real, something human. I saw her vulnerability.

The next day the girls covered me at Kell's so my mother and I could see the city. We spent hours at the Guggenheim and then we strolled through Central Park. I took her to Turtle Pond, where my father used to take me. It was a clear, warm day; the sun was low in the sky, peeking through the trees, casting large shadows on the still water. We found a bench and sat in silence, letting the natural sounds quiet our minds. I started feeling sleepy so I rested my head on her shoulder, inhaled deeply, and let the mixture of Chanel No. 5 and rose water pervade my senses as we watched a variety of birds dance about and play.

Turtle Pond has seen quite a renovation over the years: the great lawn was redesigned in '97, giving it a new, clean look, yet the vibe remains the same. Separate from the rest of the park, it's a quiet zone, free from noisy activities and music—in the traditional sense, anyway.

Growing up during those hot summers, there were times when my father would seem agitated or confined. His need for escape from the city life, with its seedy shouts and dirty sounds, was tangible. He was always so jovial, but when the pressures of running Kell's would get to him, Turtle Pond is where we would go. We would sit on the grass near the shoreline and he would say, "Can you hear it? Can you hear the music?"

I would always giggle and shake my head. "There's no music here, Pops."

"Then you're not listening."

As I sat there on the iron bench, nuzzling into my mother's warmth, I stared down at my veiny, muscular hands, my long, bony fingers, and cringed. I balled them into fists. I hate the look of my hands; they're devoid of femininity; the skin is taut against bulging blue veins, my nail beds are wide, my knuckles are thick and heavy. My hands belong to a man, yet they are my most prized possession. I thought back again to my father on the shoreline.

I am listening, Pops. I don't hear any music.

Quiet your mind, luv. I could almost hear his voice in the memory, the faint remnants of an Irish accent, the husky depth when he spoke from his chest, which always gave me the shivers. His memory ached in my soul, but his presence was still palpable in the silence. Tears began streaming down my cheeks. I stretched my hands as my fingers began to move on the illusory piano keys. I finally played the music my father had begged me to hear when I was a child; it was a song of peace and contentment, and my ugly, obedient hands could play it flawlessly.

My mother noticed my movements and smiled as if she were acknowledging my father's spirit in me. She took my hands in hers and spoke quietly, "Mia, my girl. You know I loved your father. I still love him. He was honest and kind and had a passion for life greater than any person I know. I loved his spontaneous, free spirit, and I loved how much he adored you. You know all he wanted was for you to be your most true self. He wouldn't want to see you wallowing."

In that moment, I wanted to ask her about their relationship and why it hadn't worked. I knew she respected my father, but her words were a surprise to me. I wondered why they hadn't even given it a chance after they'd found out she was pregnant, but I knew there was no sense in making her visit heavy by dredging up old, painful memories of their relationship when my father's beautiful essence was still everywhere around us.

"I'm not wallowing. I'm just trying to figure it all out."

Later that night, as I lay in bed, my mother paused in the doorway before entering. Her eyes were distant as she studied the room; she was in a trance, locked in a memory or a smell or sight that reminded her of another life a long time ago. I cleared my throat, causing her to glance down at me.

"Robert just called and canceled our date for this weekend." I sighed. I wanted my mother to meet him. I thought he would impress her.

"I'm sorry, honey. He sounds like a busy man."

"Yes. I suppose it's a good thing, though?"

"That depends on who's waiting around." She smiled warmly and then bent down and kissed my forehead.

"Good night, baby girl."

My mother continued imparting her cryptic wisdom to me over the next few days, but she held nothing back when she finally gave me the lecture I was waiting for. Although I'd expected it, but I was thoroughly shocked at which relationship she warned me of.

"Taking on someone who is loaded with baggage is no walk in the park, Mia. Just ask your stepfather. A stepchild and an ex-spouse is not an ideal situation, VP banker or not."

"Our family worked," I said, still shocked at her frankness.

"Yes, we were the lucky ones, blessed with two rare men who loved us despite the situation."

"Robert and I have only been on one date, Mom. I don't think you have to worry just yet."

"I'm surprised that you can't see what everyone else does," she said as she cupped my face in her hands. Tears touched the corners of her eyes and then she smiled. "God, you remind me of him."

When it was time for her to leave, she held me for a long time and said, "I know you're mulling things over. Remember you are your own person and you are beautiful and gifted. I'm proud of you." She squeezed me tight. "Learn to ask for help when you need it . . . learn to recognize it when you need it."

I stared blankly, trying to decipher what she was getting at without opening another can of worms.

"Have you thought about therapy, Mia, to help you get through this?"

Oh, so that's what this is about.

I shrugged and blew out a long breath. "I have Martha. She's like a therapist."

She hesitated and then in a gentle voice said, "You're right. Martha is a great listener and she has good advice. Sometimes it takes a while to figure out what she means, but it's usually spot-on."

I wondered how my mother knew that. Martha always gave these abstract one-liners, similarly cryptic to my mother's. It was like they worshipped the same self-help guru.

As soon as she was out the door, I went to Kell's and worked mindlessly, cleaning and oiling the wood as I ruminated over her words.

I came home that night to find Will sitting on the couch

with two floozies. It didn't take long for me to realize they were twins. *How cliché*, I thought. *"Hola,"* I said in a chipper voice as I eyed Will.

One of the girls jumped up and reached a hand out. "Hi, I'm Sophie."

I smiled really big, then stuck my hand up in a motionless wave and said, *"No habla inglés."* I headed down the hallway, calling back in perfect English, "Come on, Jackson!" I shut my bedroom door and sank down to pet my dog. When I heard Will and the girls leave, I went to the kitchen and found a note:

DEAR LANDLORD,
IS POLITENESS TOWARD MY GUESTS TOO
MUCH TO ASK? I'M PRETTY SURE I'VE
EXTENDED YOU THAT COURTESY.

Will didn't come home that night.

I barely saw Will for the next few weeks. I would leave mail on his bed and it would remain untouched for days. If I saw Will at all, it was while passing him in the hallway, or I would see him walk past Kell's toward the subway. I figured he was probably dating someone and didn't want to bring her home to his bitchy roommate. When we saw each other, our exchanges were polite but abrupt. He continued leaving me plenty of notes addressed "Dear Landlord," telling me that either he'd fed Jackson or taken him for a run. One note mentioned that Jackson seemed lethargic, and I knew it was another episode.

It was an extremely hot summer in New York. I spent a lot of time in the cool air-conditioning at Kell's, looking at bridal magazines and goofing off with Jenny. We sent out invitations for her engagement party that we planned to have at Kell's. I continued dating Robert. We mostly reserved our dates for every other Saturday when Jacob was with his mom. We shared plenty of fancy dinners and not-so-titillating conversations about the "good ol' days" of banking. He became a comfortable dinner companion, but little more. He got my mind off of my father and the many reminders crowding my apartment and the café.

One night after a little too much champagne, I invited him back to my place. We hadn't slept together and he probably wondered how many more tease sessions from the schoolgirl he would have to endure.

The apartment was dark. Will wasn't home, so Robert followed me to my room. We removed our clothes hurriedly like we didn't have much time. It made me feel like a teenager. Robert tried to be sexy, but he just seemed awkward. I positioned myself on the bed in a sexy pose, lying on my side with my arm propped under my head. Robert laughed—it wasn't exactly the reaction I was going for, but I could see he was clearly affected. He crawled on top of me, spreading my legs apart with his knees. His weight was on his forearms, positioned on each side of my head. He wasted no time—or shall I say, spent no time—doing anything else before he was inside of me.

"Ow," I mumbled.

"Oh, sorry, am I hurting you? I'll stop."

Don't flatter yourself.

"No, your arms are on my hair. It's hurting my neck."

"Oh, sorry." He adjusted his arms awkwardly before letting out a big moan, and then he was done.

It was anticlimactic—for me, anyway. For having waited so long with Robert, I kind of expected a magnificent, bedroom fireworks display, but like everything else we did together, it was very one-sided and I was beginning to realize that. I got up, shot him a kind smile, and said, "I'm gonna get some water. Do you need anything?"

"No, thanks."

I meandered down the hall, wearing nothing but Robert's dress shirt. I didn't bother turning the lights on. I went straight for the fridge, hoping to find a ginger ale since I was feeling nauseated after our little romp. I opened the refrigerator door and stared blankly while I absorbed the cool air. When I heard the front door lock turn, I spun around and saw Will entering the apartment. It was dark and I couldn't make out the look on his face, but I observed him quietly lean against the back of the door. I squinted my eyes for a better look, but it was useless. He was watching me stand in the light of the refrigerator, wearing nothing but another man's shirt. I'm pretty sure he knew what was going on. I felt a tinge of resentment toward Will for being gone all the time and leaving me curt notes, but I never wanted him to see me that way. Standing there paralyzed, I waited for several seconds and then slowly closed the refrigerator. In the complete darkness, I made my way down the hall with my proverbial tail between my legs. Just as I got to my room, I heard the front door close. He was gone.

I slid into bed. Robert was facing away from me, so I curled up behind him and draped my arm over his chest.

"Is your roommate here?"

"No."

He moved my arm off his chest and turned toward me. There was a small bit of light shining in through the window from the courtyard. I could tell Robert's eyes were open. He smiled and then in a low voice said, "I'm not much of a cud-

dler." He scrunched up his nose. "I get kind of claustropho-
bic. I'm sorry . . . do you mind?"

I shook my head. "No, that's fine." I gave him a small,
tight smile and then turned away and cried silently. I wondered how I could ever make it work with Robert if our relationship would only consist of a few insipid encounters each
month. Then I let my mind wander to Will. I wished that we
could go back to being silly, flirting with each other and playing music together.

After work the next day, I came home to another note from
Will:

DEAR SLUMLORD,
JACKSON HAS BEEN WALKED AND FED.

I crumbled the note and grabbed Jackson's leash to take
him to the groomer's. I decided to have him shaved that day.
Shaving a yellow Lab is not standard practice, but it was hot
and Jackson's fur was all over the apartment. He seemed like
a happier guy after the shave, even if he looked a little weird.

We left the groomer's and headed to Tompkins Square
Park for a nap on the grassy knoll overlooking the playground.
I spotted a few café regulars and hippies from days past lying
around on the tiny hill. I leaned back until I was flat in the
grass and Jackson curled up and rested his head across my
stomach. I closed my eyes to consume the ambient noise of
the park that day. I heard the faint song of a harmonica and
guitar and thought of Will. There were sweet sounds of children's voices echoing in the distance, and I thought of Will. I
dozed off, thinking of Will.

I only remember the last five seconds of my dream, which

included Will's hands on me. I felt the exquisite pulsing between my legs and sighed, which startled me awake. The feeling below, although out of my control, stopped abruptly. I was disappointed but relieved when I realized I was still in the park. Jackson was nestled beside me, sound asleep. Even though no one was close by, I could still feel my face flush as I thought about the dream. I wanted to remember more, but I couldn't. It was dusk and eerie in the park. There were fewer people around, so I decided to head home.

As soon as I cracked the door, Jackson went barreling past me and right to Will, who had gotten down on his knees to greet him. "Hey, buddy, what happened to your fur? What did this evil woman do to you?" He continued petting and talking to Jackson. There were a few moments of silence before he looked up and said, "Hey." He wore a small, sad smile. He was listening to God, but it looked as if he didn't like what he was hearing.

"Hi," I said softly.

He got up and grabbed his guitar, calling back, "See ya," as he walked out the door.

That night Jackson had another episode. It was getting to the point where I didn't even try to move him. By morning he was fine and I couldn't figure it out. At the café I did some Internet research. It seemed like Jackson was having little strokes or quiet seizures. Either way, they were getting worse and I knew I would have to take him to the vet soon. I ordered some chicken from Sam's to take to Jackson for lunch. While I was waiting for Denise to bring out my order, I heard Will playing "Pictures of You." I loved the long guitar intro and even though the sound was muffled coming through the ceiling, I could tell Will was playing it perfectly. I grabbed the chicken and ran up to my apartment, hoping to catch some of the song. When I walked in and the sound registered, I stood there with my jaw on the floor. Will's back was to me and he was singing in a perfect, melodic, and soulful voice. I knew Will wasn't tone deaf—I had heard him sing a little before—but this wasn't an impression of the vocals from the original song, it was Will's authentic, amazing voice. He sang the next part with a vulnerable fervor that was so sexy, my legs were trembling.

"Screamed at the make believe
Screamed at the sky
And you finally found all your courage to let it all go"

I lost it and stalked over to stand in front of him. He immediately stopped playing. I pointed and shouted in the most accusatory voice I could muster, "You can sing! Will Ryan, you can sing! What the hell?" It wasn't really a question. Why was he screwing around with that lame band? Why was he keeping his amazing talent from everyone? My inner thoughts were spilling out. I kept flailing the bag of chicken around. "The universe needs you, Will!" I said desperately.

He quickly unplugged his guitar. "I'm still trying to figure it all out. Please just let this go." He never made eye contact with me as he hurriedly threw his guitar in the case, grabbed his keys, and went to the door. He turned toward me with a wounded expression before looking down and muttering, "I'm not sure about anything." When he looked up, his eyes kissed mine. "You get that, right?"

Of course I got it.

Back at Kell's, Jenny was looking through bridal magazines . . . again. "What do you think about this kind of arrangement for the head table?"

"It's gorgeous," I said unenthusiastically.

"What's wrong, girl?"

My mind was going a million miles an hour. "Did you know Will before? He said Tyler was his best friend."

She chuckled. "I swear it's a total coincidence. Last year Will and Tyler met each other in a web design class at East Village Community College. Will ran into Tyler at the café one day and we put it all together. They've been hanging out a lot lately. I guess Tyler is helping Will do a website for some project." She paused and then said, "Oh, I wanted to let you know we asked Will to play a few acoustic songs at the wedding."

Will took a computer class?

"I think that's great. He's a very talented musician." I paused. "Hey, did you know Will can sing, too? I mean, like, really well?"

"Yeah, Tyler mentioned something about that. I guess The Ivans broke up and Will has been doing solo gigs at little dive bars and cafés."

"What? Why didn't anyone tell me?"

"Well, you don't exactly act like you like Will."

"Why, because I didn't sleep with him?"

"No. That's not why. Honestly, Mia, you kind of act like Will's a loser. He told Tyler that he stays away from the apartment at night because he feels like he's getting in your way when Robert's over. He cares about you, Mia. He's a good roommate and a good friend. None of us can understand why you're so resistant toward him."

"Well, he's been leaving me rude notes and the other day he called me evil. And . . . and he . . . he . . . he brings women over!" I exclaimed.

"You made it pretty clear that he's not your type. He's a man; do you expect him not to date? Anyway, he said you got all bent over the fact that he brought a friend over. I'm sorry,

I love you girl, but I think it's a little unfair the way you treat him." Jenny's words ruined me because they were true. I tried hopelessly to explain myself.

"Will has a lot of good qualities, Jenny. I hope he and I can remain friends. I want desperately to get along with him, but I'm not a fan of the whole starving-artist thing. The musician who has casual sex with all types of women. It just seems trite. I admire a man who has hopes and dreams for his future."

"Every man has hopes and dreams for his future, and Will is no exception. You know so little about him and you've already concluded that he's worthless because he plays a guitar. That seems so hypocritical of you. What comes to mind when I think of trite is the girl who spends one vapid evening after another eating expensive meals and talking about money with her rich, investment-banker boyfriend."

I crossed my arms and looked down at my feet. "Why are you trying to hurt me, Jenny?"

"I'm trying to help you. I see you meandering aimlessly through your life." She brought me into her arms for a long hug. "Every time I look at you, I see the pain from losing Pops. I know you're still grieving. I know Will reminds you of him, but I don't know why that scares you." I began sobbing in her arms. I needed to cry. "You'll figure it out, Mia, and I'll be here for you. I think maybe you still have more to learn about Pops and yourself." She paused, then whispered, "And Will."

Jenny's decisions about marriage, friends, and career seemed so rash to me in the short time that I knew her, yet she was sure of everything. Every word she said was the truth. I *would* discover more. Once I collected myself, I took a seat at the bar and faced the window. Martha came over and brought me some tea. She had been in the kitchen, so I knew she'd heard my conversation with Jenny. "Thanks, Martha."

"Hi, Mia Pia." She took a seat next to me and held my hand as we stared out the window.

"I'm so confused."

"You're twenty-five and you just lost your father. It comes with the territory," she said gently.

"Being here and living his life, it's so dramatically different from my life in Ann Arbor. My father made decisions with his heart and my mom makes them with her mind and I can't help but feel I'm more like my mom, or I should be."

She paused and looked straight ahead before speaking.

"You have to teach your heart and mind how to sing together . . . then you'll hear the sound of your soul."

It took me thirty seconds to process that single sentence, but once it sank in, I almost fell off my chair. I always appreciated Martha's warmth, but I used to think her comments were esoteric crap. As I got older, I started finding profound meaning in what she had to say. Martha continued staring out the window. When I saw a little smile play on her lips I followed her gaze to see Will, who was standing across the street. He was in front of Trax, a store that sold rare vinyl and music memorabilia. He was wearing black jeans, his usual belt and wallet chain, and a plain white T-shirt. He was looking down with his hands in his pockets, talking shyly to a woman who looked to be in her early thirties. She had short black hair and a hip outfit, and from what I could tell, she was pretty. She handed Will a piece of paper and then shook his hand; he pulled her in for a swift hug. When she walked away, he looked at the paper, then turned on his heel and trotted away exuberantly. I rolled my eyes.

TRACK 7: What Would J. C. Do?

The next week consisted mostly of me moping around my apartment alone. I wore the same outfit for four days straight. Everyone at Kell's gave me pitying looks, but other than work-related topics, no one uttered a word to me. I was starting to feel like I lived alone—Will was home for all of five minutes that week and Jackson was becoming more and more sluggish. The engagement party was coming up that Saturday, and since my standing dates with Robert were on Saturdays, I figured why not take him. It was time to introduce him to my pseudo-family. I planned to work and sleep until then, but Jenny wouldn't have it. She insisted that I go to poetry night, saying that the grand finale was going to be Will playing a few songs. How could I resist?

That night the usual poetry party showed up. When Will and Tyler walked in together, Tyler came straight to where Jenny and I were behind the counter. Will immediately took a seat without acknowledging me. Halfway through the readings, a group of college girls walked in and sat down. They were giggling and eyeing him. Then the dark-haired woman I'd seen him with in front of Trax came in. She sat at the window bar and turned her stool to face the tiny, makeshift stage where a ninety-year-old man was doing a slam about waffles. When Will spotted her, he shot her the peace sign and turned back toward the stage. I didn't know what to make of it, but she was obviously there to see Will, as was the table of giggling girls.

When it was time for Will to go on, Tyler helped him bring his amp and guitar in to set up. I had butterflies in my stomach. I could barely contain my excitement about hearing Will sing, but I was still a tad bitter that he hadn't spoken to me. He seemed nervous as he adjusted the microphone.

One of the groupie girls moved her chair in for a closer look, inadvertently tugging on Will's guitar cord in the process. "Hey, don't do that!" The girl looked shocked and embarrassed. When Will noticed, he softened his expression. "Just give me some space, okay, baby?" he said to her with his sexiest smile. She nodded sheepishly.

After he finished tuning his guitar, he leaned into the microphone and spoke hesitantly. "This is a song for my friend." He looked right at me . . . and then I fucked up again.

"Play 'Ziggy Stardust'!" I blurted out.

Looking shattered, he narrowed his eyes at me and shook his head, then quickly changed his tuning. I knew he had decided on a different song and I wondered for a second if he was going to play my request.

"This is a song for my friend, who doesn't know what she wants," he mumbled and then barreled into "Yellow Ledbetter." I have to admit, Will choosing an Eddie Vedder Pearl Jam song was very apropos. Will was the rock-and-roll type I'd swooned over my entire life and I still wouldn't give him the time of day. He knew me better than I knew myself. Will left the lyrics out; instead, he played a fifteen-minute instrumental version with his eyes closed. He was aggressive, but he played flawlessly. I was completely and utterly mesmerized watching him. Toward the end of the song he teased the audience with just one word, a pitch-perfect, lingering "oh" before the final guitar riff. He unplugged and gathered his things. People clapped but seemed dumbfounded that Will hadn't sung and was packing up to leave. The short-haired woman wrote something in a notebook before she scooted out the door, never looking back. I spotted Jenny, who was shooting daggers at me.

"Why would you ask Will to play a song about an egomaniac guitarist who breaks up his band?"

An ashamed giggle escaped my mouth. "I didn't think anyone would get it."

Tyler walked up behind Jenny and put his arm around her. "Will and I are going to get a bite." Will was already standing out on the street; I could see him cursing and acting like a lunatic.

"Will you tell him I'm sorry?"

Tyler looked at me speculatively. "There was a record exec here to see Will sing. You know he's been playing around town, right?"

"God, I feel terrible." And I meant it. I hadn't realized. I'd thought it was just another girl there to swoon over him.

"It's not all your fault, Mia. Will needs to have a thicker skin and get used to the fact that people are going to say things. He was doing really well, playing at little dives, and then when word got around that Will Ryan was something to see, he started booking shows under different names. There was The Wilburs, then Idio-Secret Agent Man, and then the last one was The Asshats. Every time he would gain a little following, he would change the name. He has a lot going on and he's trying to figure things out. I know he really takes what you say to heart. He thinks you're a brilliant musician."

"Really?" I sighed. "I feel terrible—please tell him I'm sorry." I walked away with a lump in my throat the size of a bus. I couldn't look at Tyler's and Jenny's faces anymore. I hid in the back until everyone was gone and then I locked up and went home to bed.

A peace offering was needed, so the next day I bought Will a digital four-track recorder and left it on his bed with a note.

Will, I'm sorry about how I have behaved toward you lately. You are one of the most talented people I know and I won't get in the way of that again. I care about you and I want us to be friends. Please accept this gift so you can continue making that beautiful music and know that this is your home, too. I promise to respect that.

Later that day, Will and I ran into each other on the street. He had a carefree look about him. "Hey, roomie! Thanks for the four-track and your sweet note. It means a lot." He gave me a big bear hug. "I want to jam with you soon. I have some ideas for a couple of songs."

"I would love that, Will." I felt unreasonably happy. I was relieved almost to the point of tears that he was back to himself.

"I have to work tonight, but I'll see you at the party tomorrow." He gave me another hug.

"Okay, I'll see you." When he walked away I heard him call to Sheil, whom he'd spotted standing farther down the street. I looked back; Sheil was dressed in a beautiful orange, red, and black sari. She was a stunning, exotic beauty. Will ran toward her to catch up. I had introduced Will to Sheil one day in the café but as I watched him jog toward her, I thought that they seemed more familiar. It gave me an uneasy feeling.

Jenny and I spent the entire day Saturday making food and decorating Kell's for her engagement party. We hung Chinese lanterns and twinkle lights everywhere. Then we closed the café to the public and went back to my apartment to get ready. I decided to live on the edge and wear a super-short, all-black shift. Jenny looked angelic in a knee-length, flowing white dress. Robert met us at the apartment. He wore the typical "I'm a banker" suit. He eyed my dress dismissively.

"Do you like?"

"Yeah," he said. "It's interesting."

"Okay, then. Let's head over."

We walked over to Kell's. Martha was there along with Seth, our friend from the poetry group who was going to dee-jay the party. We put some last-minute touches on the food and decorations before guests started arriving. I introduced Robert to everyone, but at times he seemed disinterested or preoccupied with his phone. Seth played wonderful big-band music while the champagne flowed. When Will arrived, I saw him shake Robert's hand and then he hugged Jenny and Tyler before making his way toward me.

"Hey, you look hot," he said as he hugged me around my shoulders.

He was wearing black pin-striped suit pants with his belt and wallet chain and a black, short-sleeved dress shirt. Black on black and smelled divine. I inhaled deeply as he hugged me.

"So do you." I laughed shyly. "I mean you look handsome."

He took a step back and drank me in. His hand went to the hem of my dress and I flinched as he grabbed the fabric between his fingers and tugged. "I like this." He winked and shot me a sexy smile. I laughed and shook my head. Some things never change . . . who would want them to?

I saw Robert observing our exchange. I elbowed Will and

winked back at him and then walked over to stand by Robert. We continued to mingle and I noticed Jenny and Tyler were happier than I had ever seen them, which made me feel more carefree than I had been in a long time. I noticed that Will chatted with Sheil for what seemed like an hour and it made me wonder, but I figured Will could talk to anyone about music for hours on end and Sheil would be a great sounding board for that. When the party was well on its way, Will stood on a chair to get everyone's attention. I scooted over so that I was standing right below him.

"I would like to make a toast to the happy couple. Jenny, you look amazing tonight, by the way. I don't know how this schmuck got so lucky," he said, gesturing his champagne glass toward Tyler. "Okay, it's an engagement prayer, if you will." He looked at me and whispered, "No pun intended." He paused and cleared his throat:

> *For each other:*
> *May your hearts always beat wildly, and*
> *May your minds always sing wildly,*
> *But most of all,*
> *May your souls always dance wildly,*
> *For each other,*
> *For eternity.*

He raised his glass higher and ended with, "To Jenny and Tyler." Cheers rang out. Everyone toasted each other. When Will stepped down from the chair I grabbed his arm and whispered in his ear, "That was really beautiful, Will."

"Thanks, baby." Then he kissed me on the cheek and headed toward Jenny and Tyler.

When the music got louder, Jenny and I got drunker along

with everyone else, I'm sure. Seth played "Live Your Life" by T.I., so I busted out my amazing (mostly ridiculous) hip-hop stylings and then Jenny and I created a medley of '90s dance moves, including the Roger Rabbit, the Sprinkler, the Running Man, and my personal favorite, the Bus Driver. I spied Will laughing at us, so I mouthed an air kiss to him and he winked at me. Robert, on the other hand, sat in the corner looking bored to death. I couldn't tell if he was antisocial or if he thought my eclectic little group of friends was beneath him. Either way, I thought maybe it would be better to keep the two worlds separate.

When the party died down, I starting drinking water and cleaning up.

"Thank you so much, Mia. This was amazing," Jenny said.

I gave her a big hug. "It was my pleasure. I'm glad you're in my life. I love Tyler and I'm so happy for you."

Before leaving, Will came up to me. "I'm heading up. Are you guys coming?"

"We're gonna stay at Robert's tonight. He has to pick up his son early, so . . . "

"No worries, I'll see you later, then," he said as he hugged me.

"Night, Will."

He waved to Robert and then walked out. I knew Will wouldn't be disappointed that I didn't bring Robert with me, but I felt like I had to explain anyway.

I got to see some of Robert's true colors in the cab on the way to his apartment. "That was an interesting group. Martha is a very strange woman, Mia."

"How so?"

"She asked me if I wanted my chakras cleansed. What does that even mean?"

"Don't be obtuse, Robert," I said, annoyed at his comment.

"Obtuse? Please. What about Will and his sappy toast? Come on, souls dancing? That loser should spend less time on the poetic nonsense and more time trying to find a job so he can stop leeching off you."

I was breathing through my nose, mouth clenched. I'd been trying hard to ignore the signs, but he was revealing his true colors to me and I couldn't let him get away with it. Through gritted teeth, I let him have it.

"How dare you! You want to know something, Robert? Will has more to offer in his little finger than you do with your Upper West Side apartment, your business degrees, and your VP job. Will is kind, sensitive, creative, determined, and he's been a good friend to me. That's more than I can say about you." I yelled at the cabbie to pull over.

"What are you doing?"

"It's not going to work between us."

Looking straight ahead, he said, "Yeah, because you're just like the rest of your friends: wannabe artist trash."

Time for the big guns. "Fuck you, you dickless, fascist fuck. I wish I could get back every meaningless, banal moment I spent with you. Ba-bye." With that, I hopped out of the cab. The taxi sped away and Robert never looked back.

I was on the corner of East Forty Second Street and Second Avenue at two thirty in the morning. If I walked one block east I would be at the United Nations. It was an interesting prospect but I decided to consider my options. Six blocks south would put me at the mouth of the Queens-Midtown Tunnel. I thought about Queens. Folding my arms, I backed up against a light pole, feeling wretched and small. What a piece of shit Robert was for letting me out of the car in midtown at that hour. I watched motionless as three taxis zipped by me. Everything around me started moving in hyperspeed.

I was standing on the sidewalk, perfectly still, staring at the constant red blur of taillights. The signal on the pole above me was changing from green to yellow to red at supersonic speed, so fast that it became one color.

The tall buildings made me feel like an insignificant shadow on the sidewalk. I could have melted into nothingness and it wouldn't have mattered. In my daze I wondered if I was more perplexed by the fact that my relationship with Robert was over or if my desire to defend Will so passionately was a sign of deeper feelings. An hour must have gone by before my shivering snapped me out of my trance. I stepped off the curb and positioned my body in front of oncoming traffic. The first car to approach was a taxi, thankfully. When it came to a screeching halt, I hopped in and shouted, "Avenue A and Saint Mark's!"

"Lady, you could have killed yourself," the cabbie shouted back to me.

"Yes, that's still an option." God, I was losing it. The cabbie shook his head and floored the gas. It was there in the safety of the cab that I really went off the deep end. I sobbed uncontrollably all the way back to my apartment. When we pulled in front of the building, I tried ineffectively to collect myself.

"Lady, are you okay?"

"Yes. I'm sorry. Can I just have a moment please?"

He gave me a compassionate nod in the rearview mirror and then turned off the meter. When I had no more tears to cry, I pulled myself together and paid the fare and then repeatedly thanked the cabbie until he finally told me he had to go.

The apartment was quiet and dark except for the hallway light. I asked the universe for a small, selfish favor. When I got to Will's doorway, I peered into the dark room. The universe did not grant my wish—there were two bodies sleeping in Will's bed. With Will lying on his side closest to the door, I couldn't see whom he was spooning. A glutton for punishment, I moved in closer, standing near the edge of the bed. My heart instantly liquefied when I saw that Will was cuddled up to Jackson, who was under the covers with his head on the pillow like a person. I took a mental photograph of the scene and then turned to walk out when Will grabbed my wrist.

"Hey, sweet thing. What's wrong?" he whispered, squinting his eyes.

"Nothing, go back to sleep."

"Do you want Jackson with you?"

"No, he's fine. I'll see you in the morning." He let go and turned back toward Jackson.

I woke up four hours later on top of my covers, still wearing the shift dress. My head was throbbing. The feeling intensified when I thought about what had happened in the cab the night before. Robert didn't give a rat's ass about me; the breakup was for the best. The clock read seven thirty and I'd told Martha I would be at Kell's by eight. I rolled off my bed and onto the floor and then practically crawled all the way to the bathroom. After a few minutes of hot water beating down on my face, I heard the bathroom door open. Through the frosted shower curtain I saw Will's figure come in and lean against the counter.

"What are you doing?" I shouted as I covered my body with my hands.

"I can't see you, there's a shower curtain," he said, chuckling.

"You can see enough."

"Well, I'm not looking. I just wanted to talk to you."

I watched him cross his feet at the ankles and lean back,

arms folded and his head down. He was making a belated attempt at manners.

"What's up, Will?"

"Are you okay? You seemed upset last night when you came in. Did something happen with Robert?" I sensed vague hope in his voice.

"No. I just felt like sleeping in my own bed. I'm sorry I woke you."

He hesitated for a long beat before speaking. "Okay, no worries. I'm going to work early . . . I'll see you later."

"Bye, Will." Once he was out of earshot I cursed myself. Why didn't I tell him the truth? Why was I being so fickle?

Over the next two weeks, I dove into the café workings. Martha and I sat down one evening and went over every line in the accounting books. The café was making a profit, albeit a small one, but enough to keep it open. We talked about the espresso machine that everyone referred to as the monster. On top of the fact that the milk steamer was slower than molasses, the machine sounded like the Tunguska meteor falling to earth.

I showed Martha some pictures of the newfangled machines and suggested we get one. She looked moderately disappointed, so I figured the old machine held some kind of nostalgic significance to her.

"It will save us so much time," I pleaded.

"Does it make better espresso?"

"Probably not. I don't know what to do. I'm just trying to think of ways to improve the business." I waited for her to beg me to keep the old machine, but I knew Martha well enough to know that she would be creative about it.

"Mia, you have to ask yourself, what would J. C. do?" She arched her eyebrows and waited for my response.

"About the espresso machine?" I asked with a puzzled look.

"Yes. What would Johnny Cash do?"

Ah, of course, my first man in black. Martha was being silly, but I think she hoped the joke would remind me that there is something to be said about character, and the old machine had a lot of it. "Okay, the monster stays."

TRACK 8: Hopes and Dreams

Will and I kept missing each other at the apartment. I hadn't seen him for over a week except asleep in his bed on the mornings when I left for work. I would leave his mail on the counter for him, and every day I would notice more and more envelopes addressed to Will from record labels. It seemed that he was getting his career off the ground. My mind would wander to him headlining big stadium shows before going back to his giant, fancy bus with a different set of groupies every night. I would think, *Good for him,* but it still bummed me out. None of that had happened yet, but I couldn't help but feel it was imminent.

One gloomy morning in July, while I was rearranging the back storage room at Kell's, I dropped a one-hundred-ounce can of stewed tomatoes on my foot. "Fuuuuuuuuuck!" All of lower Manhattan must have heard my cries.

Jenny came running in. "Oh my god, your foot." She looked both shocked and disgusted. "We have to take you to the hospital."

My foot was mangled. Who knew a can of tomatoes could do so much damage? My ankle started to resemble a giant puffer fish. My big toenail was hanging off and blood was gushing everywhere. I sat there, trying to reel in the crushing pain. Jenny hailed a cab and Martha arrived just as I hobbled out to the curb. Tears were flowing and I was biting my lip, hoping it would relieve some of the pain in my foot.

"Thank you for coming," I managed to mumble.

"Oh, Mia Pia, poor girl. That must have been some can of tomatoes," she said as she stared at my foot with a sickened look on her face. "Jenny, why don't you take her and I'll cover the café, and Mia, you shouldn't wear sandals to work!"

She had to throw in the mother-hen shit, which was laughable considering that Martha wore Birkenstocks every day of her life, even when it was snowing out.

We got into the cab and both yelled, "Bellevue Hospital!"

Jenny held my foot over her lap with an ice pack and a bloodstained towel. "I guess Martha must be squeamish. Did you see how she looked at your foot?"

"Uh-huh," I said with my eyes squeezed as tight as possible. I could barely breathe, it hurt so badly, and every bump we hit made me cry out.

"I'm sorry, Mia, we're almost there," Jenny said.

Once I was admitted at the hospital, they gave me some pain meds and took X-rays. I had a hairline fracture on the top of my foot, but other than the missing toenail, that was it. It still hurt like hell. While I was waiting to get my crutches and temporary cast, I told Jenny she could go. I knew she had to coach a tiny-tot soccer team and it was getting late. She argued with me for twenty minutes and then I said, "It's not like you're gonna drive the fucking cab, Jenny! I'm fine, they're giving me Vicodin." I convinced her to go, but not before she talked to two doctors and a nurse, verifying that I would be okay to ride home by myself.

On the way to my apartment, I asked the driver to stop at a market so I could get dinner, which consisted of wine and chocolate. When we pulled up to my building, the cabbie got out and helped me onto the curb. I stuffed my prescription, along with the wine and chocolate, into my purse and wrapped my bag around my wrist. I hobbled into the stairwell. Once inside, I looked up and saw Will sitting on the landing outside of our door. He had his legs out in front of him and his elbows were resting on his propped-up knees. His head hung down, and his hands were tangled in his tousled hair. A fragment of light streamed over his winged forearm. He looked like a fallen angel waiting to be let back into heaven. I made my way to the bottom of the stairs. When I hoisted one of my crutches onto the first step, Will's head jerked up. He got up and bolted down, arriving at my side in two seconds. Appraising me, he asked, "Why didn't you call me?" He grabbed my crutches and purse and tossed them aside.

I didn't answer him.

When he reached his arm behind my legs to scoop me up, I protested. "No, Will, just help me get up the stairs."

"You're a hundred fucking pounds; I can carry you," he said and then bent down and put me over his shoulder. He smacked my ass gently as he climbed the stairs with relative ease. "You're a stubborn woman." Will was surprisingly strong for a thin guy, and I figured it must have been from lugging the band stuff around for years. He set me down on the counter and went to retrieve my things.

When he returned, he stood between my legs at the counter with his eyes narrowed.

"How'd you know?" I said.

"Martha called me. You should have called me." He looked discouraged.

"What did she say?" I said, attempting to dodge the scrutiny.

"She just said you broke your foot and then she mumbled some crap about a breathing rose."

I laughed. "That was a one-liner on friendship."

"I guess. When I called the hospital, you were already gone. By the way, where the hell was Banker Bob?"

"Working."

He squinted and shook his head. "Of course." He looked repulsed but didn't say anything more about it. I should have told Will that I hadn't seen Robert in weeks, but I didn't.

He reached down and grabbed my leg, holding it up to look at my foot, which was encased in plaster. A shudder ran through me and I realized it had been a few hours since my last pain pill. As if he could read my mind, he reached over and opened my purse, taking the paper bag out.

"Wine, chocolate, and Vicodin? Really, Mia? I don't think this is a good idea." He was so serious it was touching, but I was really okay and I wanted him to relax.

"I'll just have one glass, but I need a pill, stat—my foot is killing me." He got me a glass of water and handed me the meds and then he poured us both a glass of wine. "I want to get into the bath, but I can't get my foot wet. Can you help me?" I could feel heat creeping over my cheeks. Will's eyebrows arched and then he shot me a sexy smile. "No funny business."

"Who, me?" he said as scooped me up. Once inside the bathroom, he set me down on the closed toilet and drew a bath. I reached over and dumped about a gallon of body wash in to make bubbles.

"Let me get undressed and I'll call you when I'm done so you can help me in there, okay?"

"Sure," he said and then walked out. The combination of the wine and pain meds was kicking in. Will was being perfect and respectful, but I wasn't going to parade around naked with my foot in a cast. I wrapped a towel around myself and called him back in.

"I'll lift you over and just leave your foot out until I can get something underneath it." Once I was standing with one foot in the bath, he positioned towels on the side of the tub. "Mia, you're going to have to let me see you so I can help you lie back, unless you want to take a bath with that towel wrapped around you?" he said with a smirk.

"No, I can do it myself. Just turn around for a sec." He shook his head and sighed. I tossed the towel and then slowly sat down, holding my broken foot out of the water. I thought it must have been some kind of amazing Olympic feat considering how much work it was to sit while suspending one leg in the air. Once I was in, I rested my head back on a towel and sank into the water, positioning my cast on another rolled-up towel propped on the side of the tub. The water felt heavenly and I luxuriated in the bubbles. "I'm in."

When he turned around, I watched him drink me in slowly. Although the bubbles mostly covered me, I realized my position was insanely erotic with my legs open that way, lying back. The warm water consumed me and I knew I must have been glassy-eyed from the meds. I studied his beautiful face as he stood there paralyzed; he was listening to God.

"Will?"

"Yeah?" he whispered.

"Do you want to get your guitar and play me something?"

"Sure . . . okay." He turned on his heel and walked out. When he came back, he had our wineglasses and his acoustic guitar. He never met my gaze; he just seemed undaunted. He handed me the glass and I took a sip and set it on the side of the tub. As soon as he hopped up on the counter, he started strumming away. He played a long intro and then began singing the words to Van Morrison's "Sweet Thing." I watched him intently. He closed his eyes and let each word linger in the exquisite tone of his voice. His face was so determined and his hands were so precise. I was feeling woozy and aroused. I made sure Will's eyes were closed and then I closed mine and let my hand travel down my body as the sound of Will's voice resonated everywhere inside of me. My hand moved in and around myself, imagining Will's perfect hands on me as he sang the words:

> *"And you shall take me strongly in your arms again*
> *And I will not remember that I even felt the pain*
> *And we shall walk and talk in gardens all misty and wet*
> *   with rain*
> *And I will never, never, never grow so old again*
> *Oh sweet thing, sweet thing oh, my, my, my, my, sweet*
> *thing."*

I felt the climbing, pulsing ache. With my other hand I grabbed at my breast, clenching my nipple between my fingers. Will's voice was peaking and falling so beautifully and I felt the intense moment between my ears and down my spine and between my legs. I arched my back and pressed deeply into myself with steady pressure. As I came, I opened my mouth wide, trying desperately to stifle the breathy "ahh" that spilled out. I felt my body curved slightly above the water. I sank back down, opened my eyes, and glanced over to Will, who had stopped singing. He continued strumming the guitar as he gaped at me, his lips slightly parted. And then with curiosity in his eyes, his mouth curled into the most sincere, small smile. It was like his expression said *I don't judge you, I want you to feel good,* and then he whispered, "Hey, beautiful."

"Hey," I said, my voice raspy. It was a moment where I thought I should feel embarrassed, but I didn't. What Will had witnessed should have made me feel like the going-to-school-in-your-pajamas dream does. You know, when you're a teenager and it feels like all eyes are on you; you're the center of the universe. Then you grow up and realize it would have been awesome to go to school in your pajamas and the only reason why you had those dreams in the first place was because you went to school with a couple of assholes who made it their goal in life to ruin you over wearing your Hello Kitty nightgown to biology class. That is what I realized in that moment. I wasn't embarrassed that Will had witnessed such a private moment, because he didn't make me feel embarrassed about it. Will was secure enough with himself to respect a moment that was so raw and personal.

Anyway, maybe I wanted Will to see, or maybe the wine and Vicodin *wasn't* such a good idea.

"Are you ready to get out?" he asked hoarsely.

"Yes." When he walked toward me, I reached my hand out and let him pull me to my feet. He only let me stand there exposed for a second before wrapping a towel around me. After he lifted me out, I hopped on my good foot to lean against the counter.

"Do you want me to grab you some clothes?"

I looked around and spotted one of Will's white V-neck T-shirts lying over the towel rack. "Can you hand me that shirt?"

He looked back, confused, but he grabbed it anyway and smelled it. Shrugging his shoulders, he said, "Smells fine, I guess." I pulled the T-shirt over my head and then shimmied the towel out from underneath. The shirt fit like a dress and smelled like Will. I inhaled deeply.

"Ready?" he said. I nodded. He grabbed me around the waist and hitched me up a little on my good side to help me hop to my bedroom.

It was a warm evening; the windows in the apartment were open, letting in a light breeze. The warmth and the street noise reminded me of the summers with my father. I lay back on my bed, propping my head and foot up on pillows while Will perused a stack of CDs sitting on my dresser. He held up the self-titled CD from the band Shine, a post-progressive rock group from Detroit. My friend who worked in a music store in Ann Arbor had recommended the CD years ago. It had become one of those albums that I kept close by. I would forget about it for months and then pick it up and fall in love all over again.

"I worked on this," he said.

I stared at him in disbelief. "What do you mean?"

"I used to know these guys. Years ago, they asked me to sing on two songs for this album. It's just the obscure backup vocal on"—he looked at the back of the CD—"track three, 'Lie, Paula,' and track five, 'Mission.'"

I couldn't speak. "Lie, Paula" and "Mission" were my two favorite songs on the album simply because I loved the ethereal backup vocals. I spent many nights daydreaming to those two songs, wondering what kind of angelic being could produce that sound. I was gawking and completely bewildered.

He smiled. "Mia, you're high as kite, huh?"

"Yeah, I guess." I didn't explain why I was so shocked. For all Will knew, I was loopy from the pain pills.

He put the CD in the player and lay back next to me, stretching his legs out and propping his hands behind his head. And then out of nowhere he said, "Did you name Jackson after Jackson Pollock?"

"No. It's a long story."

"I've got time."

I gave him a long look before deciding to launch in. "When

I was ten, my mom and stepdad got me the cutest little black Lab puppy for Christmas. Being an only child, they figured I could use the company. I decided to name him after my hero, Johnny Cash." Will shot me a surprised look. "I know, weird hero for a ten-year-old, but I loved the songwriting. The little puppy was quite the escape artist—he tried to jump over the gate and dig under the fence almost every day while I was at school. One day, while I was doing my homework at the kitchen table, my mom ran in crying and called my stepfather at work and whispered, "Johnny Cash hung himself." I didn't know if she was talking about the person or the dog. It didn't matter either way, I fell apart."

He reached down and grabbed my hand and kissed it; I contemplated pulling away, but I didn't. I realized we were friends and Will was just being sensitive to my dead-puppy story, so I continued with my hand in his. "Anyway, my mom took the lifeless Johnny Cash to the vet, but it was too late. They basically told us it was our fault because we left the collar on too loose and that's how the poor little guy hung himself. It took us all a while to get over it. A few years later, my stepdad brought home little Jackson. I asked if I could name him Johnny Cash, but they told me it wasn't a good idea, so I named him Jackson after the song that Johnny and June Carter Cash sang." I looked over at Will, who was smiling sympathetically.

"How old is Jackson?"

"He's thirteen. He's been having more episodes; I'm really worried about him."

"I know . . . me, too." We both looked over at Jackson, who was lying on his doggy pillow near the door. He wagged his tail at us and a brief thought ran through my mind. I wondered if it made Jackson happy to see Will and me like that.

Like the wish I might have had for my mother and father to be together. It was an obscure thought that was gone as soon as it arrived, but it made me think about Will and my life and the possibilities.

"Hopes and dreams, Will?" I said, changing the subject.

"What are my hopes and dreams?" he asked, clarifying. I nodded. "Well, my hope and maybe also my dream is that you'll need another bath soon," he said with a mischievous grin. I elbowed him. "There is actually this one dream I keep having where I'm sitting at a table in a fancy restaurant. Across from me at the table are Jack Black and Jack White. Jack Black is dressed in head-to-toe white, top hat and all, and Jack White is dressed the same, but in head-to-toe black. I sit there motionless, staring at the Jacks, totally confused. They don't move; they just stare right back at me. It's fucking weird," he says, laughing.

I shook my head at him and laughed and then thought it was impossible for Will to be serious. He sat up, still looking straight ahead, and put his hand on my leg. He rubbed my thigh up and down, all the way up to where the bottom of the T-shirt rested. Then he turned and looked at me solemnly and said, "I have them, Mia. That's all you need to know," and then he bent over and gave me a swift kiss on the lips. "Night, pretty baby." He didn't linger for one second; he got up and headed to his room. In the hallway, he called back, "Let me know if you need anything and stay off that foot."

"Night, Will," I whispered, but he didn't hear me.

Will's kiss and the way he touched my leg was so intimate and sweet. Not sexy, just intimate, the way you kiss or touch your best friend, with kindness and love and without judgment.

Every opportunity I had over the next several weeks to tell Will that I had broken up with Robert passed me by. The questions kept coming about where Robert was, and I continued being evasive. I wanted to tell Will, but I felt like it would change things with us and we were getting along so well.

My pseudo-family helped me out a lot during my broken-foot era. By mid-August I was off the crutches and out of the cast. Jenny was busy planning her wedding every second of the day. With Tyler's support, I talked her out of having it on Halloween. They decided on an outdoor wedding in September.

I was starting to settle into my life, even though at times I still felt like I was an observer, looking from the outside in. I saw people around me really living; Will was working a lot and still playing his secret shows, which he wouldn't tell a soul about until after the fact. The only time I felt present and alive was when I played music. Will and I worked on a bunch of piano tracks for his songs. He was never short on praise when we played together, which gave me the confidence to really explore music. He started bringing home other instruments; I dug out my father's guitar and banjo and Will and I would spend hours goofing around in our little makeshift studio. I really enjoyed those sessions and I knew he did, too. One night, after a little tequila and a lot of jamming, Will told me he thought we shared a "mystical alchemy" when we played. I couldn't agree more. He never shared any details about record labels courting him, but I knew there was hype over Will because there were countless calls and meetings. I didn't want our sessions to ever come to an end, but I knew Will would eventually move on.

TRACK 9: Mystical Alchemy

Your mom and dad made those," Martha said as she washed dishes in the big sink in the back of the café.

I was dusting off some handmade pottery mugs that I had found hiding deep in a cabinet. Each one was beautiful and different, with its own unique pattern. I paused and wondered how that was possible. Then I shouted over the clanking dishes and faucet noise, "When? Those five days back when my mom was nineteen?"

Martha looked at me but didn't say a word. I think she realized her slip and so did I.

One of the mugs went crashing to the ground when I absentmindedly set it on the edge of the counter. "Dammit!"

Martha came over to help me pick up the pieces. When I picked up the bottom part of the mug, I saw a heart inscription between my parents' initials. I set the piece down and jumped up. "I'll be right back." I ran out the door and bolted to my apartment. I ran past Will, who was standing at the kitchen counter. I went straight to the closet and yanked the big box of my father's pictures and documents down. Kneeling on my bedroom floor, I hastily sifted through the contents of the box until I came across a manila envelope. I pinched the metal prongs, opened the flap, and turned it upside down. Two tiny boxes fell out, along with a file of documents and a stack of letters and pictures. I don't know how, but I realized right away that I was holding proof of some kind of history that had been kept from me.

I went to the pictures first. There were three black-and-white photos. The first picture was an artsy close-up photo of my father lying on his side, shirtless, and looking down. My mother is peeking up from behind him, staring right into the camera lens with a seductive look. They were both very young and it could have easily been taken during the notorious five days. I imagined my father's version of Andy Warhol's Factory. My mother looked so different, so vibrant and uninhibited. Her hair was long and straight and contrasted beautifully with her fair skin; she was clearly the muse. The second photo was of my mom lying in a bed, shirtless and nursing her baby. My eyes welled up when I realized the picture was taken in the very room I was sitting in. That photograph with my mother, the peaceful look on her face, was a gift in itself, but it was a gift that was hard to appreciate because at that moment I was still very torn and confused. The third picture was of the three of us lying on the same bed. I must have been six months old, lying in between my mother and father, both of them looking serenely at me.

By the time I got to the fourth photograph, I was a blubbering mess. It was my mother and father standing in front of the courthouse. My father was dressed uncharacteristically in a suit and my mother was in a white, knee-length, A-line dress. I knew immediately it was their wedding photo. The photos were images of events I had wished were real my whole life, and now they were.

I started sifting frantically through the file of documents. I saw their marriage license and the divorce decree. They were married six months before I was born and it lasted one year, almost to the day. The boxes held two gold wedding bands and a beautiful pair of diamond earrings.

I looked up through blurry eyes to see Will standing quietly in the doorway. "Go away, Will," I said, sniffling. His expression was pure compassion, but I raised my eyebrows at him like *what are you waiting for?* He turned slowly and walked out as I continued sobbing. There were two letters, one addressed to my father and one addressed to me. I opened the letter addressed to my father and glanced down to the bottom. It was signed "Lizzie." It was the name my father had called my mother.

> *Dearest Alan,*
>
> *I've decided to go back to Ann Arbor; I know you sensed that it would come to this. I don't fit in here; this life is not for me. I love you, but we want different things and you said yourself that we create our own destiny. You've been so good to me and it breaks my heart to hurt you this way. I know you will be a wonderful father to Mia. I promise that I will make you a big part of her life. Please understand. I'm so sorry.*
>
> > *Love you always,*
> > *Lizzie*

I cursed my mother, then opened the letter addressed to me.

> *Luv,*
>
> *I knew one day you would start asking questions, so I am writing this letter from my heart. Your mother and I never wanted you to feel that our marriage failed because of you, so we chose to wait to share this information. We shared a deep love for each other, but we realized that we wanted different things in life. We hope you'll understand our choices. We love you more than anything, Mia,*

*and we love each other and always will because of what
we share in you. These rings and earrings belong to you as
a memento of your parents' love.*

All my love,
Pops

By the time I finished the letter, my head was pounding
and my shirt was drenched with tears. I felt Martha's warm
embrace around me. I hadn't noticed her walk in, but she
knew I was hurting. She held me silently for a long time. I
realized it was my mother who made the choice, not her parents. It wasn't because my father couldn't be faithful, it was
because they were too different and my mother didn't want
this life.

"How will I ever forgive her?" I whispered.

"You don't have to forgive her—you're not Jesus. Your
mom was still figuring out who she was when she met your
dad. She didn't do anything wrong except try to protect you.
Your parents loved you so much, but your mom wasn't happy
here," she said gently.

"I'm just like her; that's why I can't be happy. I'm just like
my mom, and here I am in my father's life," I said between sobs.

"Yes, you're like her, but not just like her. Do you follow me?" I thought I understood what she was saying, but
I shook my head and waited to hear the explanation. "You
are your mother *and* your father. You are your experiences
and your fears and the love you let yourself feel. You are your
degree and your talent and your passion. You are your pain,
your joy, and your fantasies. You are me and Sheil and Jenny
and Will and every person that touches your soul . . . but most
of all you are you, whoever you dream that to be." She looked
at me, eyebrows arched.

"Yes," I whispered. "I guess I'm still trying to figure out the dream."

"Just remember what I told you about listening to your soul. What I see in you is very different from what I saw in your mother twenty-five years ago. You belong here, Mia."

I hugged Martha for what seemed like an hour. When she finally left, I knocked on Will's door. He opened it and leaned in the doorway, his eyes sympathetic. He was wearing black jeans and a yellow T-shirt that said "Everything is Rad." I wished I felt that way.

"Hey," he whispered. I wanted to dive into his arms, but I held strong.

"I'm sorry for snapping at you. I just learned something about my parents and . . . it was tough."

He uncrossed his arms and took a step toward me, but I stepped back. He paused at my reaction, looked down for a long second, then back up into my eyes and gestured with his head toward the front door. "Come with me?"

"I have to go back to Kell's."

"Jenny will cover for you. I'm playing at the string festival Sheil put together. Come on, you could use some musical therapy," he said, his expression hopeful.

Nothing in the world sounded better than seeing and hearing Will play. My decision was easy. "Okay, but we should stop by the café on the way."

He grabbed his two guitars and a dulcimer while I put my shoes on. When we got to the front room, Will stood in front of my dad's banjo. "Let's bring this for you."

"No way, Will," I said abruptly. "I'm not playing anything, I'm just going to watch."

"You mean listen?"

"Whatever."

"You can play any Bob Dylan song you want," he said with a cute smile. On the banjo I only knew the handful of songs my father had taught me and they were all Dylan songs.

"Okay, fine," I said with mock irritation. I was actually excited.

We lugged the instruments over to Kell's so I could ask Jenny if she would cover for me. She told me if I didn't go with Will, she would never speak to me again.

We took a cab to Prospect Park in Brooklyn. When I saw all the cars and the huge stage, I freaked out. Sheil had told me about the festival she puts on every year, but I had no idea it was that big. "Oh my god, Will, this is a huge deal!"

"Yeah, I'm nervous," he said, voice shaky.

Before we got out of the cab, I put my arm around Will's shoulder. "You're an amazing musician."

He turned to face me. "There are record execs here to see me tonight. . . . It's unnerving." He swallowed and shook his head slightly.

"You're gonna do great, I promise." He looked at me like what I said was the gospel.

We grabbed the instruments and headed toward the stage, both of us a little apprehensive.

Right away I spotted Sheil backstage, gracefully running the show. She was dressed in a gorgeous maroon-and-gold sari and her long, shiny black hair was woven into a perfect braid running down her back. When she spotted us, her face lit up and her mouth curled into a warm smile. She came over and kissed Will on the cheek before taking my face in her hands. "My darling, I'm so glad you're here." Sheil could say nothing and everything with just a look. She made you feel like the only person in the world. She turned to Will and asked if he would accompany her with his electric guitar on another song, and they chatted about the details.

When Sheil left, Will turned to me. "Okay, we're doing our song last, so be thinking about which one you want to do, okay, baby?" I nodded.

There was a whole slew of musicians standing around back-stage and it seemed like Will knew everyone. He was in his element; his nerves calmed as the passion came out. I tagged along from group to group while he discussed specifics about different styles of music. It seemed like every other person thanked him for helping out with a song or a recording. It was becoming clear to me that Will was well-known and respected within that community of eclectic musicians.

When it was time for the opening number, Will and four other men took their places in a line of chairs at the front of the stage. Sheil came out and gave a short speech about stringed instruments and the passionate musicians that the audience would see that night. She introduced the five men as talented artists who would be playing a medley of varying styles. Will had a dulcimer across his lap; the other men had assorted guitar-like instruments. As the show began, I stood offstage in the shadows, completely absorbed by the sound. I decided that playing the guitar should be a prerequisite for manhood.

I looked out to the audience made up of a large group standing near the stage. Farther back were scattered blankets and people in lawn chairs. The lights from the stage projected onto the faces in the audience, creating a magical ambience. Listening to the sweet sounds in the warm summer night air was enchanting. Will was unyielding on the dulcimer as the group played a familiar bluegrass tune reminiscent of my fa-ther. A lump started forming in my throat when I thought about Pops and the discovery I had made earlier that day, yet my pride for Will's performance was greater. He played with such ease, but with thorough focus and respect for the sound. It was as though he was paying homage to the instrument as his hands moved gracefully over the strings. Another act went to the stage as Will came running toward me.

"That was amazing!" I said as I opened my arms for a hug. He hesitated a beat and appraised me before hoisting me up with his free arm and hugging me.

"Thanks, baby. Those guys are rad," he said, gesturing to the four men he performed with.

"Everything is rad," I said, poking him in the belly.

He looked down at his shirt and back up at me. "I know, right?"

The next song was an original that Will played solo. It was a moment for the execs to see, and the moment for Will to really prove himself. He had calmed a great deal after the first number, so I knew he wouldn't disappoint. He grabbed his electric guitar as Sheil made her way to the microphone again. "I would like to introduce you to my personal friend, a very gifted artist who I believe you will be seeing much more of in the months to come. Will Ryan, everyone!"

He turned and gave me his cocky grin, shooting his eyebrows up. I laughed as he strolled to the center of the stage. He gave Sheil a kiss on each cheek and approached the microphone. "Everybody okay so far?" The crowd cheered. "Good, that's good," he said and then drove into a powerful guitar intro. When the song started to take shape, I heard the familiar melody. It was one The Ivans played a lot. Will was playing a bluesier version; I knew his soulful voice would lend itself perfectly to it. He sang almost the entire song with his eyes closed; his passion was inspiring and his voice resonant. He ended the song with the same powerful guitar lick it started with, and when the sound ceased, you could hear a pin drop.

His eyes shot open, he looked terrified, and then the crowd erupted. Even people lounging farther out in the grass, sitting on blankets or in chairs, stood up and began clapping wildly. There were whistles and cheers, and then Will leaned in with mock shyness and spoke softly into the microphone, "Thank you, I'll see you again in a bit." Wearing a cocky grin, he scurried offstage toward me. The moment he reached the side of the stage, he was swarmed. I stepped back and let Will absorb the attention from everyone around him. He glanced over at me and mouthed, *Hold on one minute.*

It was more than a minute. I saw record executives monopolizing Will every chance they had. I realized this was the beginning of a life for him that I probably wouldn't be a part of. I suddenly felt a selfish pang of sadness. I watched as Sheil motioned for Will to get ready to go back out with her. He glanced back at me and surveyed my expression, then pointed and mouthed, *You okay?* I nodded. He went back onstage with Sheil where they started tuning their instruments. They began playing a classical Indian piece; Sheil's sitar playing was exquisite and Will complemented the sound delicately by playing just the neck of his guitar. He tuned the Telecaster to the point where he was able to play the Eastern-influenced, bizarrely out-of-tune notes perfectly. Will's musical acuity did not go unnoticed that night; the crowd went wild again.

When they were through, he looked happier than I had ever seen him. Another act took the stage as he approached me. "Okay, baby, what's it gonna be?"

I stared into his eager eyes and said, "'You're Gonna Make Me Lonesome When You Go.'" He nodded approvingly. He knew the song and I think he knew why I chose it.

When it was time to take the stage, I was shaking. Will took my hand and held it all the way to our chairs. We sat down and began to play, me on the banjo and Will on the acoustic guitar. It was an out-of-body experience. I knew we played the song well; Will sang with a country twang, but there was a blurriness in my vision that prevented me from savoring it the way I wanted to. It was over too soon and my memory of it already felt like a dream. At the end, the crowd cheered and we walked offstage, waving.

"That was exhilarating," I said to Will. He wrapped his arms around my shoulders and pulled me in for a long hug.

After the show, Will continued getting pulled in twenty different directions by all kinds of people who wanted to talk to him or offer him a spot in their band or represent him as his manager. There was no sign of his usual neurosis or spontaneous behavior—he remained gracious and attentive to everyone he came in contact with. After we said good night to Sheil, we headed out from the back of the stage where we ran into Frank Abedo, a well-known talent manager. I recognized him from an article I'd read in a music magazine. He was featured talking about the changes in the music industry over the last twenty years. He was widely respected as a manager with integrity and a real knowledge and passion for music.

"Will, can I speak with you for a second? Frank Abedo, Artistry Management." Will shook his hand and smiled genuinely.

"Nice to meet you. This is my . . . " Will paused, stumped at how to refer to me. "Mia."

"Your Mia?" Frank said to Will.

"No, I'm Mia," I said, giggling.

"No, my Mia," Will finally said as we all laughed at the awkward exchange. Even though it was a slipup, Will referring to me as his gave me a warm feeling.

"Nice to meet you, Will's Mia. Where are you guys headed?"

Will told Frank that we were headed home, so he offered us a ride. When we got out to the parking lot, we realized it was a very nice ride in a stretch limousine. Will didn't skip a beat, and I wondered if maybe he was getting used to being courted by industry people. Once inside the limo, Frank told Will how it was unusual for an artist to have the kind of hype Will did without even so much as submitting a demo tape. He said Will's name had been swirling around the business for a while and it was time to get serious.

"You definitely need management, Will. There is no way you can navigate this industry on your own."

"I already have deals on the table," Will said, shaking his head. I was shocked; I'd had no idea Will had already been offered a deal. I listened to every detail, not wanting to miss a thing.

Frank continued, "I know every A&R person in this town. I know what they're about. Artist development is practically unheard of today in this industry. What they're offering you is a death sentence. They want one hit on one album and they want it fast. They'll give you a tiny budget and a deadline, and then when the album is finished, they'll promote the shit out of it, dress you up like a clown, make you cut your hair, and then fuck you in the ass if it doesn't go platinum."

I gasped. Will looked over at me and smiled, totally unaffected.

Frank was really on a roll now. "Then, if that's not bad enough, they'll make you go on tour in every godforsaken country until you can make enough money to pay them back for the second-rate studio work they paid for on an album that nobody cares about because they wouldn't let you do it right in the first place." Frank raised his eyebrows at me, then at Will, and waited for the response.

"What do you suggest, then?" Will asked, finally serious.

"Let me manage you. You'll keep doing what you're doing, building the hype. I'll book more solo shows so you can develop your songs in front of an audience. You'll keep writing and building a good catalog. We'll get into a studio and cut a quality demo and then we'll shop you out and stand our ground. I know you're the real deal. It's rare these days and I don't want a label turning you into their monkey."

It was the whole "stick with me" speech and it was convincing as hell. I was sold and somewhat shocked when Will said, "Give me a month."

Frank smiled. "Okay, guy, but you're not getting any younger." Just like that, the conversation was over.

As we pulled up to our building, Will took Frank's card and we both took turns shaking his hand and exchanging pleasantries. Once inside the apartment, Will plopped on the couch and patted the cushion next to him, encouraging me to sit. I was happy to. He pulled my legs up, removed my sandals, and started rubbing my foot. With all the craziness, I had forgotten that I was still nursing an injured foot, and although I was out of the cast I was supposed to be taking it easy.

"How's your foot?" he asked, his voice low and gentle.

"It's fine," I lied.

"You've had quite a day, haven't you?"

"Me? I think you've had quite a day, buddy."

"Yeah, I guess so." He stared into space, then rested his head on the back of the couch and continued rubbing my foot.

A few moments of silence passed before I could no longer contain my curiosity. "Why didn't you tell me you were offered record deals and why don't you want Frank to be your manager?"

Will took a deep breath before answering. "Remember when I told you that I was still trying to figure things out?" I nodded. "Well, I'm still trying to figure things out," he said, smirking.

"Figure what out? Everybody wants you and you're sitting on your thumbs."

He turned his head and looked at me, eyes narrowed. "No, not everybody." He abruptly got up and headed toward his room.

I followed, somewhat shocked at the turn in conversation. "You're my friend, Will. You're my best friend. I'll always be here for you. I want you in my life, just not in that way," I said, pleading.

When he reached his doorway, he turned toward me. "I know, Mia, you've made that abundantly clear." Then he slammed the door and yelled "Good night!" through the closed door.

I pressed my forehead against his door, took a deep breath, and then said in a low voice, "Will, you can have anybody you want. You'll get a record deal and go on tour and everyone will be falling at your feet." My eyes filled up. "Please, Will, I care about you. You're my family; this is the way it has to be."

He opened the door and drew me into his arms. "Okay, then," he whispered and held me against his chest. "You must really be into that guy."

What? I realized Will thought I was still with Robert. Why did everything have to be so complicated? If I told Will that Robert and I were over, it would hurt him even more that I didn't want to be with him. I wasn't entirely sure Will wanted to be with me anyway. Will was just a lover through and through, and he prided himself on being true to any sponta-neous physical desire he had, or at least that's what I thought.

I imagined that Will slept with all his friends with no commit-
ment and that it wouldn't be long before he was partaking in
the perks of being a swooned-over rock star. I had no desire to
be in his humdrum history on *Before They Were Famous*. Yet,
I couldn't deny that I loved being with him and it took every
fiber of my being to refuse his touch in that way.

TRACK 10: TGIF

Over the next two weeks, I spent almost every waking moment with Jenny finalizing the wedding plans. She and Tyler decided on a small, private wedding at her uncle's cottage in Southampton. The wedding was a couple of weeks out and Jenny asked if I would spend a weekend with her out at the cottage getting everything in order. I agreed. We were to leave Friday night after I closed up Kell's. I packed my bags in the morning and left Will a note asking if he would take care of Jackson until Sunday. I hadn't seen him much that week. He was busy figuring things out, I guessed, or maybe he was avoiding me again, which made my stomach ache. I took Jackson for a walk through the park before I went into the café. Just my luck, I ran into Robert and Jacob eating doughnuts on a bench near the children's playground.

"Mia!" Robert called out to me. I glanced over and immediately wished I could disappear. Robert told Jacob to go play as he stood up to approach me.

He smiled kindly and gauged my expression before he spoke. I had to make a concerted effort to mask my hostility.

"You look good," he said shamelessly, his eyes glancing down at my chest.

It was so nauseating that I couldn't for the life of me spare him at least a little of my wrath. "Yes, I am alive, after being left in midtown at two thirty in the morning."

There was a long pause.

"There's no shortage of cabs in that area, Mia," he said, "and if I recall, you chose to be left in midtown at two thirty in the morning. On top of it, that's not a dangerous area."

"Actually, Mister Native New Yorker, contrary to popular belief, there is more crime in midtown than in Harlem or the Bronx, so it's miracle I wasn't murdered and dumped in the East River," I said, smirking.

"Well, I guess that makes you the naive one for traipsing around midtown in the middle of the night." The back-and-forth comments were reminiscent of our fateful taxi ride. I was stumped, fumbling for words, when I thought, *Why the hell am I standing here talking to this assclown?*

"Good day, sir!" I spat at his shoes and hurried away. *Great start to my Friday,* I thought. *TGIF.*

I cut Jackson's walk short and headed to the corner market, where I grabbed a chocolate bar to eat for breakfast. It was going to be that kind of day. As I stood at the register, I noticed a variety of those little airplane bottles of liquor. I decided on the tequila—no surprise there. I stood outside of the market and tied Jackson's leash around my waist. I had the open chocolate bar in one hand and the open mini bottle in the other. I took a bite of the chocolate and then slugged back the tequila. I'm not going to lie, the combination was growing on me. I headed home, wearing Jackson's leash like a belt and enjoying my breakfast. When I got back up to the apartment, I peeked in Will's room. His bed was made and the stack of mail I'd left there the day before was untouched. I thought maybe he'd stayed at Tyler's, working on whatever secret website project they had going.

I headed down to Kell's. As I walked through the door, Jenny held up the phone and yelled, "There she is! Hey! Your mama's on the phone." She was a little too cheery for the early morning hour. I shook my head frantically, but Jenny just smiled at me and nodded, saying, "Oh yeah," over and over again. She was being bratty; she knew I was avoiding my mom and probably thought I needed a little nudge. Her antics would have been hilarious if it wasn't my life she was messing with.

"Hello, Mother," I said with my tequila-inspired confidence.

"Mia, I talked to Martha. Let me explain."

"I'm all ears."

"Your father and I didn't want to confuse you as a child. It's as simple as that," she said in her determined lawyer tone.

"Whatever."

"I'm sorry, sweetheart. I would never do anything to hurt you. I was young and I didn't understand your father's world. I got nothing out of the lifestyle; it was a party trick to me back then. I would rather have had my head in a book than sit around singing songs. Your father knew that. We weren't wrong for being ourselves; we were wrong for each other." There was a long pause. "I see the way you are when you play, Mia. I see the passion, so like your father's, and I think it's time for you to be honest with yourself. All the time you spent in college trying to fight it, and look where you are? In the East Village, giving music lessons, living with Will."

"I had no choice."

"I think you did."

"I gotta go, Mom. I forgive you." I hung up the phone, told Jenny I would be right back, and headed to the corner market. I set a chocolate bar and mini bottle of tequila on the counter for the second time that morning.

This time Benton, the eighty-year-old cashier, eyed me and

shook his head slightly. "Miss Mia, you know it's ten a.m.?" I nodded. "You're too young to be so unhappy."

"I'm not unhappy. I'm concerned about the economy. I figure consumerism is the key, right?" I said it with a ridiculous amount of glee.

He rang me up and took my money, still shaking his head. I don't think he bought my story.

Once again I stood outside and pounded back the tequila on the street, which I'm pretty sure is illegal. When I got back to the café, I told Jenny to zip it about my mother and then I went about my day. At dinner I insisted on ordering salads from Sam's to offset the chocolate bars and tequila. We closed Kell's early to eat our salads in the back. I told Jenny I'd had an awful morning, but left out the details about Robert. She assured me we would have a fun weekend in Southampton. When I told her I felt bad for leaving Jackson, she suggested that I bring him.

"Really? You don't mind?"

"Not at all. I love that pooch. I had to park my dad's Jeep a couple of blocks away, so I'll go run and grab it while you get Jackson and I'll meet you on the street in fifteen minutes?"

"Perfect." I leaped up the stairs to my apartment, taking two steps at a time.

When I opened the door, Jackson greeted me. All the lights were on, the stereo was blaring, and the shower was running. I needed to tell Will that I was taking Jackson. We had gotten used to walking into the bathroom while the other person was in the shower, so I opened the door and froze. Through the frosted curtain I saw, not to mention heard, what could only have been Will fucking a girl in our shower. I quickly sucked in a breath of air, inadvertently making a squeaking noise. The motion and sound behind the curtain immediately stopped.

"Sorry!" I yelled and then backed out and shut the door. My heart was in my throat. I tried to calm myself and prevent any more tears from gathering in my eyes. I clenched my jaw and stood paralyzed in the hall. When I heard them shuffling around, I turned and abruptly headed for the kitchen.

The bathroom door opened as I walked away. "Mia?" he said in a low voice behind me.

Don't turn around. Don't cry.

I reached the kitchen counter just as the lead singer of the Black Keys began chanting something about a psychotic girl. For some reason that song reminded me of the movie *Deliverance*. I promised myself there would be no murder in the apartment that night. I was too crushed to do anything, and I had no right. I greeted him with a huge smile. "Hi, Will! I've had a fucked-up day!" I said cheerily as a rogue tear spilled from my eye. I looked away and concentrated on putting Jackson's food in a bag.

Will put his hands on my shoulders and turned me around to face him. I kept my head down, defeated. "I'm sorry, Mia. I'm sorry you had to walk in on that. I thought you were . . . going . . . " He couldn't finish his thought; he just lifted my chin and searched my eyes until I was sure he saw the hurt in them.

I swallowed the lump back and held my head up. "Yes . . . I *am* going . . . to the Hamptons. I just decided that I wanted to take Jackson, so here I am . . . picking up Jackson . . . and there you are . . . in a towel . . . postcoital . . . interestingly enough . . . time to go . . . it's time to go." I stumbled over every ridiculous word with watery eyes and a smile.

When I turned to walk out, he grabbed my arm and stepped toward me with a pitying look on his face. We were mere inches apart. I fixed my gaze on the "Soul Captain" tattoo over his heart. I couldn't look up at him. He hesitated and then in a low voice said, "I want you to meet Audrey."

I took a deep, cleansing breath. "How long have you been dating her?" I whispered.

"Two weeks, but I've known her a while."

I nodded and smiled. He was so sweet, so easily in love, and he wanted to share it with me.

"Please, Mia, I like her and I care what you think."

"Okay," I said. And then, as if on cue, Audrey came into my peripheral vision. She was gorgeous, a couple of inches taller than me with long, golden-brown hair. She had an all-American girl look about her with her cutoff jean shorts and long, tan legs. She was wearing one of Will's old Ramones T-shirts. I appraised her, hoping to find a flaw, but I couldn't. I couldn't find one blemish; she even had perfect feet and pretty toes. So then I hoped that she would be really dumb or shallow or conceited or mean. Any of those would do.

"Hi, Mia. It's nice meet you. Will has told me so much about you and I've seen your pictures all over. You're even prettier in real life—I didn't think that would be possible." She reached out to hug me and I hugged her back awkwardly. Damn, she was nice! I couldn't hate her or I'd for sure have the karma police on me. You know when someone just seems so put-together and kind, even their speaking voice has a nice sound to it and you want to hate them or find a flaw but you can't, so you have to like them, as painful as it is? That's how I felt about Audrey.

"It's nice to meet you, too. You're very pretty yourself, and Will is a good guy and great friend. Have a happy weekend," I said. "I'll see you Sunday, Will." I gave him a curt nod; he was leaning back against the counter with his arms and feet crossed.

He flashed me a tiny, sympathetic smile and mouthed the word *bye*.

I ran dangerously fast down the stairs with Jackson in tow. When I got out to Jenny, she was giving me a dirty look. I opened the Jeep door and motioned for Jackson to jump in. "What the hell took so long?" she said. I held my finger up and said, "One more minute?" I slammed the door and ran across the street to the corner market.

Benton was still working. I set three tiny bottles of tequila on the counter. This time he smirked and said, "No chocolate?" I got out to the sidewalk and drank each bottle over a trashcan while I stared directly at Jenny, sitting in the Jeep. When I finally got in the passenger side, she didn't say a word; she patted my leg and then blasted Cat Stevens. I cried all the way to Southampton.

By the time Jenny and I arrived at her uncle's cottage, it was late and we were both exhausted, so we called it a night. The next day I woke up and decided that I wouldn't talk about my terrible Friday while I was with Jenny. She was stressed about her wedding and I wanted to be a good friend. Her uncle's cottage was mostly used for weekend getaways, so it needed a little sprucing up. It sat back from the street on a large piece of property overlooking a storybook pond, complete with a wooden dock and little white rowboat. The grounds around the house were meticulously kept, so we were relieved that the brunt of our work that weekend would be just cleaning the inside of the cottage and meeting with the florist and caterer. We were completely consumed with wedding details until Sunday, when we headed back home.

"Okay, Mia, talk to me," Jenny said, her gaze never leaving the road.

By her reaction when I'd gotten into the car Friday, I had a feeling Jenny already knew something.

"Did you know Will was seeing someone?"

"Yes. He brought her to Tyler's on Thursday. . . . He asked if he could bring her to the wedding." She finally glanced over at me, gauging my reaction. I nodded. "I was going to tell you, but I wasn't sure if you already knew. I mean, after all, you live with him. What does it matter anyway?" There was hint of irritation in her tone.

"I walked in on him screwing her brains out in the shower."

Jenny sucked in a breath and bit her lip as she looked over at me. Her expression was complete and utter pity, then it changed. I took a deep breath, knowing I was in for some tough love.

"You know what, Mia? You want to know something?" Her voice got strong and intimidating. "I swore I wouldn't say anything, but I am through with the craziness between you and Will. He has not dated a single soul since he met you—he was holding out on some pathetic hope that you would break up with Robert to be with him. He had it bad for you, Mia. He wrote a goddamn song for you! But you decided to parade around with Banker Bob in your skivvies and rub it in his face." She glanced over, eyebrows raised.

"I broke up with Robert ages ago!" I yelled before lowering my voice. "Will wrote a song for me?" I was sullen and shattered.

"You mean you broke up with Robert and didn't tell anyone? Why, Mia? Why would you do that?"

"I don't know. Please stop yelling at me," I whispered and focused my gaze out the window.

Jenny took a deep, long breath through her nose and lowered her voice to a more sympathetic tone. "Audrey met The Ivans at a show last year. I guess she was hounding Dustin to hook her up with Will for months. She seems nice."

"Yes, she's very nice. Perfect, in fact."

"He was torn, Mia. Will said you told him it was never going to happen between you two and that he should find someone else."

"That's not exactly what I said. It doesn't matter, though. Will's right, I don't know what I want, but neither does he. He has record labels offering him deals and he's just sitting on them. He wants to live on pennies and play music and screw around." I knew there was no truth to what I was saying; my real fear was that I would fall in love with Will or that I already had and then he would just leave me alone, broken and pathetic.

"Is that what he told you?" she asked.

I knew what she was getting at, so I ignored her question. "Will wrote a song for me?" I whispered.

"Yes, he was going to play it that night in the café when you yelled out Ziggy Stardust." As if I didn't feel bad enough about that night. It didn't matter; I'd blown any chance I'd had. Will was with Audrey, the beautiful sweetheart. I was just a bitter bitch who would probably be alone forever, living in my father's life with my sickly dog.

"Quit feeling sorry for yourself, Mia, I can see it on your face."

"Let it go, Jenny, it's done. I'll be a good friend to Will and to you. That's what I'll concentrate on. I've been selfish and it's not right."

She gave my hand a squeeze and turned up the radio; we were silent the rest of the way home. When I got back to the apartment, there was a Will note on the counter:

HEY MIA,
HOPE YOU HAD FUN IN THE HAMPTONS. I'M

*STAYING AT DUSTIN'S TONIGHT. CALL ME
IF YOU NEED ANYTHING.*

MUAH, WILBUR

*P.S. THE ASSCLOWNS ARE PLAYING TOMOR-
ROW NIGHT AT DROPZONE IN PARK SLOPE.
YOU SHOULD CHECK THEM OUT.*

It was no doubt one of Will's secret shows. As much as I loved seeing him play, I knew Audrey would probably be there. The whole thing made me feel like crap about myself, but I'd told Jenny I would be a good friend so I guess I had to go.

TRACK 11: Benediction

The next night I rode the subway alone to Park Slope. I must have missed my stop or looked at the map wrong because I ended up walking about two miles to the damn bar. Once I reached the street, I saw the marquee from the corner. It read:

TONIGHT ONLY . . .
WILBUR GROWS A BEARD

I laughed. Will was getting really out of hand with the name thing. I thought with a name like that, he was either paranoid or he wanted to prepare everyone for a really boring show. Inside the bar I noticed he was already onstage, midsong. Dustin from The Ivans was also onstage playing a single snare drum. I spotted Audrey at the front of the crowd standing next to a busty blonde. They were swaying to the music, dressed in short dresses with stiletto heels. I rolled my eyes and thought, *What am I doing here?*

I took a seat at the bar and ordered a drink, then turned my stool to face the stage. When the song was over, Dustin jumped down and Will exchanged his acoustic guitar for the electric. He approached the microphone. "This next song . . . it's a slow one." And then he tore into a bluesy guitar riff. It was the familiar melody I remembered from one day at Sam's

when I'd heard it through the ceiling. It was the song I saw
The Ivans play when Pete said he needed to write lyrics for it.
When Will began to sing the words, I knew immediately it was
my song . . .

With my eyes wide open
I see the secrets in the rain
I see the loss, see the pain
I see you've lost your way again

No lines drawn
No boundaries made
Dance with me tonight, pretty baby
and let me pray

Don't let me hear you cry
Starve your dream
Feed your fear
I'll hold you forever here

I need the rain to cleanse my soul
It tortures me, it's makes me whole
I need the rain, I need it all

No lines drawn
No boundaries made
Just stay with me tonight, pretty baby
And let me pray

With his eyes closed and his head tilted up to the heavens, Will sang the song like it was a holy benediction. Tears
streamed down my cheeks as I wiped them away frantically.

When he finally opened his eyes, he was looking right at me. I think it startled him; his eyes opened wider and his head shot back slightly. He didn't smile, he just mouthed *hi* at me and I did the same back to him.

I glanced over to Audrey; she was laughing at Dustin, who was climbing awkwardly back onstage. I didn't know if I wished she had caught my exchange with Will or if I was relieved that she hadn't. On the last song, Dustin played the spoons into a microphone; I have to admit he was quite the gifted spoon player.

After the show, as I headed toward the stage, Audrey spotted me. "Hey, Mia! Come over here. This is my friend Kara—she's Russian . . . from Russia." Audrey was a little too chipper for my taste, but how could I complain? Will could have done worse.

I stuck my hand out. "Oh, you're one of those Russians from Russia?" I smiled. Audrey didn't get it. "It's nice to meet you." Kara shook my hand and smiled.

"We're gonna take Kara to Sokurov in the East Village. You should come with us—Frank has the limo." Two instantaneous questions ran through my mind. What is Sokurov? And how does she know Frank?

I pondered the questions while Audrey looked at me like, hello? And then I felt someone's breath on my neck. "Come with us." It was Will's voice, low and sexy. *Ahhh, why does he do that to me?* I turned to face him; his lips were pressed together into a tiny smile, but the expression in his eyes was familiar to me. It was the listening-to-God look and it made my legs tremble.

"God, Will, don't pressure her." Wow, Audrey moved fast. I guess she was getting comfy in the relationship because she was already telling him how to act. The thing is, Audrey didn't know Will the way I did. He wasn't pressuring me or intimidating me, he was asking, pleading, begging me to go with just a look.

"Okay," I said. He winked and flashed me a cocky grin. A group of young girls began gathering behind us, so we started to make our way toward the door where we found Frank chatting with the bouncer. Although Frank was on the short side and a little heavy, he still had an intimidating look about him. He could have been taken right out of a scene from *The Godfather*. He wore nice suits with no tie and he was never seen without a black fedora. He seemed much younger than his sixty years; I figured his job required him to stay pretty current.

As we approached, he reached out to me first and kissed my hand. "Ahh, Will's Mia." I practically choked on my tongue.

"Hi, Frank." I looked back at Audrey, who was oblivious.

"Let's hit it," he said and then he ushered the group to the stretch limousine waiting at the curb. Frank, Kara, Audrey, and Will sat on the bench running down the side of the car behind the driver, and Dustin and I sat between the doors. I could see all the way up Audrey and Kara's dresses, though luckily they weren't channeling Britney that night. Still, the view I had—with the talent manager and the artist basically sandwiching two leggy bombshells in the back of a limo with black leather seats, mirrors everywhere, and little blue lights— made me wish I had stayed home. Frank started talking to Will about something called the Big Four while Audrey and Kara giggled between them. I turned to Dustin after what seemed like ten straight minutes of seeing him staring at me in my peripheral vision.

"Hi, Dustin," I said, expressionless.

"Mia." He said it long and seductively.

"You're pretty good with those spoons, buddy."

A tiny smirk played on his thin lips. "You should see what I can do with my stick . . . sss."

Dustin wasn't a bad-looking guy. He was maybe five-ten, with shoulder-length, light brown hair. He wore his bangs sweeping across his forehead, Justin Bieber style, and he always had a backward baseball cap on. I thought it was a bit juvenile for a thirty-year-old, but other than the smarminess he was nice, so I didn't hold it against him.

"Mia, do you want me . . . to demonstrate that for you tonight?" He put his hand on my thigh and gave it a little squeeze.

"Shut the fuck up, Dustin, and get your fucking hands off her!" It hadn't even occurred to me that Will was listening.

"Relax, Will, she's not yours. She can speak for herself." Will looked at me like *go ahead, speak for yourself.* He arched his eyebrows, waiting for me to say something. I put my hand over Dustin's and slowly removed it from my thigh, my gaze never leaving Will's.

Audrey giggled inappropriately and said, "It's gettin' hot in here," and then I saw her wink at Dustin. It was a bizarre reaction, but I figured maybe she thought Will was just trying to protect me from Dustin's wild ways.

"Everybody cool off; we're here," Frank said and then we all piled out of the limo.

Sokurov was a kitschy Russian bar with tall, round, red leather booths and a hundred different kinds of vodka. Kara jumped up and down with excitement but quickly got disappointed when she realized there wasn't a soul in the place who was actually Russian, not even the owner. She said the place wasn't authentic but the vodka would do. I sat on the end of the booth next to Kara and Dustin. Audrey, Will, and Frank sat on the other end. Frank and I talked across the table to each other for an hour about recording studios in New York. He told me about the need for good studio musicians and suggested I look into it. I thought I could ask Sheil and I knew Will had connections, too. The idea excited me.

Out of the corner of my eye, I could see Will's arm around Audrey's shoulder. He was leaning into her neck, whispering something in her ear. Then I saw him take her earlobe in his teeth and give it a little tug before planting a kiss on her jaw. I stood up. "Well, I think I'm gonna call it a night," I said, smiling. "You guys have fun."

"Have the limo take you," Frank said.

"I think I'm gonna walk. It's less than a mile to my apartment." I looked at Will, who was staring intently at me.

"I can walk you home," Dustin said with a smirk.

"No, really, you guys, I'm fine. It's like four blocks." Will shook his head slightly and narrowed his eyes.

I said good-byes, Frank kissed my hand, and then I left. My foot ached as I headed down the street. I heard someone yelling my name and turned to see Will jogging toward me.

"Mia, wait up!"

"What's wrong?"

"Nothing is wrong. I'm gonna walk you home."

"You don't have to do that, Will."

"I know. I want to. Anyway, I'm staying at Audrey's tonight so I wanted to make sure you got home." I bit the inside of my lip hard and nodded at him with a little smile. "Hey, I heard what Frank was saying. You should seriously look into doing some studio work."

"Yeah, I really want to," I said.

"Really?" He looked surprised and elated.

"Definitely," I said and then a shiver ran through me.

There was a chill in the air that night. Will reacted without hesitation, putting his arm around my shoulder and pulling me into him. I wrapped my arm around his waist and took a deep breath, inhaling his body wash and sandalwood smell. I wanted to commit everything about Will to memory before I lost him to Audrey and the fame that was surely on the horizon. In that moment I also desperately wanted Will to bite my earlobe. I shook my head to clear the thought. We walked in silence for a moment before I said, "Will, you don't have to protect me from Dustin." There was a long pause.

"I . . . just didn't think the banker would appreciate where Dustin's hand was headed, that's all."

"I broke it off with Robert," I said quietly. Will stopped walking and turned toward me.

He looked me in the eye. "I'm sorry, baby. Are you okay?" I nodded. When we reached the apartment, he turned to me again. "I feel bad now for leaving. Do you want me to stay here tonight?"

"No. Seriously, we broke up a while ago. He was an ass; I'm better off. Don't worry about it, go ahead and go. I'm over it . . . really."

He brought me in for a long hug. "Okay, call me if you need anything." Still holding me around the shoulders, he leaned back and appraised my face. "You're beautiful and amazing and you have a special soul, Mia. You deserve the best." Then he planted a swift, chaste kiss on my lips before letting me go.

"Bye, Will." I turned and rushed up the stairs as tears fell from my eyes.

Over the next two weeks, I became insanely productive and determined. I talked to Sheil about doing some studio work, Jenny and I had our final dress fittings, and I bought a violin and practiced day and night on it. I hardly saw Will; he was spending a lot of time at Audrey's. One day in passing he told me that he had agreed to let Frank manage him. He said there would be a lot more shows coming up and then he asked if I wanted to accompany him on the piano or violin at certain shows. I told him I would absolutely love that. It seemed like a departure for me to want to play live shows or to be involved in the music scene at all, but I started embracing it when I realized how truly excited I was at the prospect of playing more. The business degree still lingered in my mind, but, as Martha had said, I needed to teach my heart and mind how to sing together.

One night while I was alone in the apartment I took Will's four-track recorder and his laptop and started recording some music I'd written. I completed one song, which sounded like it could be a piece from a movie score. The piano track was slow and simple, with very fast rhythmic intervals. I created a haunting tone with the Wurlitzer, which I used to accent the piano track. During the fast intervals, I played a dark, driving violin riff. When I was happy with the finished song, I burned it on a CD and left it on Will's bed. I scribbled with a Sharpie,

One piece from the soundtrack of my life

The next day was Friday, the day before Jenny's wedding, and I planned to head out to the cottage with her that night. It was slow at Kell's for a Friday. As I stared out the café window, I saw Will come out of the record store across the street. He took a cigarette from behind his ear and lit it. When he saw me in the window, he smiled really big, then threw the cigarette down dramatically and stomped on it. He swung his backpack around and pulled out a CD. He pointed to it and yelled, "It's fucking awesome!" I loved that he liked my song. Right then

Audrey came strolling out of the store as a cab pulled up. She waved to me while Will yelled, "I'll see you at the wedding." And then they hopped in the taxi and sped away.

Jenny and I rode out to Southampton that night along with Jackson. We danced in our seats and sang at the top of our lungs the entire way there; it was Jenny's sad excuse for a bachelorette party. I'd tried to plan one for her but she'd told me the last five years of her life had been one long bachelorette party. Tyler must have felt the same way because he didn't have a bachelor party either. Jenny didn't even want a wedding shower; she was satisfied with one day at the cottage with thirty of their closest friends and family.

"So what is Will gonna play?" I asked Jenny, realizing we had never talked about it.

"Just ceremony music, some acoustic guitar. He wrote us a really beautiful instrumental piece, so I'm going to walk down the aisle to that."

"That's wonderful. He's so good and I can't wait to hear him play."

"Yeah, he is. He asked if we cared if Audrey played the finger cymbals on one of the songs. I guess she told him that she always feels left out 'cause she's not a musician, so he taught her how to play the fucking finger cymbals." She said the last part giggling.

I started laughing. "God, I know it's terrible to be mean 'cause she's so nice, but, man, she is way, way too happy. She's happy and nice to the point where I feel like an asshole just being around her."

"Yeah, I'm sure she has flaws, everybody does," Jenny said and then turned up the radio.

Once we got to the cottage we went straight to bed. The next morning Jenny's mom showed up along with Karen, a friend of Jenny's from high school. The four of us had the task of setting up the tables and chairs. The wedding was to start at three; we had our work cut out for us. Jenny wanted to be back in the cottage by noon so we would all have plenty of time to get ready.

It was a beautiful morning; the pond glistened behind a rose-covered wrought-iron archway set up for the ceremony. Once the florist arrived, the setting really started to come alive, with rose petals lining the aisle and gorgeous centerpieces made of Casablanca lilies and pastel-colored flowers on each table. After sweating for hours, we took a little water break.

"Why aren't Tyler and Will here doing this?" I asked.

"Tyler can't see me today, duh, and I like being in control of this stuff anyway. I guess Will and Audrey are staying at a little bed and breakfast this weekend, making a mini vacay out of it, so I didn't want to ask them."

"How adorable."

"Stop," Jenny said, stretching the word out. Just then a truck came backing into the side yard. Jenny yelled at the driver, "I want it right there under that trellis! Thanks!"

Two men wheeled an old upright piano on to the back lift gate of the truck.

"You rented a piano?" I said with excitement.

"I couldn't let my piano virtuoso BFF get overshadowed by Finger-Cymbal Girl."

I laughed. "Thank you, Jenny, but I didn't prepare anything."

"It's just for fun after the ceremony. You and Will can mess around on it." I smiled mischievously at her. "Musically, I mean. Get your head out of the gutter, Mia Pia, we got a wedding to put on," she said as she pulled me toward the house.

TRACK 12: Prayer for Each Other

Y ou look incredible!" I said to Jenny as she stood in front of the mirror in her wedding dress. It was a simple ecru gown with long, straight lines. The thick straps hugged the outside of her shoulders, showing off her whole neckline. She wore her curly blond hair in an updo with a few stray strands hanging down. Her friend Karen and I had matching coral knee-length dresses that echoed the bodice of Jenny's dress with thick off-the-shoulder straps. We both wore our hair in simple updos.

Jenny's wedding colors were shades of coral, pink, tan, and burnt orange; it was very summer-cottage inspired and very romantic. There were roses everywhere and the cake was simply a tower of macaroons, each tier a different whimsical color. Guests were starting to arrive. Through the window I saw Jenny's mom giving orders like a drill sergeant. I finally saw where Jenny got her spunk and assertiveness. The caterer was ready, the seats in front of the archway were filling up, and I saw Will and Audrey seated off to the side of the aisle. Will was strumming the black Gibson and I could see a shimmer in Audrey's hand from the finger cymbals. *How cute*, I thought sarcastically.

When I saw Tyler standing at the front of the aisle with Jenny's little brother, I knew it was time.

"This is it, Jenny. You ready?"

"I was born ready." Jenny was by far the calmest bride I had ever seen.

Karen went first and then I followed, walking out of the cottage and down the aisle. I smiled as I walked slowly toward the archway. Will was seated at the front, off to the side, playing an acoustic version of "At Last," accompanied by Audrey clanking the finger cymbals at all the wrong times. Clearly Audrey was musically challenged, but she looked cute in her pink chiffon dress and stiletto heels. When I reached the front, I noticed all the guests except Will had turned to watch Jenny come down the aisle. He started playing an original song I didn't recognize and I figured it was Jenny and Tyler's, but he was looking right at me while he played it. He winked and I smiled and then he finally turned toward the aisle. He always wanted to make sure I knew he was acknowledging me. I definitely noticed him; how could I miss him? He looked like the cover-model love child of *GQ* and *Rolling Stone*. He wore a gray suit with a white shirt and a thin black tie. His hair looked like he'd run his hands through it with a touch of gel. Then I thought maybe Audrey had run her hands through it in their cozy room at the B and B. Ugh.

As Jenny walked toward the aisle, I looked at the crowd and recognized the back of a few heads. Dustin for one was easy to spot; he had the same suit as Will except he had a matching gray baseball cap on backward. Ridiculous. I saw Sheil wearing a beige sari and Martha in a flowy hippie dress.

Jenny came walking down the aisle on her handsome father's arm. She was every bit the beautiful bride. She looked extremely self-assured and radiant. I glanced over at Tyler, who was on the verge of jumping up and down; he was smiling from ear to ear with satisfaction and happiness.

Although Jenny and Tyler were not the traditional type,

they'd decided to have a traditional ceremony with the standard vows. That morning I'd told Jenny I was surprised Tyler didn't want to read a poem. She said they had each written a private wedding prayer that they planned to read to each other later that night. She said Will gave her the idea; that made my heart melt.

After they said their I do's, we all clapped and cheered. Will played their song as we followed them to the tables on the grass overlooking the pond. There were Chinese lanterns and little round carnival lights everywhere; it looked magical as the sun set. The DJ set up and started playing some Frank Sinatra while our dinner was served. I sat with the wedding party across from a table where our little East Village crowd sat.

Will came up to me during dinner. "You look stunning." He hugged me and whispered, "As usual." I smiled and kissed him on the cheek.

"I love the song you wrote for Jenny and Tyler. It was really sweet."

"Thanks. Save me a dance, okay, pretty baby?"

"I'd love to."

After dinner Jenny's little brother, Kevin, who was the best man, gave a nice speech about wanting a big brother and how he sure got one in the almost seven-foot-tall Tyler. When it was my turn, I looked out to the small crowd of guests and felt a lump form in my throat. I was really happy, and even though I hadn't known any of those people long, I realized they were my family.

"Jenny and Tyler, you're a lovely couple and I am so thrilled and honored to be a part of this. I'm not great at speeches, but I love you guys and I want to play you something, if that's all right with everyone?" The crowd clapped and cheered me on, but I heard Will yell the loudest, "Yeah, baby!" The guests crowded around the upright as I started playing "All of Me," a new-age classical piece by a guy named Jon Schmidt. It's a fast, vibrant song with dizzying movements and spiraling notes, but it's an eternally happy song and that's why I chose it. It's a hard piece to play because it's so fast; my hands literally blur in front of my eyes. It's such an electrifying feeling that I find myself lost in it, playing frantically and moving to the rhythms. I wanted to express to Jenny and Tyler everything I would have liked to say in a speech but couldn't, and I think I did with the song. When I was finished, the group surrounding me was literally stunned.

"Wow, Mia, that was epic!" Tyler shouted. I looked up at Will, who had a huge grin on his face, as if he always knew I had it in me. Jenny was crying happily, so I stood up and gave her a big hug and then I pushed the piano bench out perpendicular to the piano.

I looked at Will. "You have your harp?" He nodded and pulled a harmonica from his pocket. I gestured for him to sit on the bench. "Let's have some fun." We sat back to back as I began playing some loud boogie-woogie blues. Will added dramatic and soulful riffs with the harmonica. The guests clapped along as we played, getting faster and faster. Will turned and straddled me, then kicked his leg up on the high keys and started banging his heel to the beat. Everyone was laughing and cheering us on. He pulled his leg down and then there were four hands on the piano and he was playing with me, his chest flush with my back. His hands started on the outside of mine and then when the tune changed, he reached one hand under my arm, brushing intimately close to me. Our hands alternated as he played right along with me on the same keys in a lower octave. We were so connected. I felt his warm breath on my neck. When I leaned back against him and closed my eyes, the cheering got louder; the crowd understood the difficulty of what we were doing. When it was over, everyone clapped. I turned and gave Will a big smooch on the cheek. "You're rad," I said to him.

"Everything's rad," he said, smiling.

"I know, right?"

I followed Jenny around a little and made sure she had everything she needed. The DJ played some hip-hop music, so of course the wedding party had to have a dance-off on the little makeshift dance floor we'd created on the grass. After Jenny kicked everyone's ass by pulling out all the stops and yanking her dress up to do the Michael Jackson splits, I ran up to the cottage to grab a sweater. There were only two bedrooms in the cottage—the smaller one I was staying in and the one that Jenny's parents would stay in that night. Jenny and Tyler were getting swept away to some secret spot his parents had paid for, and most of the other guests were either going back to the city or staying in a hotel nearby.

I opened the door and noticed right away that a couple was in the room. They didn't notice me because they were partially hidden by an old-fashioned privacy screen, plus they were . . . occupied. I squinted my eyes but couldn't make out exactly what I was seeing and then I heard what was sadly becoming a familiar sound: Audrey and Will having sex. I backed out of the room, begging the universe to let me remain unseen. I shut the door and turned around to walk away when I ran smack into Will's chest.

"Have you seen Audrey?" he said. I did a double-take. I must have looked as confused as I felt. Who the heck was in there with Audrey?

It wouldn't be long before I found out. "What, Mia?"

he said seriously. Then Dustin walked out of the room and stood behind me, closing the door behind him. Will glanced at Dustin and then back at me. He looked dumbfounded and ruined, like he was going to cry, and then he whispered, "Oh no. Really? Really, Mia? You and him?"

Dustin and I stood there frozen, and then with perfectly shitty timing Audrey opened the door and walked out. It was only a matter of seconds while we stood there, but it felt like an eternity. I couldn't find the words to tell Will that I wasn't part of it. His voice suddenly got loud and high. "What?" he said through crazy laughter. He was laughing and it was scary and then his expression turned to bewilderment and then disgust. "The three of you? What the fuck?" He turned on his heel and headed down the hallway, waving his arms around and mumbling something I was sure none of us could understand.

I turned and looked at Audrey and Dustin. "You guys are serious assholes. You should leave." They looked blankly at me, like idiots. I ran after Will, but I was a ways behind him. Every one of the guests watched as Will grabbed a giant bottle of whiskey and headed toward the dock. "What are you doing, Will?" I yelled after him.

I noticed Audrey and Dustin hadn't taken my advice yet because they came rolling out behind me. When I got to the top of the dock, Will had already rowed himself to the middle of the pond in the tiny wooden boat. "Come back, Will, let's talk," I said, pleading with him.

"I'm not. Talking. To. You. *Ever!*" It was lunatic Will.

He stood up in the boat, looked at me, Dustin, and Audrey, and flipped us off with both hands, then yelled, "Fuck all of you!" And then he lost his balance and the boat started rocking. He fell but sat right back up and started rowing away.

"Don't look for me!" he yelled as he rowed farther into the darkness.

All the wedding guests looked on with amusement. I looked at Jenny and mouthed *sorry*. As I turned to head back toward the cottage, I stopped in front of Dustin and Audrey. "Come on, the screw-happy drummer? So cliché, both of you. Just leave." They turned and headed for their cars without a word.

I went to the cottage, where I finally got that sweater, and then I exchanged my heels for some Converse, grabbed a flashlight, and headed back out. The pond was only about the size of a football field and there was an easy-to-navigate footpath around the entire thing. I walked around to the other side where I found Will sitting in the boat on the shore, taking continuous swigs of whiskey.

"Will?" I said in a low voice.

"Don't fucking come near me, Mia. I swear to God, I will row myself into the middle of that goddamn pond and stay there till next year."

I stood still and spoke calmly. "I walked into the room and thought you and Audrey were having sex. I couldn't see who it was behind the screen. I tried to sneak back out and that's when I ran into you. I was confused."

"Go away, Mia."

I knew Will believed me because he knew me, but he was hurting and I wished I could comfort him. I looked back at the wedding, where I could see the party winding down and people leaving. Seeing the lights from a place so dark was enchanting, but it made me sad that two people who were supposed to care about him had ruined such a beautiful day for Will. I went back to the wedding where everyone was cleaning up. I worried about Will, but he was surprisingly responsible for someone who sometimes acted so erratically. I knew he wouldn't do anything stupid.

We sent Jenny and Tyler off in a fancy old car, and then it was just Jenny's parents and me. I said good night to them, showered, and then crawled into bed wearing my underwear and Clash T-shirt. I was asleep within minutes.

Hours later, I started awake and glanced at the clock. It was five thirty a.m. Whenever I drink or stay up late, I always wake up way too early and then I get anxiety over the fact that I didn't get enough sleep, which prevents me from going back to sleep. It's a vicious cycle and it's annoying as hell. My mind also wandered to Will; it was getting light out. It was also the coldest time in the morning before the sun came up. I turned over and gasped when I found him next to me, fully clothed in his suit and shoes, lying on top of the quilt and sound asleep. He smelled like a whiskey distillery but looked like a pallid child. My heart ached for him. I crawled out of bed, careful not to make any noise. I untied his laces and gently pulled his shoes and socks off. He moaned and mumbled something in his sleep. I lifted his loosened tie over his head and then I reached for his belt. The moment I touched it, he grabbed my wrist and held it. He looked at me through squinted eyes. "I got it," he murmured. "Come back to bed."

He stood up, stripped down to his boxers, and then slid back into bed, curling behind me and pulling me tightly into his chest. He slid his hand under my shirt and clutched my side. His long fingers easily wrapped around me and came to rest centimeters below my breast. When he hitched his long leg over me, I was completely cocooned by him. It felt like heaven.

"Are you okay?" I said quietly.

"I am now." There was a long pause, and then I felt him

kiss my hair before whispering, "It hurt more when I thought it was you." I smiled, perfectly tranquil, and then within minutes we were both asleep again.

When I woke up, I was lying on my back; Will was on his side curled up next to me, his body dovetailed with mine and his head resting on my stomach. I was mindlessly running my hands through his hair when I realized how incredibly intimate our positions were. He stirred sleepily and then his hands moved to my hips, where he twisted his fingers in the waistband of my underwear. When I felt him hard against me, I jerked away, sat up, and threw my legs over the side of the bed. He rolled over, away from me, and mumbled, "Sorry, baby." His voice was strained and raspy.

Leaning in, I kissed his shoulder and whispered, "Get some sleep."

Don't complicate things! I chanted that line over and over in my head as I gaped at Will's arms and hands and imagined them everywhere, all over me.

I threw on some sweats and headed for the tiny cottage kitchen to start coffee when I found a note from Jenny's parents saying that they'd headed back to Jersey. They'd left the Jeep and directions to their house where I could drop it off. While I made coffee and cleaned up the cottage, I heard Will get into the shower. He came out dressed in the only clothes he had—his gray suit pants and the white dress shirt, the tails tucked in and the top buttons open and sleeves rolled up on his forearms. If it weren't for his sparkling new pair of black Converse, his style might have resembled the banker's; he even had a typical suit belt on and no wallet chain. He ran his hand through his wet hair as he watched me survey his appearance.

"Weird, huh?"

"Kind of, but I like it. Coffee?"

"Please. Thank you." I handed him a mug. As he sipped his coffee, I noticed he seemed distant, distracted. "I need to get my stuff from the place Audrey and I were staying." There was a vague sadness in his tone.

"Of course. I can take you there. Let me just straighten up and jump in the shower and then we'll go." He nodded.

After my shower, I threw on a sundress and flip-flops and decided to let my hair air-dry. Will and I put all the windows down on the Jeep so we could enjoy the warm September air. He looked at me and stuck his hand out for the keys.

"Do you know how to drive?"

"Of course. You're in luck—I have a commercial driver's license. I used to drive a school bus in Detroit," he said with a beaming smile.

I laughed at the image of Will driving a bus. "You're kidding me. I can't see you driving a school bus. When?"

"About five years ago, right before I moved out here. I love kids; I had so much fun. I had a lot of odd jobs in Detroit." After Will lifted Jackson into the backseat, I handed him the keys.

"Okay, I trust you."

As we got on the road, I looked over at him. He was wearing his black Wayfarer sunglasses and bobbing his head to the Cars, playing on the radio. Like everything else he did, he was a completely self-assured driver.

"So what other kinds of odd jobs did you have in Detroit?"

He laughed to himself. "The first job I ever had was in a newly remodeled mall when I was sixteen. They had a lot of publicity and promotional garbage going on because of the new stores, so I got paid to walk around dressed as a giant soccer ball and wave to all the kids and stuff like that." I was stifling a giggle. "There was a football and a baseball and a couple of other characters. People from my high school used to come and push us over. The costumes were so bulky that it was practically impossible to get back on your feet without help, so I would just lie there flailing around, going, 'Come on, guys, help me out.'" I was laughing hysterically at that point. Will was never too proud and I loved it. He glanced over at me and started laughing, too. "What about you? What kind of jobs did you have in Ann Arbor?"

"I never really worked before Kell's; my parents and grand-parents supported me through college. Before my dad died, I was studying for the GRE to go to grad school, so I gave piano lessons, but that was it." He nodded. "Why didn't you go to college, Will?"

"I don't know. It just wasn't in the cards. My brother and some of my sisters did, but it would have been tough on my parents. I audited a ton of classes at Adrian College, so I kind of got a free education."

"What kind of classes?"

"Music, sound mixing, media technology, and a few others along those lines."

"That's cool. I wondered how you knew so much about that stuff."

Will turned up the radio and accelerated as I leaned back and absorbed the sun on my face. He smiled warmly at me and for a few minutes I think we were both completely content.

We pulled up to a beautiful, bright yellow colonial house; the sign said MERRY WAY INN. It was charming and cheery, but the look on Will's face was anything but. He looked like he was going to be sick.

"Do you want me to go in and get your stuff?" I asked gently.

"No, I should go. Fuck Spoon Guy and American Pie," he said.

"Yeah, totally. You're better off."

"I guess. Will you come with me, though?"

"Of course."

We walked in through the front door and up a small staircase. A woman who I assume was the innkeeper eyed Will, but he smiled and waved as if it were usual business. When we got to the room, he ran his hands through his hair nervously before knocking. There was no answer. He fished a key from his pocket, unlocked the door, and walked in. The room was large and decorated in various floral patterns. The comforter and pillows on the king-size bed were strewn about. I thought I heard Will dry heave before he walked to the window to gaze out.

"There they are. Sunbathing on my dime . . . fucking assholes," he said in a low voice. I stood behind him and looked out the window to where Audrey and Dustin were lying by the pool, sharing a chaise longue. I wrapped my arms around him from behind and gave him a squeeze. He brought my hand to his mouth and kissed it. Turning, he picked up his bag and headed for the door, never letting go of my hand. We held hands all the way to the Jeep. As we headed back to the city, I closed my eyes and dozed off to the sound of the wind in my hair.

I didn't wake up until Will was halfway up the stairs to our apartment with me in his arms. I hooked my arm around his neck and let him carry me all the way up. He looked down at me and smiled. "Hi, sleepyhead. You were out for the count."

"Yeah, I was exhausted."

He set me down on the landing and opened the door. "I'll take the Jeep to Jenny's parents'. Go ahead, go to bed.

I'll see you in the morning," he said and then waited for me to respond. I hesitated a moment and thought it would have felt perfectly normal to reach up and kiss him, but I knew that would be blurring the lines, so I didn't.

"Okay, thank you. Will, you're the best." He winked at me and then trotted down the stairs.

The next morning when I heard Will in the shower, I got up and headed to the kitchen. I poured myself a cup of coffee and leaned against the counter while I flipped through *The New Yorker*. I flinched when he wrapped his arms around me from behind.

"Easy, jumpy cat; just wanted to say good morning." And then he kissed me behind the ear.

"Morning. Why are you up so early?"

He walked over and poured himself a cup of coffee. "I have a meeting with Frank."

I turned around and hopped up on the counter in my usual sweats and T-shirt. Will was wearing nothing but a towel. It hung low, showing off the cut lines of his lower abdomen. I gaped at him until I noticed he was watching me. He tilted his head to the side and smirked. "Hi, friend," he said in a low voice.

I shook my head and took a deep breath through my nose. "Okay, so are you going to fill me in on what Frank says?"

"Absolutely. I have work the next five days, but let's make dinner here on Saturday night and then we can jam a little. What do you think?"

"Yes, let's do that." He walked over and stood between my legs, running his hands up my thighs. I took a deep breath and placed my hands over his. "I have to get in the shower," I whispered.

"How 'bout a bath?" he said, arching his eyebrows.

I smiled shyly and shook my head.

"Have a good day, then. I'll see you later." And then he made kissy lips, so I leaned in and gave him a peck.

"You, too."

He lifted me off the counter and then smacked my butt as I walked away. I huffed and pretended it annoyed me while I tried unsuccessfully to hide the permanent grin on my face.

Wednesday afternoon Jenny called me drunk from her honeymoon in Cozumel, wanting to know what had happened to Will after the wedding, so I filled her in on the details.

"What? You're kidding me? For Dustin? What the hell was that girl thinking? Well, at least the door is open for you to jump his bones." Her voice was slurred.

"There will be no bone jumping, Jenny. We're friends and I'm really starting to feel close to him. I want it this way . . . for a long time."

"Okay, girl, whatever you say. Tyler and I are workin' on babies over here, so you better put on your auntie pants," she said, giggling. I could hear Tyler in the background telling her to hang up.

"I love you guys. Have fun!"

On Saturday when I got home from Kell's, Will was already cooking. He was making my favorite pasta dish. I noticed there was wine on the counter and one of my father's Nick Drake albums was playing softly in the background. We sat at the table and ate while we talked about our week; being with him that way felt like home. Will always had a handful of interesting bar stories to share. I told him about Jenny and Tyler trying for a baby.

"That's awesome—they love each other," he said. It seemed that simple to him, just like it was that simple to Jenny and Tyler.

"Well, they've only been together for a few months—they haven't even lived together," I argued.

"Listen, my sister was married for ten years before she and her husband decided to have a kid. They were divorced three months after the baby was born. You never know—it's a crap-shoot, a leap of faith."

"No such thing," I said with a wry smile.

"How can you say that? You can't predict how others will behave in certain situations."

"Cause and effect. The decisions we make for ourselves have the most impact on where we end up in the future. Your sister should have seen the signs, or maybe she did and that's why she waited ten years to have a kid. It's not a crapshoot; the writing's on the wall long before we take that so-called leap of faith."

"The problem with that theory is that you're assuming everyone is a perfect judge of character. The leap of faith is giving it a chance and not projecting your own crap on some-one else because you're afraid of failing." It was the first time Will had ever really talked seriously to me about life, and even though we were talking about other people, I knew he was referring to me.

"Well, what about you? Why haven't you signed a deal yet?" I said, arching my eyebrows.

"I'm glad you brought that up. I'm scheduled to go into the studio to cut the demo next week. Can you make it in there on Thursday to lay down that piano track we worked on?"

"Yes, definitely," I said. "Forward progress, Will. Keep making it."

He narrowed his eyes and cocked his head to the side. I thought for a second that I'd offended him, and then he said,

"I have a show tomorrow night at Dropzone; do you want to come and play?" He looked hopeful but poised for rejection. I waited twenty seconds before answering.

"Okay," I said in a low voice.

"Really?" He stood up from the table, grabbed my face with both hands, and planted a hard, close-mouthed kiss on my lips.

"Will!" I protested.

"Lighten up, Mia. Come on, let's practice."

We played music into the wee hours of the morning, eventually narrowing down our set list for the show. Before heading to bed, I decided to take a shower. Through the frosted shower curtain I watched Will walk into the bathroom, brush his teeth, and then turn and lean against the counter. He crossed his feet and arms and put his head down into Will's standard *I'm being respectful* posture.

"Hey . . . do you need me to wash your hair or your back or anything?" I could hear mischief in his voice.

"Nope," I said, shutting off the water. I wrapped myself in a towel, flung the curtain open, and stepped out. I paused and turned as I walked out the door. Grabbing his face in my hand, I leaned in and gave him a peck on the cheek.

"Thanks for asking, though. Night, buddy."

"Night, sweet thing."

The show at Dropzone was a success. Even though we were performing under the name Bokononism, Will's fans were on to him, so we had a good turnout. Because of all the solo shows, he had perfected the skill of live looping. It was quite remarkable. He would have a few instruments along with a recording device that he could control with foot pedals. He'd play a guitar riff or pluck the violin and record it live onstage to play in a loop while he was strumming another guitar and singing. Because it requires so much coordination and instrumental expertise, the process really wowed the audience. His gifts were incontestable when he was performing.

The Dropzone had an old grand piano with clunky keys and a rattling string reverberation that gave the sound a rich character. Will introduced me as his little sister, which threw me for a loop, but I went with it. It reminded me of the way Willie Nelson always introduces his piano-playing sister. I thought about Willie's song "Angel Flying Too Close to the Ground" as I watched Will strumming his guitar and singing with his eyes closed and his head tilted to the heavens. I thought that song could have been written for him.

After the show, we were swarmed by people asking when he was going to release an album. His only response was "soon." I was approached by a good-looking guy named Mark who wanted to buy me a drink. Will must have overheard because he came up from behind and wrapped his arms around me. He bent down and whispered, "We gotta go," and then placed a lingering kiss over my ear. Mark looked at me, somewhat disgusted. I had gotten used to Will touching me that way, so I ignored him. I looked at Mark and thought briefly that I might take him up on the offer just to spite Will for being the overprotective roommate.

"You guys aren't really brother and sister, are you?" Mark asked with a smile.

"Yeah, we are," Will said quickly and then smacked me on the ass. "Let's hit it, sis."

I rolled my eyes at him. "It was nice meeting you, Mark. Thanks for the offer, but we better get going." Mark didn't seem disappointed. If anything, I thought I caught a look of relief on his face as we walked away.

"Why'd you do that? He just wanted buy me a drink," I said with mock disappointment.

"There are male groupies, too, Mia. Next thing you know he'll be at the next performance with your face silk-screened on his T-shirt," he said, laughing.

"I doubt that."

Back at the apartment, I stood in Will's doorway as he sat on his bed removing his shoes. "I have to be at Kell's early tomorrow so I'm gonna get to bed."

He stood up directly in front of me, head down, and took my hands in his.

When his gaze met mine, I saw peace in his eyes. "You were great tonight. Thank you, Mia."

I felt my face flush. "You're too kind. Really, you were amazing." This time I threw my arms around his neck, reached up on my tippy toes, and gave him a big, long hug. He held me tight against him.

"Good night," he said and then kissed my cheek.

I cried as I lay in my bed that night, thinking about how it wouldn't be long before Will would go off and become a famous musician, leaving this little life we created behind. There would be models and celebrities vying for his attention and I would become just a blurry memory from the early years. I would see him in some interview online talking about how he'd spent time in the East Village, playing in seedy venues and reading poetry in coffee shops. I cried because I knew that if I gave myself to Will, I would be left in pieces . . . left behind. The only way I could hang on was to be his friend, even though every part of me wanted more.

TRACK 13: The Sound of His Soul

On Thursday, I woke up feeling an unreasonable amount of excitement about going to the recording studio where Will was working on his demo. I took Jackson for a slow, meandering walk through the park. He was becoming more and more listless during our outings. Jackson always had sad eyes, but they were starting to look hollow. I knew he was growing old fast and that day I begged him to hang on for another year.

"I need you, buddy, now more than ever," I said to him. He wagged his tail and I felt my heart lift a little. It would be a good day; I could feel it, and for the first time in a while I looked forward to working hard at something, though music never really felt like work.

When I got to the studio, Will greeted me with enthusiasm. He had already completed two songs and just needed the piano track for the third to finish his demo. He was including my song, which he named "Pray," along with "All Fine" and the song "Polarize," which I would be working on.

"Hey, baby," he said, kissing me on the cheek. He quickly grabbed my hand and led me through the studio and past a few people sitting on a couch in the lobby area. "This is Mia, everyone," he said and then pulled me through a door and motioned for me to sit down at the mixing console. Frank was there with another man who I assumed was the engineer. "Mia, this is Jeff. Jeff, Mia."

"Nice to meet you," I said, shaking his hand. I looked up at Frank and smiled. He winked back at me but remained quiet in the corner. I directed my attention to Will, who was all business, moving the dials and pressing buttons. I could barely wrap my head around what he was doing.

"Listen, you have to hear this and tell me what you think," he said. It was my song playing and it sounded better than I could have possibly imagined it. As Will's vocal began to rise in the second verse, I got chills; goose bumps covered my body. He held each note so long and steady and controlled. I couldn't think of any way to make the song better.

He looked at me sharply while I listened and then he said, "What do you think? Too much on the low end?" The look on his face was intensely serious.

"No way! It's perfect. That depth makes the song," I said.

"Yeah, I agree." He worked at the board like every dial was a string on his guitar. I was astonished. Jeff the engineer literally did nothing; he was leaning back in his chair with his feet propped on a table. I'm pretty sure I saw dollar signs in Frank's eyeballs as he shot me the most self-satisfied smile I had ever seen. Will was a perfectionist and there was no doubt that he was in his element in the studio.

"Let's do this, then," he said while flipping a couple of switches. He stood up, reached for my hand, and led me into the soundproof room where I sat down at a gorgeous Yamaha grand piano. He spoke to Jeff through the window. "Okay, we're gonna go, start to finish, one take, and then we're outta here."

"What? Will, what do you mean?"

"You know the song, Mia, we've played it a hundred times. The room is already miked for it. I want to do piano, guitar, and vocal organically, like this . . . together." He paused again and assessed my look, which must have been pure fear. "We've got this, you and me, remember . . . mystical alchemy." And then he winked, grabbed his guitar, and took a seat in front of the microphone. I shook my head frantically, but he just shot me an arrogant smile and said, "It's a recording studio, they'll let us have another take if we need it, but I have a feeling we won't."

And we didn't. The acoustics in the room were magical. Will was right; recording the song that way gave it more identity. After we finished our take, he went to the mixing console and started the playback. He was ranting to Jeff about push-ins and drum tracks, so I decided I should get out of his way.

I put my arm around his shoulder and said, "I'm gonna get outta here unless you need me?"

"Yes! I need you. Why, where do you have to be?"

"Nowhere. I just don't want to get in your way."

"You are never in my way. I want you here; you're the only one who knows the sound I'm going for."

I was so incredibly flattered that Will felt that way. I stayed the entire day and into the night working with him to tweak each song. It took him several hours to perfect the drum track on "Polarize." I didn't even know Will could play the drums before that day, but he was competent enough at it that he was able to achieve the sound he wanted. When Frank and Jeff left, Will put some final touches on the last song and we listened to the completed demo tape all the way through. He was leaning back in a big leather chair. When I walked over to sit at the console, he pulled me onto his lap. I leaned against him, resting the back of my head on his shoulder as we listened to music we'd created.

On the subway ride home, he seemed truly at peace and satisfied with his work that day. He thanked me over and over and I just kept thanking him back; I told him it was one of the best days I'd had in a long time. When we got home we took turns in the shower and then went to our rooms. Will yelled at me from his bed, "Night, pretty baby!"

"Night, Will."

It was getting colder in the city, Halloween came and went without fanfare, and Will and I saw less and less of each other. He was working a lot, trying to keep himself busy while he waited to hear from the record labels. Jenny and Tyler were back, but not really; they weren't kidding about wanting to start a family right away. I'm pretty sure they only got out of bed to go to work. Sheil started dating a fellow sitar player, and although I was really happy to see her moving on, it still felt like a reminder that my father was gone forever. I kept at it with the café, even though the daily business of running it started to feel mundane. I hoped that I would find more studio work to keep me busy, so I started working on putting together my own demo tape to offer people looking for a pianist.

One morning at Kell's I noticed Jenny looking a little pale. There was a line of patrons forming, but she and the old monster weren't keeping up. Sheil popped in and started helping while Jenny leaned against the back counter, looking ill. I told her to go up to my apartment and rest, but she just covered her mouth and shook her head.

"I promise I'm fine," she said and then dry heaved into the sink.

"You're not fine." I looked at her closely. She was flushed and her cheeks were puffy.

"Are you hung-over?" Leaning in closer, I tried to catch a whiff of her breath. She put her hand out to stop me and then covered her mouth again, hiccupped, and then burped.

"Oh, I feel like shit."

"Maybe you have the flu." She just stared at me. "Hey, will you sneeze on that grumpy-ass guy that comes in all the time? You know, the one who wears that stupid floppy hat?"

"You're terrible."

"I'm just kidding. Seriously, though, Jenny, you should go lie down, you probably have a stomach bug or something. Go, get outta here."

Wearing a pained smile, she shuffled across the café and out the door.

At lunch I went to see her and found her listening to Will's demo. "This freakin' rocks!" she said, bobbing her head.

"Yeah, Will is going to be big." I feigned enthusiasm. I knew it was selfish. I wanted to be genuinely happy for him, but the thought of him moving on was becoming a giant void in my heart—a void that I tried desperately to ignore. "You seem to be feeling better." There was a long pause.

"You're going to be an aunt, Mia," she said with a huge smile.

"Oh my god!" I wrapped my arms around her for a long hug. "I'm so happy for you guys. Duh, I should have known. When did you find out?" I felt the tiniest pang of sadness that she hadn't told me right away.

"Yesterday. I was going to tell you, but it's still so early. The doctor confirmed it." She frowned. "He did one of those weird internal ultrasounds. You know?"

"No, I don't know. You mean the jelly stuff on your belly?" I had seen that enough times in movies.

"No, they shove this long, ultrasound probe up inside there."

"What?" I said, looking horrified.

"Calm down; it wasn't that bad. It was actually pretty awesome because we got to see our little peanut and the tiny flickering heartbeat."

"Really, that is so amazing. Is it really the size of a peanut?"
She shrugged. "Even smaller, I think."

"Does Will know?" I was thinking it would piss me off if they told him first.

"Tyler couldn't keep his mouth shut. He told him last night after a couple of drinks. I guess Will jumped up and down and did like three cartwheels down the sidewalk and then kissed Tyler on the mouth."

"What a dork."

"Lovable dork." She was smirking by that point.

"Yes, he is," I said wistfully. Will's reaction to the news didn't surprise me at all. I understood why Tyler was so eager to tell him. The thought of Will doing cartwheels down the sidewalk left me smiling for hours.

Jenny and I spent the rest of the afternoon together at Kell's, talking about babies and pregnancy. I realized I was extremely uninformed on the topic. I was an only child, no younger siblings, no nieces and nephews—I didn't even have friends with kids. My only experience was the small amount of time I'd spent with Jacob and a few music lessons I'd given in Ann Arbor. Jenny told me she wanted Will and me to be the kid's soul parents. I looked at her with amusement. "Is that like godparents?"

"I guess it would be like godparents if we were religious. It's like backup parents, you know?"

"I'm totally honored, but don't people usually pick a couple for stuff like that?"

"I think best friends will suffice."

I had never thought of Will and me as best friends, but we were and everyone else knew it.

"We would love that, Jenny."

I noticed an unkempt, grumpy-looking little fellow approach the counter with his iced cappuccino in hand. It was floppy-hat guy, sans his usual hideous headwear.

"Shit, what does he want now?" I said, just loud enough for Jenny to hear.

"Oh, this is gonna be good." She flipped on the old monster.

Grumpy Man set his glass on top of the refrigerator case. He had to yell over the screeching espresso machine. "Can I get a paper cup for that?"

"I'm sorry, but we don't have paper cups here."

"I've got to be somewhere and I'd like to take my three-dollar coffee with me," he said, his voice getting even louder.

"Like I said, I'm sorry, but we don't stock paper cups here." I was trying to tug at some environmental heartstrings he clearly didn't have.

"You're kidding? Well, you can expect a Yelp review from me."

What an assclown. I had no patience for his crap. "If you want a three-dollar cappuccino in a paper cup, there's a Starbucks around the corner—they'll even write your name on it." I gave him a condescending smile.

He pushed the glass over toward me, intentionally spilling the contents directly down my shirt. That's when mama bear lost it. Jenny shut the machine off and flew around the counter with a metal pitcher of steaming milk. "Get the hell out of here, you scary little psycho man!" She had rage in her eyes and I had no doubt she would have scarred that man's crabby little face if he hadn't turned and hurried out the door. When she noticed the shock on my face, she smiled and said, "What? It's the hormones. Anyway, what kind of man does that? What a crank-ass."

"Yes! I love it, Jenny. That's my new favorite word." We laughed and then I made an ill attempt at cleaning my white shirt.

"Go ahead and go home, Mia. Tyler will be here any minute; he can help me close up."

"Thanks, girl." I kissed her on the cheek. "Congratulations again. I'll see you guys soon."

I leapt up the stairs to the apartment where I found Will and Frank sitting across from each other on the couches. They were both leaning forward over the coffee table, reading documents. My heart started racing when I realized it must be a record deal. They both looked up at me and then directly to my shirt. Will raised an eyebrow.

"Occupational hazard," I said, pointing to the stain. "Hi, Frank." I shot my hand up and headed back to my bedroom to change. Will followed me and then stood in my doorway, quietly observing. I pulled my shirt over my head and threw it on the floor, then stared blankly into my open closet, wearing just my jeans and bra. I glanced up at Will, who seemed to be appreciating my bold behavior. "Nothing you haven't seen before," I said in a singsong voice as I grabbed a shirt off the hanger.

"We need to talk tonight after Frank leaves." I sensed a vague sadness in his tone, yet he was wearing his sexy, crooked smile. He leaned into my room, gripping the molding above the door with both hands. I focused on his tensing muscles as he rocked forward ever so slightly.

"Jenny's pregnant," I said as I pulled a T-shirt over my head.

"I know. Tyler told me. I think it's great."

"Yeah, me, too." We smiled serenely at each other. When I turned away toward my dresser, he was suddenly wrapped around me. He folded my arms in with his and pulled me back tight against his chest, his fingers intertwining with mine. His mouth went to the crook of my neck without caution. I tilted my head slightly, giving him access, where he trailed delicate kisses all the way up to my ear and whispered, "I gotta get back to Frank. Don't fall asleep on me, okay? We need to talk."

"I won't."

He held me with fervor, so tight I could barely breathe, and then he nuzzled his face in my hair and inhaled deeply before letting me go and walking out.

I let out the huge breath I was holding and then almost collapsed from the warm feeling running through my body. I took a shower and then sank into Will's bed while he continued his conversation with Frank in the front room. Will's gesture in my room earlier had me reeling. I thought it must have been some kind of good-bye embrace. I fought my heavy eyelids and tried to prepare myself for whatever he planned on telling me that night. When I could no longer keep my eyes open, I curled on my side and snuggled into his pillow.

I started awake when I felt him pulling me into his chest from behind. "You fell asleep on me. I like you in my bed," he whispered.

"What time is it?" I asked.

"A little after eleven." I had only been asleep for an hour or so.

"Let's talk."

"It can wait." He sighed and then pressed himself against me.

"No, what's going on?" I sat up and folded my legs underneath me.

He leaned up on his elbows. I turned the light on, crooked my eyebrows, and waited for him to speak. "I was offered a deal from Live Wire Records. They're an independent record label and they're willing to give me a lot more creative con-

trol than the others. I have until February to make a decision, but they've asked me to go to California in January and
open three shows for Second Chance Charlie. It would be San
Francisco, San Diego, and LA." I was familiar with that band,
mainly because the female lead singer is drop-dead gorgeous
and plastered on every magazine cover. I swallowed back the
huge lump in my throat.

"Okay, and . . . ?"

"Well, they want me to work on a couple of songs at a studio in LA while I'm there, so I'll be gone the whole month of
January, and I just wanted to know if maybe you would want
to go to Detroit with me for Christmas and come back here
for New Year's before I have to leave? I want to tell my parents
about the deal in person and I want you there with me." He
had hope in his eyes and it made me smile.

"Can we go see my mom and David while we're out
there?"

"Of course."

"I'll have to figure something out with Kell's and Jackson.
I don't want to take him on a plane," I said, biting my lip.
Leaving him worried me, but I really wanted to spend the
holidays with Will and meet his family.

"I'm sure Martha will watch him."

"Okay, Christmas Eve until the twenty-seventh, that's all
I'd be able to swing."

He sat up and gave me a hug. "Thank you."

When he let go, I leaned back and looked into his eyes,
trying desperately not to cry. "I'm so proud and happy for
you. Congratulations. Honestly, Will, I knew it would happen."

"Then why do you look so sad, sweet thing?" he said with
a pained expression.

"I just . . . I don't know. I want you in my life and I'm afraid . . . "

"There's nothing to worry about. You're my BFF, best friend forever; we'll always have this." He tilted his head to the side and smiled.

"Promise?"

His lips flattened and his expression turned serious. "I promise."

He remained motionless as I leaned over and gave him a peck on the cheek. In the doorway I turned to say good night and noticed he had the listening-to-God look. I wondered if this was the first time he realized how much I truly cared for him.

Will had to work on Thanksgiving—I guess hotel bars never close. I thought it was weird that he hadn't quit his job since he would be collecting an advance from the record label once he signed the deal. When I asked him why he didn't agree to the terms straight away, he simply said there was no need to rush it, but I wondered if he was waiting for something better to come along.

Jackson and I went to Jenny's parents' house in Hoboken, where they had the full holiday spread. I almost choked to death on a piece of turkey when Jenny's mom, Carol, asked me if Will and I had plans to marry.

"They're just friends, Mom," Jenny said, laughing.

"Oh, I thought . . . never mind," Carol said, smiling.

After dinner, I helped Carol clean up while Jenny sat on the couch, looking uncomfortable. She was whispering something to Tyler when Carol noticed her posture. "What's wrong, Jenny?"

"Nothing, I just feel crampy." The room went silent. Jenny's parents and I froze where we were standing. Those were not words anyone wanted to hear from a pregnant woman.

"It's normal to feel a little crampy this early, right?" Jenny said to her mom.

"I think so, but should we call the doctor just in case?"

Jenny stood up and then instantly doubled over. "Ow!" she shouted before running off to the bathroom.

I heard her cry out and then Tyler ran over and yelled, "Open up, babe!"

The lock turned and he walked in and slammed the door behind him. I didn't know what to do. I stared at Jenny's mom and dad, who were both pale and motionless. I heard a guttural moan from Tyler and then Jenny began sobbing loudly. The door swung open and he walked out, carrying his shattered wife.

"I have to take her to the hospital," he said through heavy breaths. Jenny looked like a frail child in his long arms. Tears began streaming down my cheeks as I walked behind them out to the driveway.

Tyler, Jenny, and her parents rode to the hospital together while I waited for a cab so I could take Jackson back to the apartment. Will was in the kitchen when I walked in. As soon as he saw my face, he was at my side with a look of pure concern. "What's wrong, baby?"

I let out a long sigh. "I think Jenny had a miscarriage; she's at the hospital now."

He narrowed his eyes. "Oh no, that's awful. We have to go."

I nodded in agreement.

As we gathered up our things to head out, the phone rang. It was Carol saying that Jenny had indeed had a miscarriage and they weren't going to keep her at the hospital. She said everyone was tired and wanted to get home and put an end to the horrible day. I told her to tell Jenny and Tyler we loved them and that we'd come by the next day.

On our way to Jenny and Tyler's the next morning, Will and I stopped at a market where we argued for ten minutes on what to buy them. I had flowers and Will had chardonnay and chocolate. "Flowers would be an appropriate gift, Will, especially at nine o'clock in the morning."

"It's Jenny. Trust me, this is what she wants."

"Fine, we'll get it all."

When we got to Jenny's, Tyler opened the door. He looked devastated. I hugged him and told him how sorry I was, then moved past him to Jenny, who was on the couch with a box of Kleenex and a big, cozy quilt. I handed her the flowers and bent over to give her a squeeze.

"Thanks, girl," she said in a low voice.

"I'm so sorry."

"I know," she said. She seemed to be keeping it together pretty well.

Will came over and, without a word, set the chocolate and chardonnay on the table and then knelt down in front of her. She glanced at the gifts and then looked him in the eye and smiled before breaking down into sobs and burying her face in his chest. He wrapped his arms around her and swayed slightly from side to side whispering, "Shhh. It's okay, shhh."

He was so tender and warm toward her that she was able to completely let go and accept the comfort he was offering. Watching Will like that made me want to be a better person. It made me want to be more like him, and I knew that was definitely a sign I was falling completely and deeply in love with him.

Will held my hand in the cab on the way home.

"You were really sweet with Jenny. I know they both love you," I said.

He brought my hand to his mouth and kissed it gently. "Thanks, baby. They love you, too." He seemed contemplative before he said quietly, "My sister Regina and her husband tried to get pregnant for two years and then when they finally did, she had two miscarriages back to back. They were devastated. They eventually had three kids, but my sister worried through each pregnancy. It was like she was waiting with bated breath for nine months. It really changes a woman. So I guess we just need to remember that for Jenny."

"You're sweet," I said, squeezing his hand.

"Wanna sleep in my bed tonight?" he said with a crooked smile.

"Not a chance, Wilbur."

He shrugged, laughing it off.

TRACK 14: Wait, What?

We flew to Detroit on Christmas Eve. Will was a neurotic head case about flying, so I made him a playlist and bought him some fuzzy socks. He tried to convince me to make out with him, saying it was the only thing that would calm his nerves. I knew it was a ploy. After we landed, he stood up to remove his guitar from the overhead bin and I noticed the girl across from us eyeing him. He winked and shot her a sexy smile and then looked at me with feigned confusion and mouthed *what?* We headed out to the curb and waited for his sister to pick us up.

"So, do you have a lot of ex-girlfriends in Detroit?"

"A couple. I had one girlfriend in high school, . . . Brenda. She dated me as a cover." He flashed a small, mirthless smile. "Yeah, she was having an affair with our history teacher. I had no idea at the time. She was my first and said I was hers, but she knew very well what she was doing and didn't seem too satisfied with my amateur ways, if you know what I mean." He chuckled and then grinned from ear to ear. "The summer after we graduated, she turned eighteen and broke up with me that very day. I think her and the teacher are married now. I would have been totally heartbroken except that I had already met Kate . . . who was a lot of fun. She was a nurse and ten years older than me. I learned a lot from her. We dated off and on until I moved to New York. She's married now but we've kept in touch. That's it, really. I dated girls in New York but nothing serious."

"Were you in love with Kate?"

"In a way I was, but we both knew it wouldn't work. We just had fun with it. She said she loved my guitar hands. She'd let me practice all kinds of things on her." I rolled my eyes at him and simultaneously thought Kate was a very wise woman. "What about you? I bet you had lots of admirers in Ann Arbor?"

I flushed. "Not at all. I didn't have sex until college. I didn't even have a boyfriend in high school. My first time was with a soccer player at Brown. He told me he loved me after one date, then he basically stole my virtue and stopped calling me."

"Guys are dicks, Mia, stay away from 'em." He wrapped his arm around my shoulders to keep me warm while we waited.

Will's sister Reina pulled up in a mint-green minivan. She rolled down the passenger window and yelled, "What up, homey!" Will flashed her a peace sign. I could tell she was a character. She wore a Mickey Mouse sweatshirt and mom jeans and her hair was a wild nest of curls sprouting out of a high ponytail. Her only resemblance to Will was her dark, deep-set eyes. She reached over to shake my hand as I hopped in the back. "Hi, Mia! We're so glad to finally meet Willie's girlfriend." I nodded and smiled at her and then turned and shot a peeved look at Will, who was loading our bags. He shrugged and mouthed, *Go with it.*

I squeezed between two little kids and leaned forward. "Thanks, Reina, I'm really happy to be here." The little boy and girl I was sitting between were beautiful, with red hair and freckles. They looked to be four years old and they were buckled into matching car seats. "I'm Mia, what's your name?" I said to the little girl.

"Maddie."

"Oh. Is this guy your brother?"

"No . . . I don't know that kid," she said flatly.

Reina chimed in. "Yes, they're twins. That's Conrad."

I turned toward Conrad. He smiled and said, "Hi" in a tiny monster voice.

I looked back at Maddie and leaned in toward her. "I like you," I whispered.

"I like you, too," she said. "Let's be friends."

"You bet."

Will jumped in the passenger seat and then turned around. "Hey, Freckles. Hey, Bam Bam, what's up?"

"Hi, Uncle Will," Maddie said.

Conrad started giggling when he saw Will's face.

We drove to Will's parents' house, which was located in a little Detroit suburb. After their kids had moved out, they'd downsized from what Will called the six-bedroom crap hole he'd grown up in to a modest three-bedroom tract home. The first thing I noticed when we pulled up was an inordinate number of Christmas lawn ornaments scattered across the snow-covered yard. The driveway was full of cars, so we parked five houses away and carted our stuff up the street while Reina dragged the twins along. When we got to the front door, people started pouring out to greet us. Will turned to me and raised his eyebrows. "Are you ready for this?"

I nodded. It would be a very eye-opening experience to spend the holidays with such a huge family. I felt the warmth spilling out to us as his family members embraced him with twenty minutes of hugs and kisses.

The next several hours were a blur. There were a hundred kids running around and no real organized meal, just a bunch of food on a table for people to graze. Will's mom, Rita, was a sweetheart—she complimented me over and over and seemed truly happy that Will had brought someone home. She said the next morning would be a quieter time for us to get to know each other, but she did tell me they used to worry about Will when he was younger because one of the sisters dropped him on his head as a baby. "He just always seemed different than the other kids," she said.

He clearly didn't fit in with the rest of the group. His dad was quiet and somewhat unsocial. He basically sat in a recliner while all the kids jumped around him. He was kind when Will introduced us, but he made very little effort to talk to me after that. Will's brother Ray was literally his polar opposite. I could see immediately why they weren't close.

"Mia, this is my brother Ray. Ray, this is Mia."

"Nice to meet you," I said, holding my hand out. He shook it robotically while Will stepped away to get us a drink. Ray stood a tad taller than Will and was about sixty pounds heavier. What was left of his severely receded hair was very short, and if it weren't for his dark eyes, the family trait, he would have looked nothing like Will. All the family members dressed in a kind of typical suburban, conservative attire. Compared to his family, Will seemed very edgy with his tattoos and silver-studded belt, but to me he was just Will, my sweet and sensitive Will.

"So you're the girlfriend?" Ray said with a patronizing smile. "Are you a bartender, too?" I could tell right away he was one of those people who always had a hint of condescension in his tone.

"No, I'm not. I own a café in the East Village and . . . I'm a musician, as well." My own admission surprised me, but I wanted to remind Ray that Will wasn't just a bartender.

"Ah yes . . . the music. Kind of an oddball thing to pursue, don't you think?"

"Why is that?" I said with a smile of my own.

"I don't know, just seems like more of a hobby."

I waited a long beat before responding. "Well, I disagree. I've studied music most of my life and your brother is by far the most talented musician I've encountered. It would be a crime if he didn't pursue a career in music. And, really, there is nothing odd about it."

He studied my expression. "Hmm. Well, he's always had a knack for it; I'll give him that. So what do you play?"

"Piano," I said and he nodded with a smile.

Will appeared and threw his arm around my shoulder after handing me a glass of wine. "Watch out, Ray, this one's a fire-cracker," he said as he kissed me on the forehead. Ray smiled warmly at both of us. I knew he meant well, but I wasn't sure if anyone in Will's family would truly appreciate the magnitude of what he was about to tell them.

Will glanced around the room and then cleared his throat loudly. "Ahem. I have an announcement to make." Everyone immediately quieted. I noticed several sets of eyes surveying me, first my left hand and then my stomach. Clearly most announcements in this family were either engagements or pregnancies.

"Everybody, I want to let you know that Mia here . . . has never had turducken." Huh? The first thing I thought was that Will was right, I had never had turducken; he told me it was his family's Christmas Eve tradition to roast a deboned chicken inside of a deboned duck inside of a turkey. It sounded disgusting to me, but that wasn't the point. I thought he was going to announce his record deal—instead Will threw the attention to me and then stared off smugly while his entire family started talking at once about how much I was going to love the freakin' turducken.

I elbowed him and then narrowed my eyes. "You're in trouble," I whispered.

"What are you gonna do to me, sweet thing?" He grinned.

I yanked him away into the bathroom and shut the door. "What was that? Why didn't you tell them about the deal?"

"Mia, did you see how many little kids were running around out there?"

I shot out my hands. "What does that have to do with anything?"

"In my family it's just kind of a funny thing when one of the couples goes into the bathroom and locks the door." He smirked devilishly.

I gasped, appalled. "Oh my god. First of all, we're not a couple, and second, that is ridiculous." He just shrugged and held his shit-eating grin. "Will Ryan, I am mad at you." I stomped my foot like a petulant teenager. "And furthermore, you still haven't answered my question."

He leaned in, dropping his head down near my cheek and putting his hands on my hips. Any inkling of a gap between us was closed. I took in a sharp breath and shut my eyes as I felt his body against mine. His lips grazed my jaw and then his mouth moved up along my neck. He tugged at my ear with his teeth and whispered, "We'll talk later, okay, baby?"

I pushed his shoulders away. "You have to stop touching me like that!"

He took a step back and gazed at me sorrowfully. "I thought you liked it."

"I do."

"Then what's the problem?"

"I just don't want to complicate things, Will, that's all."

"By letting me touch you?"

I nodded. "Yes."

"Listen, I changed my mind. I'm not going to tell them about the record deal now. I don't want to have to explain all the fine details to every member of my family on Christmas Eve. Let's just be together . . . okay?"

He looked so pathetic standing there, rejected. He corrected himself a couple of times when his body made involuntary movements to reach out and touch me. He was fighting the urge to just simply take my hand or kiss my cheek. I didn't know why I was being so harsh; he hadn't really crossed the line, although the soft kisses on my neck were certainly testing the limits. The charade and the constant touching created so much confusion. I couldn't tell anymore what we were to each other.

Maybe Will wanted me to come home with him and meet his family just to pretend for a few festive moments that I was his girlfriend and he was just like the rest of them: loved. I buried my head in his chest and hugged him around the waist; he wrapped his arms around my shoulders. "Okay, you're right, let's just enjoy this time off. And we can hug, like this, all you want. This is what friends do," I said as he squeezed me tighter.

When we returned to the living room everything was back to usual business. Rita displayed the cut-up turducken and everyone cheered. I wasn't sure what all the hype was about—it tasted like turkey, duck, and chicken. No surprise there, but it was charming how the entire family got so excited over it.

After everyone left, Will's dad went off to his bedroom and Rita and I cleaned up while Will made a bed on the pull-out sofa.

"Will, you're almost thirty years old. I think your father and I will be okay if you and Mia want to sleep in the guest room." Will looked over and waited for me to make a decision. It wasn't like sleeping in the same bed was anything new for us, but I think after the episode in the bathroom he didn't want to make any assumptions.

"That's fine, thank you, Rita."

She looked at me and then cupped my face and said, "I'm glad you're here."

"Thank you. I'm glad to be here." I truly meant it. I studied Rita's features. She had the same dark eyes as Will and the same full lips. She wore round glasses and her gray hair was in a bob. She was much older than my mother, but she had a youthfulness about her that I was sure Will had inherited.

In the guest room Will stripped down to his boxers, slid into bed, and rolled away, facing the window. I dug through his bag and pulled out one of his white T-shirts and slipped it over my head.

"Night, Will."

"Night, buddy." He said it with a tinge of irritation. He made no attempt to touch me.

The next morning, I woke up to an empty bed. I threw on some sweats and went to the bathroom and brushed my teeth. When I got to the living room, Rita yelled out, "There she is. Merry Christmas, Mia!" Will's parents were dressed in matching red pajama sets and Santa hats. His dad did not seem the least bit amused; it was clearly his mom who was the festive one. Will had on flannel pajama bottoms that I had never seen—they really made him look domestic and I think it turned me on. His white T-shirt was a stark contrast against his tattooed forearm and his hair was wet and brushed back away from his face. He looked unreasonably handsome for first thing in the morning.

There was a fire going and the lights on the Christmas tree

were twinkling. I sat down on the couch next to him and put my hand on his leg. "Merry Christmas, honey," I said softly and then I puckered my lips. His parents' eyes were glued on us. Will focused on my expression as I gave his thigh a squeeze.

His eyes kissed mine and then he let out a barely audible sigh as he leaned over and pecked my lips. "Merry Christmas, baby." His mom gave me a steaming mug and I wrapped my hands around it and folded my legs onto the couch, curling up into Will as I sipped my coffee.

Rita sat back on her heels, next to the tree. "Okay, it's time to open presents," she said as she handed me a box with a big red ribbon on it.

"Thank you so much—you didn't have to get me anything."

I tore the wrapping open and lifted the lid to find a gray, high-necked cashmere sweater. I put it up to my face. "Wow, I've never had cashmere. This is beautiful. Really, it's too much."

"Don't be silly, Mia. Will has never brought a girl home for us to meet, we're thrilled to have you here and we wanted to get you something you would like. I sent Will a picture of the sweater and he gave me the thumbs-up," she said, pleased. She looked at Will, who was smiling at her with love.

"Thank you so much." I got up and handed Rita the present I'd bought for her and Ray.

"Look, Raymond, a French press! I've always wanted one of these. Thank you, Mia."

Will and his parents exchanged some gifts; he bought his dad a Civil War anthology and a baseball documentary DVD boxed set . . . very Americana stuff. For his mom he had a book called *How to Write a Cookbook* and a gift card to Williams-Sonoma. When she opened it, he said, "You have to do it, Mom. Write the book. People will love it!"

Rita looked over at me and said, "I've been saying I want to write a cookbook since before Will was born."

"You should, Rita, you're a fabulous cook. Will has made so many of your dishes for me and I can't get enough. I'm really going to miss it when he's gone."

As soon as the words came out of my mouth, it hit me that Will hadn't told his parents yet.

"What do you mean, when he's gone?"

Will chimed in. "I'm going to California on New Year's Day; I'll be there for a month. I'll be opening up for a band called Second Chance Charlie."

"Never heard of 'em." Ray Sr. finally decided to join the conversation.

Will continued, "It's just for three concerts. I'll be back in New York the first week of February."

"Oh, that's wonderful, honey," Rita said with a smile. Will didn't elaborate and I knew why. There was really no point. His parents were not into music and probably never would be; it was like speaking a foreign language to them.

I jumped up and handed Will my present for him. He pulled the leather-bound black notebook out of the gift bag and slowly ran his hand over the cover.

"Open it," I said. On the inside cover I had taped a black-and-white picture that Jenny had taken of me, Will, and Jackson sitting on a blanket in Tompkins Square Park on the Fourth of July. I was leaning back on my hands with my legs out. Will was lying perpendicular to me with his head on my lap and one arm reaching behind him around my waist and his other hand petting Jackson's head. The three of us looked like a little family, completely relaxed and at ease with one another. On the first lined page of the notebook I had written a message:

Will,

　　Here is a little something to write your thoughts in, or perhaps lyrics or your inspiring poetry. All of it is amazing and beautiful and I've felt so lucky to have been privy to it. I wanted to include the picture as a reminder that you will always have us to come home to if ever you need a break from being super famous and swooned over... you know how well I can bring you back to earth... wink. But seriously, the whole group from Kell's loves you and we're so proud of you. I know I'm going to miss you like crazy. You've been the biggest comfort to me since I moved to New York. You've been a great friend; you've been the best and I won't forget it.

　　Don't forget about me, okay?

　　　　　　　　　　　　Love, Mia

Will narrowed his eyes at me and shook his head slightly. "What?" I said.

He glanced over at his parents and then back at me, swallowing before he spoke. "Thank you, Mia." As he reached in to kiss my cheek he whispered, "We need to talk."

I nodded and then sat back on the couch. He reached down and grabbed a box from under the tree and handed it to me. I opened it to find a framed black-and-white picture of Will and me onstage at the string festival. It was a timeless picture that could have been taken in the sixties and I loved that about it. We were both smiling and looking out to the crowd with magic in our eyes. The plain black frame matched so many of my father's from the apartment; I knew Will intended it to be an addition to the collection. On the cardboard back, Will had written:

MYSTICAL ALCHEMY

"There's something else in the box," he said. I looked down to find a necklace with a lotus-flower design carved into a round, silver pendant.

I looked up at him and smiled. "I love this."

"It's a lotus flower."

"I know."

"It symbolizes purity of the heart and mind."

I reached in and gave him a long hug. "Thank you. You know me so well."

"Do I?" he whispered.

I leaned back to gauge his expression. His lips were bent into a small, tight smile and there was sadness in his eyes. I immediately put the necklace on and haven't taken it off since.

We spent the next day acting like everything was fine. I knew on the drive to Ann Arbor we would have a chance to talk, so we made the best out of our time with his parents. While speeding out of Detroit in our rented car, Will blared the Adolescents, singing along to the music at the top of his lungs. I finally turned it down during the song "I Hate Children," when it occurred to me that Will was working out some of his frustrations; some that were clearly brought on by me and my harmless gift.

"What's up, buddy?"

"Yeah, what's up, buddy?"

Ah, it was neurotic Will. "What do you mean?"

"I don't understand you. There, I said it. How many times do I have to tell you? What do I have to do to prove to you that I'm not going anywhere? I'm leaving for a month; I'm coming back. I live with you, for God's sake. You're my best fucking friend, Mia. I wish it were more and I think you know that. You are the most guarded person I have ever met, yet everything you feel is right there on your face and you don't even know it. Whatever you need me to be, I'll be! Friends? Fine! Best friends? Great! I'll do it, because I want you in my life more than anything I have ever wanted. So please stop with the don't-forget-me shit!"

"Okay." I meant to say it softly, but it came out as more of a whine.

He glanced over at me and his expression softened. "Okay? I'm sorry, baby, I just . . . I don't want to leave either, and I don't want you to put up your defenses because you think I'm going to run off and forget about you."

Will knew I had always been worried about the rock star life and all the faceless, foregone conclusions that would come into his life. He was reassuring me that I wasn't that, no matter what label we gave to each other. Really, Will wasn't the rock star, at least not the stereotypical image I'd had in my mind when I first met him. He was nothing like that. Sure, he could flirt with women, but he was never smarmy and he didn't sleep around . . . per se. He liked people, he liked women, he was a lover, but he was honest with everyone he came in contact with and he was especially honest with himself—a quality I needed to work on.

I reached over and squeezed his hand; he pulled my hand to his mouth and kissed it, never taking his eyes off the road. He changed the CD, turning up Nina Simone's "Sinnerman."

He accelerated and we flew toward Ann Arbor without another word. He bobbed his head and tapped his hand on the steering wheel to the fast, jazzy beat. The music set my mind into spiraling motion, thinking about what he had said. I never considered myself guarded; I thought of myself as strong, but I was wrong. Life had thrown me for a loop when my father died. I'd gone to New York thinking I would straighten things out with the café, then go to grad school, further my education, meet some strapping doctor or businessman and let my life follow the square rules I set forth, but the moment I stepped onto that plane back in March, I'd started to feel a different pull. There was a magnetism I felt from Will, the music, my new friends, the café, and the city itself. It felt right and it felt good. How could I have been so wrong about myself before? If I was guarded it was because I was realizing how little control I had over my feelings and it scared me.

When we got to my mother and stepdad's in Ann Arbor, I gave Will a brief tour and introduced him to David, whom I called Dad. It was a Sunday and the Detroit Lions were playing, so my stepdad was wearing his normal NFL garb. Will struck up a conversation about the team and the two hit it off right away. I didn't even know Will followed football, but there were so many things I didn't give him credit for. He may not have been a sports fan, but Will read the newspaper every single day. He knew a little about everything and his own curiosity and desire to better himself and grow as a person had given him a far more valuable education than I had gotten from a fancy, Ivy League college. My mother and I caught up in the kitchen while we prepared dinner.

"Mom, I want you know that I don't blame you for what happened between you and Pops. I'm getting things now . . .

I guess I'm realizing we're all just people trying to figure it all out."

She walked over and wrapped her arms around me. "Thank you for telling me that. You'll figure it out, Mia; I think maybe you already have." She glanced over at Will. Somehow letting my mom know how I felt gave me a sense of closure regarding my father.

After dinner, Will sang and played his acoustic guitar. My mom and stepdad seemed really impressed by his ability to figure out a song in a matter of minutes. It wasn't always perfect, but he would usually get the melody pretty close. My mom requested "The Girl from North Country" by Bob Dylan. He knew the song but he needed a little help with the lyrics, which my mom knew word for word. I was surprised since I had never known her to listen to Bob Dylan. I knew the lyrics as well; Pops had sung that song a thousand times and then I realized why my mom requested it; there was no question that Will had a spirit like my father's. He sang the song passionately with his eyes closed. His soulful voice belted out the lines like they were his own. *"I'm wondering if she remembers me at all . . . many times I've often prayed."* I looked up at my mom, who immediately looked away. I wondered if my father thought about her when he sang those lines.

I made an ill attempt at the harmonica solo, but it didn't sound that great; Will chuckled at me and winked. He finished the song carrying the last line out, soft and slow: *"She once was a true love of mine."* I looked at my mom again, but this time she didn't look away and she didn't hide the tears streaming down her face. She was mourning my father, too, and Will being there was healing for us all. The old music wasn't Will's style but he didn't care; he just wanted to play for the people he cared about. He never asked if we wanted to hear an original song, even though I knew he had plenty of great ones—he just wanted to provide everyone with something that was personal. He played for hours—we laughed and cried and talked a little about Pops.

When it was time to go to bed, Will offered to sleep on the couch. "No way," I said, "I want to cuddle." He smiled and laughed.

Will looked at my mom, who shrugged and said, "She wants to cuddle."

I curled into Will under the covers of my childhood bed. I was asleep in minutes and I got the most restful sleep I'd had in months.

Opening my eyes, I realized I was using Will's chest as a pillow. I peeked up and found him wide awake, staring at the ceiling. "You talkin' to God?"

"Something like that," he murmured.

"What's wrong?" I asked.

"I have a lot on my mind. We need to get home. I want to put another dead bolt on the door and make sure the smoke detectors have batteries and the furnace is working before I leave. Plus, I need to get all my equipment together. I'm just stressed about the next couple of days."

"Will Ryan, are you worried about me?"

"I'm always worried about you."

"We'll get it done. I'll help, and don't worry about me; I'll be fine. Do you want to spend New Year's Eve at the apartment? We can have Jenny and Tyler over to give you a proper sending off."

"I'd love that," he said with a conflicted look on his face. He smiled bleakly and then kissed the top of my head before rolling out of bed.

TRACK 15: Hallelujah

We flew home that day and got right to work on preparing for Will to leave. Over the next couple of days we were completely consumed with chores. Will did a whole crazy safety check on the apartment while I was at the Laundromat doing his laundry. I stole two T-shirts out of the pile; I figured I would need them to cuddle up with in the weeks to come.

On New Year's Eve, while Will was out with Frank, I made a cake and got ready for our little party. I told Jenny it was going to be a California theme, whatever that means. I cranked up the heater in the apartment and put on a sundress and flip-flops while the snow was falling heavily outside. I drew a palm tree and wrote "Surf's Up, Wilbur" on the cake. Jenny and Tyler showed up before Will got back.

After they both stripped off three layers, Jenny revealed her Hawaiian-print dress. Tyler had a matching print shirt. "It was the closest thing we had," she said, pointing to her dress and laughing. She pulled a joint out of her little purse. "Look what we brought. Let's get stoned—it's totally California."

"Oh my god, Jenny, you guys kill me. Will could definitely use that, he's been a loon the last couple of days. He really hates flying."

"No . . . he's worried about leaving you," she said, smiling at me.

"Oh, well, it will be fun at any rate."

Will came through the door looking beat. He patted Jackson on the head before looking up at us with a huge smile. "You guys look ridiculous—it's twenty-four degrees outside."

"We got pot," Jenny said in a singsong voice as she waved the joint around.

Will wrapped his arms around her and lifted her off the ground in a bear hug. "Oh, sweet, sweet Jenny."

Tyler came over and high-fived Will. "Congratulations, man! You better make us proud."

"It's not that big of a deal, you guys, seriously. I haven't signed a deal, I'm just doing three shows."

"But it's a start. Quit being so freakin' humble, Will. You deserve to celebrate—you've worked hard for this," I said as I reached up to give him a peck on the cheek. "Now go strip down, you must be boiling in that."

He came back out dressed in a white T-shirt, long black shorts that hung low on his hips, and the silver-studded belt. With his natural olive skin and disheveled hair, I thought he would fit in perfectly in California.

The four of us ate and had cake and champagne. None of us had any desire to fight the crowds in Times Square, but we thought we should at least watch the ball drop on the Dick Clark special. Our small little TV that we never used was on low as we sat talking at the kitchen table. When we heard the name Second Chance Charlie, we all jumped up and ran over to watch the performance. I knew the music and recognized the lead singer, Sonja, from the many magazine covers she graced. The band reminded me of a cross between the groups No Doubt and Paramore. Sonja jumped around a lot but had a really strong, sensual voice. She was beautiful, small, and graceful, and clearly the fantasy of many a teenage boy, which was the core of her audience. The band appealed mostly to the high school emo crowd. It didn't really make sense for Will, with his white-boy rock and roll, to open up for them, but I figured his music wasn't that simple to define and maybe he would capture a younger audience if he were marketed that way. After all, he was not only extremely talented, he was also good-looking and he had that whole sexy, brooding thing going for him. After the performance, Sonja was interviewed, and she mentioned she was flying to California first thing in the morning and that it would be a long night.

"Are you guys on the same flight?" I asked.

"Yeah, we're flying private. The record label chartered a plane."

"Oh," I said, wondering why he hadn't shared that little tidbit with me.

"Hey, Will, why is the label having you open for them? It seems like kind of a different crowd," Tyler said.

"I guess it is. I don't know, the girl saw me play at the string festival and asked the label if they could get me to open for her. I kind of agreed to it just to buy more time before I have to make a decision."

"I didn't know she requested you—why didn't you tell me?" I narrowed my eyes but tried to hide my jealousy.

"It seemed irrelevant," he said, straight-faced.

Tyler tried to intervene. "So do you have a band you're going to play with?"

"Yeah, basically pickup musicians and Nate. I got him, so I'm happy about that, but the other guys I barely know except from the few practices we've had."

"Good for you, man. It sounds like a great opportunity; you have to keep us posted."

"Definitely," he said, but he was looking at me, trying to decipher the look on my face when he said it. I went into the kitchen and Will followed. "She's a child, Mia; she's eighteen years old. You have nothing to worry about."

"Eighteen is an adult, not a child, and you can do whatever you want. We're not together—I don't even know why you're saying this to me."

"I'm saying it because it seemed like it bothered you."

I looked into his eyes for a long second. He seemed troubled and concerned. "It doesn't bother me, I promise." I smiled and walked past him, grabbing the joint off the counter. "Let's do this, people—it's eleven o'clock. We have one hour until 2009!"

We sat on the couches and passed the joint around while Will dropped the needle on Patti Smith's *Horses* from my father's collection. He sat down on the couch next to me, taking the joint and inhaling. He blew a lungful of smoke out while simultaneously tapping his foot and singing the line *"Jesus died for somebody's sins but not mine."* We all burst into laughter.

"God, this is like fucking high school!" Tyler said.

"Except that this album was made before any of us were born." Jenny giggled.

"All I would need is a Mickey's forty and an empty football field and I'd be right back in my high school days," Will said.

"Boone's Farm, Strawberry Hill for me. What about you, Jenny?" I said, laughing.

"Wine coolers and nacho cheese Doritos . . . yuck. Tyler, your turn."

"Mad Dog 20/20 and Taco Bell."

"Why were we so gross back then?" I asked.

"No money," Tyler said.

"We still have no money, but at least we have some dignity."

"What are you talking about, Mia? Will has money." Tyler looked at me, stupefied.

"Well, he will, if he'd ever sign that deal."

Will jumped up. "Let's dance!"

We danced around like fools for a while and then I noticed that the countdown to the ball drop had started. "It's time!" I yelled.

We all chanted, "Five . . . four . . . three . . . two . . . one." I watched Jenny jump up and wrap her arms around Tyler, kissing him.

I glanced over to Will, who was watching me with the listening-to-God expression in his eyes. Looking down, I grabbed his hands in mine, and then with a small smile and no words, I looked up and asked him for a kiss. His lips met mine gently; he lingered there, but didn't ask for more. He tugged ever so slightly at my lower lip before pulling away. "Happy New Year, sweet thing," he whispered.

"Happy New Year, Will."

I glanced over to Tyler and Jenny, who were still making out. They stopped abruptly when they noticed us waiting for them. "Happy New Year, guys!" Tyler said.

We exchanged hugs and then Jenny caught Tyler's eye again. "We're gonna head out," she said. I figured I knew why: honeymoon phase.

We said our good-byes and walked them out to the landing. Will went to his room and started throwing stuff in a bag as I watched him from the doorway.

"Have you seen my white T-shirt? The longer one?"

"I'm keeping it," I said, grinning. He looked up and laughed once.

His hair had gotten quite a bit longer since I'd first met him. It was a disordered mess, falling in his face. "Do you want me to cut your hair?"

"You?" He said it like it was the most preposterous idea he had ever heard.

"Yeah, I used to cut my father's hair. I can do it."

He appraised me. "Did you cut your father's hair while you were stoned and drunk?"

"No, but I can do it," I said, laughing. "Come on, buddy, I'll get the scissors." I grabbed the scissors from the bathroom and kicked off my shoes. Will followed me to the kitchen. "Take off your shirt," I said as I pulled a chair away from the table. He obliged but stood in front of me before sitting down. I sucked in a breath as I let my eyes trail from his chest down and back up again. "Sit," I said in a raspy voice. I put Damien Rice on the iPod dock, hoping it would help me concentrate. I really didn't want to mess up Will's hair, but his shirtless chest was causing a bit of a distraction for me.

He shook his head and stood up. "I can't let you do this; it's crazy."

"It's just hair. Sit down, Wilbur, or I'll tie you to this chair." He raised his eyebrows and shot me a sexy half smile.

I was very careful as I cut the back and sides. I combed his hair down over his eyes and trimmed as much as I could while I stood on each side of him. When it was time to trim the front, I threw my leg over his, straddling him on the chair. He sucked in a breath but kept his eyes closed. "Tell me you didn't cut your father's hair like this?"

"Quiet, silly, I'm concentrating. Almost done . . . " His hands moved to my thighs. I trimmed the last little bit and then put the comb and scissors in one hand while I brushed his hair off his face with the other. He opened his eyes and simultaneously gripped my legs. Searching his face, I saw a vaguely defeated look wash over him. His eyes kissed mine and then his hands moved higher under my dress; I thought I heard him moan softly as his lips parted. I dropped the scissors and comb and rested my forearms on his shoulders while I continued running my fingers through his hair.

The champagne and pot, not to mention Damien Rice, were creating a heady atmosphere in the kitchen. When I leaned forward slightly, I felt him hard beneath me and my body took over. I pressed down onto him and sucked in a breath. He gripped my hips and pulled me against him. I moved, grinding harder as I let a breathy "ahh" escape. With my dress riding up around my waist, he leaned forward and placed one hand behind my neck, holding me as his mouth went to my collarbone. I let my head fall to the side while he trailed kisses up my throat. My inner thighs were quivering and I could feel the heat between my legs spreading up my body. He pulled me tighter against him, and then with a heavy breath he whispered, "What are you doing to me?"

My dress strap fell off my shoulder. He seized the moment, pulling the top down on one side. I arched my back, offering myself to him as he kissed my breast, his tongue toying with my nipple. I squirmed in his arms but he pulled me even closer to him. He moved so fluidly that I felt myself lost in a rapture I had never experienced. This time the "ahh" had a sound I couldn't stifle as he kissed my body urgently. I continued to grind down on him while my hands moved frantically in his messy hair. I held him close to me and allowed myself to relish the all-consuming feeling of our bodies melding together. There was a quickening pulse and dampness between my legs as I felt him pressing harder against me. His skilled fingers moved seamlessly from my stomach down the inside of my panties, and when he touched me there I lurched forward involuntarily and then jumped off.

He quickly reached out for me. "Just let me kiss your

mouth," he whispered, his eyes pleading. I pulled my dress back into place and squinted my eyes in disbelief. I felt like the last three minutes were the most erotic moments of my life, yet somehow there was no kissing on the lips . . . I blame the pot.

I stood there transfixed while he sat in the chair, searching my face for something. I was breathing heavily when I turned and ran off to my room. I slid down the back of the door and began to cry. When I heard him walk down the hallway, I tried to stifle my sobs. He stopped at my door; I could hear him breathing on the other side and then he said in the most heartrending voice, "I'm sorry, baby."

"Me, too."

It wasn't his fault, he didn't need to apologize, but I knew him well enough to know he didn't want us to leave each other that way. I had never wanted anyone so badly—my body ached for him as I sat on my floor wondering how I could make things right. I couldn't give myself to Will mere hours before he would be leaving, but it was wrong of me to lead him on. I didn't know how to fix it, so I curled up into a little ball next to my bed and went to sleep, feeling utterly wretched.

I woke up from the early morning light accosting me through the window and found myself lying in my bed, under the covers, wearing the wrinkled and scrunched-up sundress around my waist. My bedroom door was open and it occurred to me that Will must have come into my room and put me in bed after my pathetic ass passed out. Staring at the ceiling, I wondered how the independent and shrewd Mia of one year ago could find herself drowning in the pitiful depths of a quarter-life crisis. It Just. Seemed. So. Dull. I was running away full force into a plain old ordinary existence when I had angels-singing, heart-thrashing love reaching out for me. Why couldn't I allow myself to let him in?

I heard the front door close and the familiar sound of Will skipping down the stairs. I knew I had to do something quickly. I flew with supersonic speed down the hallway to the kitchen window to yell, "Stop!" to Will before he left. When I reached the window, I swallowed hard at the sight of Sonja down the street, leaning against a town car, waiting for Will. Her platinum hair and ruby-red lips could be seen from space. I blinked away tears so I could get a clearer view of Will walking toward the car. He bent down and gave Sonja a swift kiss on the cheek; she smiled and opened the door for him. *In what parallel universe does my Will have a celebrity opening doors for him?* I thought.

I felt bile rise, and my bad choices from the night before were not helping my situation. Frank moved into view and I watched as he hopped into the front seat after holding the back door open for Sonja to get in. Will and Sonja sitting in the back of the town car, headed toward their private jet. How nice. I wondered if he had his hand on the little sprite's leg as they drove off.

TRACK 16: Lies, Lies, Lies

Days went by without word from Will until finally I came home to the message light blinking.

"Mia, I'm here. It's warm, but feels colder ... I miss you guys. Call me."

Will was rarely that curt, which left me with a sinking feeling. I couldn't sit around the apartment anymore and debate whether I should call him, so I went back to Kell's to help Jenny close. The café was empty and Jenny was mopping the floor when I walked in. "What are you doing back?" She looked at me, eyebrow raised.

"I was bored. I've been meaning to ask you, are you and Tyler going to keep trying for a baby?"

"Of course. Some things are just out of our control, you know? That wouldn't stop us from trying to have a family." She said it almost as if my question was offensive.

"Yeah, you're right."

"It wasn't meant to be, otherwise it wouldn't have happened." Once again, Jenny was able to simplify something that seemed like a labyrinth of thoughts, feelings, and hard decisions in my mind.

"Will called here looking for you right after you left. Did he catch you at the apartment?"

"No, I must have just missed him. He left a message, though."

She walked around to my side so she could see my face as

I washed the dishes. "Did you call him back?" It was like she was asking a child.

"No."

"Did something happen between you two?"

"What did he say?"

She sucked in a loud breath. In slow motion her mouth curled into the largest, most smug grin I had ever seen. "What did you guys do?" Her eyes were bugging out of her head.

"Nothing! I just wanted to know what he said when you talked to him."

"I don't believe you. Anyway, I knew I sensed something from my conversation with him. He just asked how everything was going for me and Tyler, then he asked about Jackson, and then he got really quiet before saying he needed to talk to you."

A shiver ran through my body as I swallowed hard.

"You need to call him. And you should tell me what happened so I can help you pull your head out of your ass."

"Geez, Jenny, take it easy on me. We had a moment, we didn't even kiss . . . really."

"What does that mean? I saw you guys kiss at midnight."

"We didn't kiss kiss, though. But later on, when I was cutting his hair." Her mouth fell open again. "I sat on his lap and things got a little crazy . . . I stopped it and ran off to my room . . . and then I passed out and didn't even get to say good-bye."

"So you led him on again and rejected him and then couldn't even roll your ass out of bed to say good-bye?"

"I heard him leave in the morning, so I ran to the window. I saw Sonja waiting for him with a town car."

"Sonja was at your apartment? Oh my god, how awesome!"

"Jenny, please, she's probably in the process of seducing Will as we speak."

"Don't be silly; Will is no dummy." She paused for long second. "He's in love with you." She said it deadpan as she stared into my eyes, waiting for a response.

"How do you know?"

"I can tell and, anyway, he told me. I believe his exact words were 'cosmic, soul-shattering, air in your lungs kind of love.'"

That sounded like something he would say, but it hurt to hear it from Jenny. "Why didn't he tell me himself? Why are you telling me now?"

"He asked me not to; he said he wanted you to figure things out. He wants you to be happy."

"I know he does, but Will loves everyone. Don't you think?" I searched her eyes for a tell.

She boldly looked me straight in the face and slowly said, "No, Mia, not like this."

My eyes welled up and I tried in vain to swallow back the huge lump in my throat.

The following week flew by like I was watching it on a movie screen in fast motion. I still had not called Will back. I received a postcard of a fishbowl with one tiny, lost goldfish soul in it. There was a line on the back in Will's handwriting,

WISH YOU WERE HERE.

He didn't sign his name. Later that day at the café, I let my curiosity get the best of me. I went into the back office, which was a glorified broom closet with a computer, and I did an Internet search. I typed in "Will Ryan" and immediately found a video link titled "Sonja and new guy Will Ryan sing a duet."

The video was from the concert that had taken place the night before in San Francisco. It was posted by a Sonja fan, so I doubted they had the inside track on anyone's personal life, yet the title still caught my interest.

The video started with Sonja at the microphone introducing Will. "Hey, everybody! If you were here to see this guy open the show, then you know how much he fucking rocks!" I rolled my eyes at that line but continued watching the torturous spectacle. "I talked him into coming back out to sing a song with me, so here he is, my new favorite person, Will Ryan." The crowd cheered. Will sauntered onstage sans guitar, which was completely out of character for him. When he took a seat at the piano, I gasped. He proceeded to play the opening riff of The Rolling Stones's "Wild Horses." It was a song I'd played for Will many times. I knew he could play the piano a little, but he was a much better guitarist, so I could only deduce that he was somehow playing the song to me, at least I hoped that was the case.

His voice sounded pained while his eyes focused fervently on the piano keys. He played a beautiful and extremely slow version. When he sang, he held out the words until there was no music, it was just the sound of his voice slicing through the silence. He increased the tempo and volume on the piano as Sonja stood at the front of the stage and sang the second verse, quite well, I must admit, even though it seemed like Will was trying to drown out her voice. No matter what was going on or how innocent the intention, these two people were singing an intensely romantic song; people were going to make assumptions. When they were through, Will got up and Sonja walked over to him, stood on her toes, and gave him a kiss on the cheek. He didn't react, which was unusual for Will, who made it commonplace to kiss his friends on the lips. He blew a kiss out to the audience and waved as he walked out of view. He never once smiled the entire time he was onstage. Even through the jealousy, my heart still ached for him.

The video ended as the intrusive ringing of the café phone startled me out of my seat. "Kell's," I said abruptly.

Will let out a long breath. "Baby! How are you?"

I hesitated. "I'm good." Lies. Lies. Lies. What I should have said was that I missed him like crazy after only a week and a half.

"I played 'Wild Horses' last night on the piano, but it didn't hold a candle to your version. Sonja sang it with me." He said the last part with zero enthusiasm.

"How is Sonja?"

"She's a pain in the ass."

"Oh?"

"Yeah, she's a spoiled little brat and I'm starting to think this whole arrangement was made to appease her and not the label."

"Well, she seems to really like you, doesn't she?" I said with feigned excitement.

Will was silent for a long beat. "Who cares, Mia?"

"Are you mad?"

"No. Just tired." He took another long breath. "I don't like it here; everyone on this tour sucks. The label wants me to be something I'm not and it scares the shit out of me. I miss you—I miss my friend and you act like you couldn't care less."

"That's not true. I miss you, too. I was just worried because of what happened the night before you left."

"We were both fucked up. Okay? It was a little slip, one I don't regret. You're beautiful and amazing and I've never wanted anyone more in my entire life and I wouldn't even call it a slip if it weren't for the fact that you want nothing to do with me in that way."

"You're being irrational and a little melodramatic."

"Am I?" His tone was icy at best.

"I don't want to fight with you while you're away. Please. Let's talk about the shows."

In a completely pragmatic voice he began spewing information. "We've done San Francisco and now we're in LA so Second Chance Charlie can shoot a video. We'll do a show here in a few days, then San Diego and back to LA for the studio stuff. I don't even know why we're here, we could have come home between shows. It's a joke. The drummer they got me sucks and Nate is being a whiny bitch about it. The food we eat is terrible, everyone on this tour is fake, Sonja being the queen of fakeness, but still everyone kisses her ass. She wanted me to go onstage and play guitar on some stupid fucking song she wrote when she was twelve and I said no, so she stomped around before the show until Frank finally told her that I couldn't play the song, which was a lie. I could play that fucking song in a coma, I just refused. And that's it, nothing to write home about."

"Hang in there, buddy, you'll be headlining your own shows soon."

"I have to go. Say hi to everyone for me. I'll call you later."

There was silence. I think we were both searching for the right words. "Bye, Will. Be careful."

"Bye. You, too. Lock up, and pet Jackson for me." And then he hung up.

Another week and a half went by where I barely spoke to him. Apparently he was busy having dinner with the spoiled brat who annoyed him because it was all over the gossip magazines.

I stood in the corner market staring at a picture of him leading Sonja out of a swanky restaurant in LA. His head was down, and although it was nighttime, he was wearing his sunglasses. Sonja was smiling happily at the cameras. The caption read:

Sonja seen with her older man at LA hotspot, Fray.

His name wasn't listed in the caption, but there was no question it was Will. I stared at the picture, hoping that his face would come to life and look up so that I could see he was pissed off for having to drag the little brat out. Instead, I had to live with the possibility that she had grown on him and he was protecting her from the photographers.

My eyes welled up. I glanced behind the counter at Benton, who looked at me compassionately. He slid a mini bottle of tequila across the counter toward me and then pointed to the chocolate bars and nodded. I took my tequila and chocolate home where there was a voice mail from Will waiting for me: "I've been trying to get ahold of you. Call me, okay, baby? I talked to Jenny—she said you're fine but I want to hear your voice."

I ignored it. I drank my tequila, ate my chocolate bar, and went to bed.

At the café the next day, I told Jenny about the magazine and she told me to get over it, but I didn't . . . and I didn't call him back.

A couple of days later, as I walked home from the bank, I passed a familiar face on the street. I stopped in my tracks, turned, and scanned his features while he did the same. It was Jason Bennett, but all grown up. He was the one and only kid in the East Village I'd hung out with during those summers with my father. He'd lived across the street from Kell's until I was twelve, when his whole family moved to South Africa. I was heartbroken when they left. We remained pen pals for a couple of years, but eventually lost touch.

"Mia Kelly?"

"Jason? Oh my god, I never thought I would see you here again."

I reached up and gave him a hug and then leaned back and studied his face. I grabbed his chin. "You're handsome." Jason was short and very skinny with dark brown hair. He didn't have any standout features, but he had a chiseled jaw and he was a much better-looking adult than he was a kid.

"You're gorgeous, but you always were."

"Thanks. It's so good to see you. How are you and what are you doing here?"

"I'm fantastic. I wanted to bring my fiancée here to show her where I grew up." Just as he said that, a striking Asian woman walked out of the corner market and stood next to him.

"Laura, this is the Mia I told you about. Mia, this is Laura."

"Hi, it's nice to meet you." She stuck her hand out and I shook it and smiled. I noticed she had a very prominent English accent and Jason's accent was similar but more subtle.

"It's nice to meet you, too. Have you guys been over to Kell's?"

"We were just headed there. How's Pops?"

It was like a knife being slowly pushed through my heart. "He passed away last year." I tried to say it with as much composure as possible, but my voice cracked at the last second.

"I am so sorry, Mia," he said. Both of them stood there with sympathetic looks.

"Thank you." I took a deep breath. "Hey, if you guys

don't have dinner plans tonight, why don't you come to my apartment and I'll throw something together?"

"You live here now? Permanently?"

"After Pops died, I came out to run the café and I just fell in love with this place and the people here. What about you? Where do you live now?"

"London. Been there for five years."

"That's wonderful. So what do you say to dinner?" Jason looked over at Laura, who smiled and nodded.

"Yeah, that sounds great!"

"Okay, come over around seven."

Jason and Laura were a charming couple, absolutely in love. She was studying to be a philosophy professor and he ran a nonprofit organization that helped get computers to schools in South Africa, where he'd lived with his family for several years before moving to London. We caught up while I cooked one of Will's pasta recipes. While I sautéed vegetables on the stove the phone rang, so I told Jason to grab it.

"Hello?" He paused and looked over at me. "This is Jason, Mia's friend." Right at the most unfortunate moment I burned my hand and immediately ran over to the sink to run it under water. I heard Jason say, "She's busy right now. Can she call you back?"

He hung up and walked over to me at the sink. "That was a guy named Will; is he your boyfriend?"

"No, roommate."

"Oh, he seemed pissed."

"He's a lot nicer to women." I was being facetious for no reason since Jason didn't even know Will. Will was just as nice to men as he was to women, but I was feeling a little pissy after seeing the picture of him and Sonja on the magazine, so the comment just slipped out. Anyway, I knew he must have wondered who the heck Jason was, and I'm sure his imagination was getting the best of him, but I didn't care at that moment.

Later that night after Jason and Laura left, Jenny called. "What did you do tonight?" she blurted out without even saying hello.

"Nothing."

"Oh, you're gonna pull that bullshit? Will just called Tyler and asked if you were seeing someone. He said he called the apartment and some guy answered."

"Jenny, just leave it alone. Will shouldn't be involving you guys."

"Well, okay, Mia, we'll leave it alone. I can't help you, anyway. Stop playing games, that's all I'm gonna say."

We said good-bye and that was that. She didn't bring it up again.

TRACK 17: Angels' Wings

On January twenty-sixth, exactly one week before Will was scheduled to come home, Jackson died. I took him for a walk through the park that morning. I threw the ball for him and he chased it like a puppy. We took a nap on a blanket overlooking the children's playground; he seemed so happy and content. When we got back to the apartment, he went and curled up on his bed while I took a shower. Coming out the bathroom, I glanced into the doorway of my bedroom and noticed that he was lying in a different position. He was facing the wall, which was unusual, and he was very still. Too still.

I knew he was gone without getting any closer. "No, no, no, please no." I ran straight out of the apartment, wearing nothing but a robe. On the street, I was blasted by freezing air, which caused me to scream loudly. I was hysterical by the time I walked through the café door. Martha and Jenny swarmed me.

"It's Jackson!" I said, sobbing.

Martha wrapped me in her arms then turned toward Paddy and Joe. "Can you boys man the counter?"

They stood up, proudly saluted Martha, and dashed behind the counter like it was the most important job they would ever do. "Thank you," I mumbled, barely loud enough for them to hear.

"Of course, luv," Joe said sympathetically, sounding just

like my father. Pain shot through my heart again. I winced and then buckled over. Jenny rubbed my back and urged me toward the door.

Once on the street she called Tyler, asking him to come over immediately. When the three of us got to the landing outside my apartment door, I turned toward them. Hyperventilating, I tried to get the words out. "I can't . . . go . . . back in there." We slumped into a pile at the top of the stairs, both of them holding me tight as we waited for Tyler. I cried softly into my hands until I felt him moving past me. He bent down, leaned toward my ear, and spoke slowly. "I'm sorry, Mia."

"I know," I said, voice raspy. "Thank you for helping." He kissed my temple and went into the apartment.

He brought Jackson out, wrapped in a blanket. I stood up and put my hand on him. Through sobs I spoke to my dead dog. "I'm sorry, buddy. I love you—you were the best." And he was. He didn't even make a fuss about dying; he just curled up on his little bed and went to sleep. *Man's best friend. I get it.*

Inside the apartment, Jenny hugged me. "Tyler will take care of everything—he has a friend who works for a vet."

"What are they going to do with him?" I asked, squinting. In Ann Arbor we buried our dogs in the backyard. In New York, that wasn't an option.

"They'll cremate him and bring you the ashes, but don't worry about that right now. Do you want me to call Will?"

"No," I said sullenly. "I'll call him later." I knew Will was going to take it hard, too, and I wanted to spare him that while he was away. I had no intention of calling him later.

I looked at Martha and Jenny and thanked them as tears continued pouring from my eyes. "You guys can go. I'm okay. I just want to be alone."

"Don't be ridiculous. We're not leaving you alone," Jenny said.

"No, really, I'm serious. I just want to cry alone, please." They looked at each other and then back at me. "Please," I said again.

They stood there, paralyzed, until Martha broke the silence. "We'll be in the café, close by." I fell into her arms and sobbed on her shoulder. "Oh, my Mia Pia, poor girl. First your Pops and now Jackson."

I let out a loud cry. When I could finally speak, I said, "Please, I'm fine, I just need to be alone. I love you guys."

After they left, I went and threw on some underwear and one of Will's white T-shirts. I could barely handle being in my room where both my father and Jackson had died, so I went and curled up on Will's bed and cried myself to sleep at two in the afternoon.

I woke up several hours later, surrounded by darkness and feeling as desolate as the apartment looked. It was nine o'clock and I wondered how I would get through the night. I yearned for Will and it was worse being in his bed, surrounded by his things.

I went to the kitchen and opened a bottle of wine, attempting to numb the pain. Of course, half a bottle down, and nothing was numb. If anything, I had become more of a raw nerve. I sat at the piano and played "Wild Horses" over and over, sometimes fast, sometimes slow, while the tears ebbed and flowed. Just before midnight, I closed the cover on the piano and put my head down. I cried tears I didn't know I had. My head ached. I drenched tissue after tissue as I cried for my dog and my father and for Will, too.

I was in that moment right as you fall asleep, when your body relaxes slightly and your hazy thoughts become a dream. I jolted awake when I heard someone coming up the stairwell. Without looking or caring, I swung the door open and stood face-to-face with my angel, except that he looked like a mere mortal that night. He was thinner than before, his eyes were bloodshot, and he shivered beneath his thin black sweatshirt. His head was down; the top of his hoodie came to rest just above his sad, dark eyes, which peered at me through narrow slits. His hands were shoved deep in his pockets as he shifted nervously.

Taking a deep breath, he leaned to the side, looking past me into the apartment. "You alone?" I nodded and took a step back. He must have felt awful, wondering if I had another man over, comforting me. He picked up a small bag and walked in, kicking the door shut as he stared into my puffy eyes.

"Aw, baby, I'm so sorry," he whispered as he wrapped his arms around my shoulders, bringing me into his chest.

I tried to form a coherent sentence. "How . . . why . . . how are you here?" I thought I must have been dreaming, but he felt so real and he smelled like Will and he sounded like Will and, God, how I wanted it to be Will.

"Tyler called me. I got on the first flight back. You should have called me."

I broke the hug and reached my hands up to his face. He sucked in a sharp breath and bit his bottom lip. Pushing his hood back, I studied his beautiful mouth while I tried to collect myself enough to talk. But I couldn't—I just stood there expressionless, in shock, as tears ran steadily down my cheeks. I wasn't sobbing. In fact, I was barely breathing, but the tears wouldn't stop.

He looked at me with a pained expression. "Why didn't you call me?"

"Shhh . . . I just want to feel good . . . make me feel good . . . okay?" I whispered.

His mouth was on mine in an instant, kissing me deeply

with fervor and need. It was the kiss I had thought about so many times, but it was better than I imagined. I unzipped his sweatshirt and pushed it off his shoulders, onto the floor. His hands were frantic, grabbing at my side and then moving to my neck as he deepened the kiss. He kicked off his shoes while I pulled his T-shirt over his head. We paused and looked at each other for just a moment and then he reached behind me and lifted me from the back of my legs to straddle him as he made his way toward the bedroom. Breathing heavily and moving frantically, he pushed me against the wall in the hall-way. "God, I want you," he hissed and then his mouth went to my neck, where he violently kissed and sucked, tugging at my skin with his teeth. I was aching for him to be everywhere and he was trying desperately to do that. I pulled my shirt off and then we pressed our bodies into each other. He moaned deep from his chest, trailing kisses across my collarbone as he continued toward the bedroom. I moved my hands through his hair, pulling his head tightly into me. "Your room," I breathed when he hesitated at the end of the hall.

Inside his room he set me down on the bed; I reached for his belt and yanked his jeans open but he stopped my hands. "Lie back." I obliged as he hooked his fingers in the waist-band of my underwear and pulled the last stitch of clothing off me. I was completely naked and vulnerable while he stood above me and drank me in. There was a pale light from a street lamp shining through the window. "I like you in my bed," he said, just above a whisper. I could see he had the listening-to-God look in his eyes and then his mouth curled into a sweet smile before he knelt down between my legs. He trailed kisses up the inside of my thigh and whispered, "Let's go slow. I Want. This. To last. For . . . " And then the whispers stopped. A tremor ran through my body as the heat consumed me. I sucked in a breath and moved my fingers through his hair while he kissed me . . . everywhere.

I arched my back and let out a breathy "ahh." When the quickening became too much, I gripped his shoulders and felt the intense release all the way down to my toes. I pulled him up toward me; his hand went to my hip as his mouth went to my breast. Will knew what he was doing, there was no question, and even though he seemed overwhelmed with passion, he took his time. His hands were gentle but determined, like when he played music. Never second-guessing himself, he just moved purely from feeling. He stood up and stripped away his clothes and then climbed on top of me, reclaiming my mouth. As he buried himself inside of me, forcing the breath from my lungs, I dug my fingers into the bunching muscles in his back.

"You are so beautiful." His voice was primal and raw, but his motions were graceful. Leaning on his forearm, he moved his other hand from my hip, up my side to my breast where his thumb brushed the sensitive, firm skin of my nipple. I writhed, arching my back, letting myself get lost in the feeling. He smiled between breaths and the words "mystical alchemy" came to mind again. I realized how perfect our bodies matched and moved together—it was utterly divine.

I hadn't believed that people could be made for each other until that moment. "I love you." My voice was soft but full of conviction as I stared deep into his eyes. He stopped, mid thrust; his hand gripped my hip hard and his mouth went to mine as his body tensed. When he drove back into me, we cried out as we came together. He collapsed beside me and fell asleep with his head on my bare chest. My sweet Will, in my arms, like a dream.

Time was irrelevant as we slept tangled in each other. The sun came up and filled the room with a hazy light. I looked down at Will, who was sleeping soundly, with seraphic contentment on his face. The phone rang, but I ignored it and pulled the sheets over us as I dozed blissfully back to sleep.

I woke up squinting at a figure standing in the doorway. I gasped and blinked my eyes frantically until Jenny came into view. She immediately held her finger to her mouth to quiet me and then she blew me a kiss as she gazed at Will's body wrapped around mine. I smiled lovingly and she did the same before turning and walking out. I knew Jenny was checking on me, and although I don't think she expected what she found, I'm positive it made her happy.

Sometime later that morning, Will stirred. "Mia?"

"Yeah?"

"Last night . . . when you said . . . "

"Yeah?"

"Did you say that . . . because we were . . . ?"

"No."

We dozed off again, still tangled in each other.

The bed was empty when I woke, but I could smell French toast cooking and I heard Will singing faintly to a Pearl Jam song. I became positively turned on by the combination of those things. My shirt was nowhere to be found, so I darted across the hall in my underwear.

"I saw that!" he yelled.

I giggled and grabbed a T-shirt from my collection before heading to the bathroom to brush my teeth. When I got to the kitchen, I hopped up on the counter. Will came over and stood between my legs, resting his hands on my thighs. He was shirtless, with his jeans hanging low on his lean, narrow hips. I followed the dark happy trail down to the silver-studded belt; there was no sign of boxers.

"Good morning, baby," I said with a brazen smirk. He

grinned and then closed his eyes and kissed my lips delicately, for a long time.

He pulled away just an inch and whispered, "Morning," before kissing me again. "Time to eat."

"I can't wait!"

We sat at the table and ate the best French toast ever made. Andrew Bird was plucking away and serenading us with weird words over the iPod speaker.

"I think this song is about one of those tumors that has teeth and hair," Will said.

"That's disgusting. I think it's about love and kittens."

"Nope, it's about a teratoma," he said, smiling.

"Well whatever . . . let's not think about that. Are you done in California?"

His mood dropped through the floor like an anchor. "Let's not think about *that*."

"What happened?"

"Nothing happened, but I have to go back and finish what I started in the studio." He turned toward me and grabbed my hand in his. "Come with me."

It took me a millisecond to decide. "Okay."

He seemed calmer than usual before our flight to LA, except that he insisted on being one row behind the exit aisle. After we got off the ground, he was back to his usual shenanigans. Leaning over me, he said, "I need to make sure the landing gear is retracting," but he didn't look out the window. He took a deep breath through his nose and then kissed me deeply. We kissed for minutes or maybe hours before resting our heads on each other and falling asleep.

At LAX we were whisked away in a town car while Will updated me on the current status of his career.

"Honestly, I don't understand why they're paying for the studio time. I haven't even signed a deal; it makes no sense. Frank finagled some sign-your-life-away contract with them, I know it."

"They really want you. I think that's why."

"No, it's something else, it has to be. I hate feeling indebted to these people and I'm tired of their fucking input. They want a hit, that's all. They keep asking me to change lyrics and simplify whole parts of the song. Who does that? If they think I'm so great, then why do they want to change everything?"

"Don't screw it up, just do what they say," I said, opening my eyes wide to urge him further.

He narrowed his eyes and jerked his head back. "Why? What's going to happen if I don't?"

"Go ahead, throw your life away because the label wants you to take out a couple of swear words?"

"I don't even know if this is what I want."

"What?" The *Twilight Zone* theme song was on repeat in my head. "People would die to be in your position. Isn't this what you've been working toward your entire life?"

"NO! I have not been making music to get famous and have shitty things written about me, or to be stuck on a bus for months, or to be told what to do by some schmuck in a suit who listens to fucking modern jazz all day. I've been making music because that's what I love doing. What's going to happen, Mia, if I turn my back on this shit now?"

"Career suicide. You'll probably have to work at the Montosh for the rest of your life."

"No! I mean what's going to happen with us?"

"I don't even know what *us* is yet."

With his mouth open in awe, he shook his head frantically.

Here comes neurotic Will. "Singing a different tune now, are we? I seemed to recall you saying you loved me, but maybe that's only when you're on your back."

"How dare you," I said, trying to prevent tears from welling in my eyes. "I just lost my dog . . . and my father. I'm not capable of making any decisions right now."

"I know . . . I'm sorry," he said immediately with a purely penitent look on his face. His eyes darted back and forth, searching mine. I let him squirm for a few minutes while I thought about what could have happened to the real Will. I considered asking the impostor what he had done; if perhaps my sweet Will was in danger somewhere or maybe the impostor was actually wearing Will's body like a suit. I burrowed my laser gaze into his corneas and waited a good thirty seconds before speaking. He must have anticipated some catastrophic meltdown on my part because he took a deep breath and held it. But instead of anger, I just felt disappointment.

"I think you're the one who's singing a different tune. You got me in bed, so now you can be a jerk, right?"

"I'm sorry, I'm so sorry, I didn't mean it. Please, Mia, I'm crazy about you. I'm under a lot of pressure and I need you on my side."

I stared out the window without a response. When we pulled up to the studio, he ran around and opened my door, but I didn't take his hand. I was surprised to see so many suits in the place. Live Wire was sending in the big guns to set Will straight, and it looked like Frank was eyeballs deep in apologies when we walked in.

"What's she doing here?" Will said to Frank, gesturing toward Sonja, who was sitting in the corner with her entourage.

"Will, we need to talk. Let's go outside."

My stomach dropped. There was a doomsday atmosphere

in the room; people barely acknowledged Will and I was definitely getting the stink eye from all directions.

Right outside the door, Frank grabbed Will by the shoulders, getting his full, undivided attention. "Listen to me closely." He looked over at me and winked as if he had just noticed my presence. "Hey, Will's Mia." He abruptly brought his attention back to Will. "Rady and some other execs from Live Wire are in the building. There are lawyers here; your lawyer is on his way."

"I have a lawyer?" He was genuinely surprised. I tried my best to follow the conversation. I knew Rady was the A&R guy from Live Wire that Will avoided at all costs, and I knew that Will was in hot water because of his lack of cooperation with the genius they'd hired to produce the song.

Supposedly Brent Blackton was a studio savant who had produced more hits than Jimmy Jam, but Will thought he was fake, in part because on the first day they met, Blackton asked what kind of music he played. Will told me he his response was, "Christ, I'm fucked. You don't know what kind of music I play. I play Swedish fucking folk music—get your goddamn clogs." Needless to say, Blackton wasn't amused and first impressions can mean everything in the music business.

"They want you to sign the contract before they spend another dime on this song. Blackton wants Sonja to sing backup, and the label is behind him one hundred percent."

"No! No fucking way! You have to fight for me, Frank. That's what you're getting ten percent for."

"I haven't seen a dime, Will, and I won't unless you sign this deal and cooperate with these people."

"What happened to artistic freedom? I'm getting fucked!" He was screaming at that point. "You people are blowing me wide fucking open, you're gonna make me sell my soul to the devil. I won't, Frank, I won't sell my soul." Then he looked at me and pointed in my face. "I won't!" Neurotic Will in full force.

"Calm down," I said with authority. "I mean, who has final say? He hasn't signed anything yet."

"Listen, there's a lot of hype about Will because of Sonja. The label wants to ride that wave."

I could see Will splintering. He was on the cusp of making an irreversible and rash decision. "Give him one day. Ask the label if we can meet tomorrow. He's been on a plane for five hours—let him sleep on it." I smiled and shamelessly batted my eyelashes at Frank.

"It's not up to me, sweetheart, but I'll try."

Frank left us outside. A bead of sweat trickled down my forehead. I was dressed way too warm for Southern California, even in wintertime. "It's freakin' January and seventy-five degrees—what a joke." I looked at Will, who was clearly experiencing some sort of cosmic mental breakdown. His face was flushed and then he shivered as he stared aimlessly at the ground. He was wearing black jeans, steel-toed boots, and a gray T-shirt over a black, long-sleeved thermal. I couldn't understand why he wasn't roasting. When he crossed his arms and shivered again, I put my hand to his head.

"You have a fever." I looked into his eyes, but he fixed his gaze on the empty parking space behind me.

His shoulders were slumped and his face defeated. "No, this happens when a man's heart is ripped out of his chest and then kicked around by the people he trusts."

I wanted to wrap him up in a blanket and put him in my pocket for safekeeping.

Just then Sonja sauntered out and threw her arm around Will's shoulder. She glanced at me and smirked before addressing him. "Willie, what's wrong? Are you mad?" Her speaking voice was shrill, nails on a chalkboard. I threw up in my mouth a little and then shook my head. Will kept his head down and ignored her. She wore a tight, pink, lacy dress that left nothing to the imagination, but her shoes were what really got me. She had on white platform wedges that were at least twelve inches off the ground. The angle of her foot was so steep I thought she must have been double jointed or something. I gawked, wondering how it was even possible. Her short little body almost met Will's at six feet tall.

"I think Will wants to be left alone."

"Well, you're out here." She had a cute doll face, pudgy red lips, brown eyes, and thin black eyebrows that looked like strings. For having a decent singing voice, her speaking voice was barely tolerable. She arched the strings, waiting for my response.

"Well, I'm his girlfriend." The moment I said it, Will looked up with just a tiny bit of hope in his eyes. One side of his mouth curled into an unabashed smirk. If I had to guess what he was feeling, I would say two things: he was happy that I said I was his girlfriend and, more than that, he was intrigued at the prospect of a catfight between Sonja and me. I rolled my eyes at him.

"Sonja, this is Mia. Mia, Sonja."

"Hi," I said with an obligatory smile. "I like your shirt."

"It's a dress."

"Whatever. Ready, Will?"

He slowly took Sonja's arm from around his neck and stepped away from her like she was a cobra about to strike.

"Wait! Hold on. I just wanted to say thank you for opening the shows. You did a great job and"—she looked at me and smirked—"thanks for that night back in San Diego. I won't forget it." She said the last part in a sultry voice.

The way Will's eyebrows pointed together like he felt sorry for her made it obvious that she was full of shit.

Frank came barreling out the door. "You're good to go, kid. He handed Will a disk. "She already cut a vocal track; just listen to it." He looked at Sonja. "It's not bad, sweetheart, but I think Will wants to debut something more original."

"Frank, you know you can't talk to me; that's what I fucking pay people for. Talk to my manager." And then she made a shooing motion with her hand before turning on her giant heel and walking away.

"Let's get outta here—I feel like crap," Will said, yanking me toward the car.

In the back of the town car he nuzzled against me and began trailing light kisses across my collarbone. "What do you want to do?" I asked.

"I just want to get wasted with you and find out if there *is* a God," he murmured into my neck before tugging on my earlobe with his teeth.

I shivered. He moved his hand between my legs and then kissed me gently, teasing my bottom lip with his tongue. "What was last night, then?" I whispered.

"Progress, but I think I need more convincing."

The car pulled up to our hotel overlooking the Santa Monica pier. As soon as I saw the giant Ferris wheel, I grabbed Will's arm. "We need to get on that thing! Now!"

"Is it safe?"

"Come on!"

When the big red bowl swooped us off the ground, Will's grip on my hand tightened. We were silent and spellbound by the orange and white Creamsicle-like sunset taking place over the ocean. The crashing waves were like glorious movements from some unfinished musical masterpiece. We sat transfixed as the sun played the ocean like a Steinway.

We looked at each other at the very same moment and then just stared into each other's eyes, perfectly content. "Did something happen with you and Sonja?"

"No. Do you want to tell me who Jason is?"

"An old friend. He and his fiancée came over for dinner." He huffed and I knew it had tortured him until that moment, but just like that, things were straightened out and we were finally communicating. I was a little hesitant to approach the Live Wire subject because it seemed like he was feeling better, definitely over the fever and chills. "Are you going to sign the deal and let her sing on the track?"

Without hesitation he said, "No," then kissed me passionately, pulling me onto his lap. His mouth was urgent and his hands gripped my face like a vise. It was a theatrical display that got everybody on the ground clapping as we swooped by.

Will was avoiding the topic and it sent me reeling. We were expected to meet the Live Wire execs the next day, but Rady had arranged for Second Chance Charlie and Will's band, the managers, and whatever friends or family wanted to join to have dinner in a rented-out restaurant that night. It was sort of the period at the end of the sentence for the two groups who were parting ways. If Will didn't show, it would be a real slap in the face, regardless of what his decision was going to be the following day. Plus, I think everybody wanted an opportunity to work on convincing him to sign the deal, me included.

TRACK 18: A Violin

I explored our gorgeous suite, complete with a baby grand piano and a stone fireplace. The marble floors were freckled with ornate Persian rugs and everything in the bathroom was white and smelled like lily of the valley.

"Wow, Will, I can't believe Live Wire paid for a room like this."

"They didn't. It's my way of thanking you for coming with me."

"You paid for this?" He nodded slowly, like he felt a fraction of doubt about telling me that tidbit.

"Thank you. This is amazing and you're sweet," I said. "I think we should go to dinner with the group."

"Fine, but first this . . . "

By that point we were mindlessly removing each other's clothes. I pushed him down on the bed and lowered myself onto him. He sucked in a breath and smiled, so I leaned down and kissed him sweetly and then tugged at his lower lip before sitting up and moving on top of him. I went slow and savored the feeling of him filling me. He met my movements with the perfect amount of resistance. One hand gripped my hip while he ran his index finger down the center of my chest, slowly inching his thumb down to the bundle of nerves above where our bodies connected. He knew exactly what to do with his adroit guitar hands, and I made a mental note to thank the nurse if I ever saw her. I jerked, writhing from the intensity; his other hand gripped my hip tighter. I arched my back and let my head fall while I got lost in the feeling of Will in me and all over me as we both cried out. A moment later he sat up, still inside me, and wrapped his whole body around mine.

"I love you, Mia."

"I know."

I couldn't say the words because the feeling had unearthed a new sensation that I had no experience with in a relationship . . . fear. It's a plaguing, unruly affliction that clouds any happiness born from real love. It's a fool who thinks love will set him free. Love equals a morbid and relentless fear of losing the other person. It's a freak-accident fear, a piece of space junk falling from the sky and obliterating him, leaving nothing but his smoking boots. It's the unfortunate-organ-defect fear—suddenly, on his thirtieth birthday, the little crack in his heart that's been there since birth will rear its ugly head and take him in his sleep while he's spooning you. It's the only way to know you're really in love, when you ask the question: Would it be harder to watch him die, or to know he'll watch me die? Is there more mercy in being the one who does the watching or in being the one who does the dying? It's when you realize what mercy killing actually means: it's when you actually care to the point of tormenting worry. It's not roses and white horses, it's fucking brutal, and it can send a person running for the hills. To love is brave, and Will was the bravest person I knew.

When we got to the restaurant, Rady came stalking toward us in his black mohair suit with Ray-Ban Aviators peeking from the pocket. He was good-looking in a clean way, but he was fat. He looked like he'd eaten Ryan Seacrest for breakfast. He waddled up to Will, holding the black Gibson.

"What the fuck are you doing with my guitar?"

"Shut up, Will. Give the execs something."

"Why, you guys having second thoughts?"

"No, of course not—it's a nice gesture. They've made concessions; we all have. Pull your head out before you fuck yourself into obscurity."

"Charming," I said to no one in particular.

"I came here to have dinner. I brought my girlfriend. I'm not a circus monkey."

"Hey, doll." Rady finally acknowledged me before looking back at Will. "One song, blow 'em away, it'll get everyone off your back." Will begrudgingly snatched the guitar from Rady and walked away. I stood there, not knowing what to do with myself until I spotted Frank sitting at a table nearby. He motioned for me to come over and then he stood up and pulled a chair out for me.

"Are you working on him?" he said, gritting a cigar between his teeth. He was pickled in Polo cologne, which I loathe. I squinted, trying to prevent the smell from permeating my space.

"I don't know what to say. He has his own agenda. Maybe he thinks he'll get another deal."

"Maybe, but once word gets out that he's difficult to work with, labels will keep their distance. What's this master plan he keeps ranting about?"

"Never heard of it." I searched my mind for some mention of a master plan, but there was nothing. While Will tuned his guitar on the tiny stage, I looked around the dimly lit room. The walls were painted blood red, which caused me to repeat *REDRUM*, like the kid from *The Shining*, over and over in my head. Then I imagined Will decapitating everybody but me with his guitar like it was a machete. I spotted Sonja ogling him; I hoped he would get to her first.

I felt a hand on my shoulder and turned to see Nate. "Hey, how are you?" I said as I stood up from the table.

He hugged me and whispered, "I'd be a lot of better if he would sign the deal."

I yanked my head back. "What's in it for you?"

"They'll keep me on and send me on tour with him. I'll get paid, for once. I hope you're not the reason he's fucking around with this," he said derisively.

"I can assure you, it has nothing to do with me. It was good seeing you," I said sarcastically before sitting down. I finally understood what Will was fretting about. Bloodsuckers coming out of the woodwork, pressuring him to do this and that—it was frightening.

Will cleared his throat into the microphone. In his soft, sweet voice, he spoke. "Hi, everyone." People clapped and cheered and a few said hi back. It was a very casual atmosphere except for the elephant in the room, which was the table of execs from Live Wire. I half-expected Will to burst into a punk-rock rendition of the Rolling Stones's "Schoolboy Blues," a song written as an eff-you to their label, but he didn't. "This is the song we've been working on and it's evolving still, so bear with me. It's called 'Lost on You.'"

No apologies for what I've said before
I've told you time and time again
I'd sell my soul for something more.

You've left me standing here
A thousand times
Waiting on this big world to make up your mind
But I promise I won't get lost on careless thoughts
'Cause love's lost on you this time.

So put me out, don't put me down
I can't wait another minute to be found
When no words have been spoken
They say still waters run deep
But not when mislaid plans are broken

With nothing left to give
I'll fall fast out of my mind
But I promise I won't get lost on careless thoughts
'Cause love's lost on you this time.

He sang a saccharine and predictable version of the song the way he knew the suits wanted to hear it. He couldn't massacre it even if he tried, but there was little passion behind his performance and it may have only been evident to the people who really knew him, because most of the crowd clapped wildly. Without acknowledging the applause, he immediately went into another song with a slapping motion over the neck of the Gibson. This time there was passion and he didn't strum smoothly; he played with disconnected movements and dramatic passes over the strings. It gave the song a melancholy vibe with bluesy undertones. I decided I wanted to be eulogized over that type of guitar playing. When he started humming, I found the melody vaguely familiar, but I couldn't place it. The humming went on for several minutes, albeit perfectly euphonic humming, but I saw a few bewildered expressions throughout the room. I thought it might have been a strange version of "Amazing Grace" until Will uttered the first words.

How many times have you heard someone say
If I had his money, I would do things my way.

It was the song "A Satisfied Mind" and he was making a statement or a declaration, maybe to me, maybe to the suits, or maybe just to himself, because he didn't open his eyes once. He had no restraint when he sang and I thought he might miss a note, but he never did; he was always right in tune, completely effortless, like it was impossible for him to sing badly. The words gave me pause; I feared Will had made up his mind about the deal and that it wasn't a favorable decision. I chose denial at that point; I wouldn't interfere with his decision-making process like everyone else. I wouldn't pressure Will—I loved him too much, and if he wanted a satisfied mind over his own page on the iTunes store, more power to him. If he could see the value in having dignity over money, then I would love him more for that. At least that's what I told myself.

If the tone of his voice wasn't so perfectly mellifluous, it might have seemed like he was screaming when he sang:

Money can't buy back your youth when you're old
Friends when you're lonely, oh peace to your soul
The wealthiest person is a pauper at times
Compared to the man with a satisfied mind.

When he was finished, he smiled from ear to ear and then whispered, "Thank you," like he was talking to God. He darted off the stage and out the door. I found him outside smoking cigarettes with Tony, the drummer from Second Chance Charlie.

"Mia!" He called to me and motioned with his hand for me to come over. It was jovial Will. He was lighter, like the five-ton weight of his future had been lifted. He was a man with answers now, one who had experienced the glimpse, as I liked to call it; someone had slipped him a copy of the Cliffs-Notes to his life and I could see it all over his face. It was the look of a man who knew exactly what he was destined to do. I envied that look the way I envied people who had a strong faith in God.

Once my grandmother told me I needed to find God and I said, "Why don't you just tell me where to look and save me the trouble?" I was dead serious. Faith, destiny, all the shit you can't see, yet people are so willing to take the leap. Not me.

I guess it was during the song when Will was singing those words that he became the man with a satisfied mind because I never saw him waver again.

"This is Tony, the most talented guy in the whole bunch," he said, pointing back dramatically at the restaurant. "Seriously, he's gonna be big one day; he's just gotta get out from behind that drum kit and Sonja's bullshit."

"Hi, nice to meet you." Tony looked to be in his early twenties. He had big, round, liquid, topaz-colored eyes and brown, shaggy hair. He smiled with this innocence that made me think he must have had a really wholesome childhood even though he was standing outside smoking and listening to the ranting of a lunatic.

I smiled at him but turned my attention to Will. "Can I talk to you?"

He stared at me for a good twenty seconds before speaking. He had a way of tapping a direct line to my heart by simply squinting his eyes slightly as he gazed into mine. It was a kissing effect and it turned me to Jell-O. "Baby, no heavy stuff tonight, okay? Let's go eat."

I huffed but decided that was the best damn idea Will had had all day. Denial, remember?

We sat at the bar and avoided Frank and Rady and all the

other suits. Sonja took up residence on Nate's lap two bar-stools down. When I saw him stick his hand up her dress, I turned my back and faced Will. "How many girls have you slept with since you met me?"

He said, "Two," but held up four fingers.

"Which is it? Come on, this is normal girlfriend stuff. I realized we skipped right over it and went straight to comfort sex after our dog died."

"I like that you called him *our* dog. He was the best, huh?"

"Yeah, Will, he was the best dog in the world and he died the best freakin' doggy death, but I don't want to talk about that 'cause it's gonna make me cry, and anyway, you're avoiding the question. How many?"

"I like that you said 'girlfriend,' too." He was adorable.

"Come on, tell me."

"Three . . . okay, four."

"Who?

"Well, there was Audrey . . . and her friend." I choked on my vodka-soda-cran.

"The Russian? At the same time? With Audrey?"

"Yep," he said with arched eyebrows and a cheeky grin.

"What about the other two?"

"You don't know them—girls I met at work. It might have been spite sex after I walked in on you and the banker." Smiling, he playfully threw his hands up in a defensive gesture. "What? I'm not proud of it. Anyway, I thought I said no heavy stuff."

"Were you careful?"

"Of course." He said it like it was a ridiculous question.

"Well, you weren't with me."

"It's different with you."

"Well, I'm on the pill, in case you're wondering."

He shrugged. "Doesn't matter to me. I trust you." I didn't know what he meant, but I didn't press. I wondered if he was saying it didn't matter if I got pregnant, but I thought the last thing Will needed on the back of his tour bus was a Pack 'n Play and a wailing baby.

"Don't you want to know about me?"

"Yes, I want to know everything about you, but I don't care about who you've slept with. It's in the past and I don't want to think about you with anyone else. You're mine now." He said it with surefire confidence.

Normally, possessiveness would repulse me. I remember in high school when I discovered feminism. I would beg my friends to let me take pictures of them in all kinds of artsy statement photos. I made my friend Ruthy stand naked with a frying pan on her head while I snapped away. I wrote "Fuck Your Kitchen" across the photo with a big, black Sharpie and then I projected it on the wall at the talent show while I covered PJ Harvey's "Sheela-Na-Gig" on the piano. Everyone thought I was a lesbian after that, which explains why I never had a boyfriend. I thought it was very avant-garde, but it just got me in a heap of trouble. I had to write a ten-page explanation to the principal about how I didn't fully understand the impact of projecting a picture of a naked girl along with the word "Fuck" on the gymnasium wall. Needless to say, everyone got the wrong message and Ruthy got a bad reputation.

That time is what I will refer to as the deafening era. It's when I learned that being artistic came with a price, the price of being misunderstood. It's probably around the time that I tuned my heart out of what Martha would refer to as the soul-harmonizing shit. Still, I remained a die-hard feminist until my feelings for Will took over. All I wanted to do was wash his underwear and fold it into neat little packages that smelled like Snuggle and remind him that he was loved. I wanted to take that frying pan and make food that I would regurgitate and feed to him like he was a baby bird. I wanted to be his; I wanted him to own me. I would nourish his body with mine. I would feed his heart, his mind . . . his soul, and I wanted to do it while screaming, "What do you think of me now, Gloria Steinem?" That's how bad I had it for Will, so I guess it's sort of ironic that I was willing to throw it all away . . .

"Wake up, sleepyhead." I yawned, peering at Will through squinted eyes. He looked invigorated and way too sunny for seven a.m.

"Jesus, what kind of vitamins do you take?"

"I prefer Lord and Savior, but Jesus is fine," he said with no trace of humor.

"Ha, ha. Why are we up so early?"

"I'm taking you somewhere special before I have to meet with the label."

"Where, where? Tell me. I hate surprises."

"Not telling, but I'll give you a hint: *Irises.*"

I jumped out of bed. "We're going to the Getty?"

He hugged me from behind and trailed kisses up my neck. "Or we could stay in bed all morning?" It was a tempting offer . . .

The Getty Museum is a palatial spread that sits atop a massive hill overlooking the 405 Freeway in Los Angeles. When you arrive in the parking lot at the bottom, people in white shirts usher you onto a white tram that zigzags up to the top of the hill. It reminded me of the movie *Defending Your Life* where Meryl Streep and Albert Brooks ride a white tram to heaven. I pretended that Will was my angel and that he was going to give me a guided tour. Inside the museum all the dead artists would stand next to their works to answer my questions, except their answers would be void of any artistic narcissism. I would ask van Gogh why there is one white flower in *Irises* and he might say something like he ran out of blue paint.

Will caught me spacing out once we were there. "Penny for your thoughts, kitten."

"Meow."

"That's it? I thought you were deep," he said, shaking his head with mock disappointment.

"Is that song about me?"

"Which one?"

"'Lost on You.'"

"Not anymore." He kissed me and then pulled me toward the Man Ray exhibit.

We stared at *Le Violon d'Ingres* for ten minutes. It's a photograph of f-holes superimposed on a woman named Kiki's naked back; her arms are folded in front so that you can't see them in the photo. The armless shape of her body is that of a violin and it's hard not to consider for a moment that Man Ray liked to play with Kiki in the same way. I pondered whether or not the photo was an example of female objectification or if it was simply admiration of the female form. "I totally get that," Will said. There was my answer.

We moved from exhibit to exhibit, agreeing on everything. It was refreshing and a far cry from my time with Robert or visiting the Guggenheim with my mother. It was like we saw everything through the same lens.

Back at the hotel, Will said he thought the meeting would be boring. "Why don't you just stay here and relax? I have to finish up the studio stuff anyway."

"So you've made up your mind?"

"Yes. It was an easy decision." His gaze moved to my lips.

"Did you think there would be a better deal out there from another label?"

"No, there's not going to be another deal." He kissed my nose. "I'll see you later, sweet thing."

After he left, I took a walk on the beach and found myself wandering into the boutiques located off the boardwalk. I found a store with European lingerie—really beautiful, elegant, lacy pieces. I was more of a T-shirt kind of girl, but I thought it would be nice to give Will a treat, so I picked up a delicate black satin and lace camisole set. Back at the hotel, I took a long bath in the oversized tub. I thought about Will signing the paperwork, being a bona-fide professional musician, not that he wasn't already, but the world was going to know his amazing talent. For the first time, I was genuinely excited for him. I was with a man whose dreams were coming true and I would get to be right by his side through it all.

I sat on the veranda looking out at the ocean, savoring the peace I felt for what seemed like hours. Seven turned into ten and when he still wasn't back, I decided to lie down. I dozed off to the sublime sound of the waves crashing against the beach.

I was startled awake and glanced at the clock: it was two a.m. The bright moonlight shone through the wall of windows that looked out onto the ocean. My eyes darted around the room until I saw Will, who looked to be asleep in the chair next to the bed. He was shirtless but still wearing the jeans and boots. His head was resting on the back of the chair, his legs were spread, and he was slouching. His hand sat on the arm, clutching a highball glass with brown liquid—whiskey, I assumed. His face was completely shadowed so I couldn't see his eyes, but I thought he was sleeping because he didn't make a sound or movement and his posture was thoroughly relaxed. I sat up and kicked my legs over the side of the bed, then pushed my thick mane of hair away from my face. I took a breath, looked down at my lacy, satin piece and thought, *Oh well, there's always next time.*

Right before I stood up to take Will's shoes off, he whispered, "So beautiful."

My heart jumped to my throat; I slowly walked toward him until I was standing between his legs. He didn't sit up; he didn't speak. He just reached his hand out and ran it across my rib cage, playing with the satin between his fingers. I pulled his boots off, then his jeans, then . . . I was on my knees between his, and his hands were in my hair, pushing himself deeper into my mouth. He stood up and simultaneously pulled my face up to his and kissed me hard, then whispered, "I need to be inside you." He spun me around toward the bed while he pulled my satin shorts off and practically tore off my camisole. He pushed himself inside me aggressively from behind; his hand cupped my breast as his mouth went to my neck. He held me against him, making subtle but strong movements. He eased up for just a moment and mumbled, "You're mine."

I whispered "Yes?" but knew it wasn't a question.

He reached around and pressed his hand into the space just above where he and I connected. The aching was unbearable, the pulsing, then quickening. He whispered, "Come for me," and I did.

I collapsed onto the bed. Will positioned himself beside me and traced f-holes on my back. "Le Violin de Mia."

I turned and smiled. "So I'm just a hobby?"

"No, you're everything."

"What just happened?" I rolled over on my stomach and propped myself up on my elbows so I could see his face.

"What?" he said playfully.

"That was a little rough."

His expression turned somber. "Did I hurt you?"

"No."

"You didn't like it?"

"No, I loved it."

He rolled me over onto my back and spent twenty minutes kissing every inch of me. When he got to my stomach he paused. "Are you going to give me lots of babies?" His voice was smooth and wistful.

The sound of a car screeching to a halt played in my mind, or maybe it was a needle being pushed off the record right in the middle of my favorite song. Whatever the case, my body tensed up. I lifted his head to look into his eyes. It was undoubtedly the most romantic thing anyone had ever said to me, but it freaked me out.

"Whoa, whoa, buddy, slow down."

"What?" he said, looking dejected.

"No. I'm sorry, that was really sweet, but there are a few things that should happen before that, don't you think?" I said it gently, but he still looked crushed.

"I know, Mia; I want to marry you first." He said it like it should have been obvious to me, but that wasn't my concern.

I literally had the two most conflicted feelings in that moment. I wanted to have a million of Will's babies, but at the same time I couldn't believe that he would expect me to raise him a tribe while he traveled the country on tour.

"Will, don't you want to see what it's like to be on tour before you start bringing children into that world?"

He looked completely baffled. "What are you talking about? I'm not going on tour. I turned them down. I thought you knew that."

"What?" My voice suddenly got high. "Well, then, what were you doing in the studio and where the hell have you been?"

"I gave the song to Sonja. I helped produce it. I'll still get paid for the writing. I'm so confused. Are you mad?"

"People would die for the opportunity you were given. You won the fucking lottery and you're gonna throw it all away?"

"If this is about the money, Mia, then I don't know you at all. You said you were worried about me getting big and forgetting about you; now you're yelling at me for turning down the deal?"

My jaw dropped. "You turned it down for me? How stupid are you?"

He winced at my words, then his expression turned to anger. "Don't fucking flatter yourself. I turned it down because I don't want to be, what did you call it . . . big and famous? I just want to make music."

"Oh good, so now you want me to give you lots of babies while you live in my apartment and work for pennies at the Montosh?"

He didn't say anything; he just narrowed his eyes and slowly shook his head back and forth. I wrapped myself in a blanket and stormed off to the bathroom, slamming the door behind me. Falling asleep on the bathroom floor, I thought about the hurtful words I had just spoken. I didn't apologize because I didn't know how I was going to move forward with Will. I felt like the earth had shifted on its axis—I was trapped in the gravity of my own mind, spinning out of control. I love him; he loved me. It's too bad I didn't believe love was ever enough. Throw love in the pile with faith and destiny and it would pretty much sum up how I felt at the time.

I stumbled out of the bathroom the next morning and noticed that everything "Will" was gone except for some words
scribbled on a napkin.

*A CAR WILL PICK YOU UP AT 10 AND TAKE
YOU TO THE AIRPORT.*

—W

P.S. YOU'VE RUINED ME.

Tears began pouring from my eyes. The last thing I wanted
to do was hurt him. I picked up my phone and dialed his cell,
but it went straight to voice mail. I called Frank and he told
me Will had gotten on the first flight back to New York.

TRACK 19: A Cautionary Tale

My flight was delayed due to a mechanical failure. It was the first time I felt an irrational fear of flying. I thought for sure that I would be going down in a fiery ball of flames and never get to tell Will how sorry I was. I called his cell phone twenty times while I waited at the gate. Every time it skipped to a message saying that his voice mail was full. I couldn't wait to get back to the apartment and apologize, but I still wasn't sure what I would say and I didn't know if I was willing to stay with him after his catastrophic decision to throw the deal away.

It didn't matter; I wouldn't get a chance to make that decision. When I got to the apartment, all of Will's things were gone. There was a check for five thousand dollars on the counter. In the memo he wrote "For whatever." I fell to my knees and sobbed.

Over the next few weeks, I called his phone hundreds of times with no luck. I kept replaying the words "You've ruined me" over and over in my head. I did nothing but the bare minimum in the café. I showered rarely and wore the same clothes practically every day. I had no energy, my apartment was a mess, and I didn't even open my mail. Every day just blurred into the next and I fell deeper and deeper into a surreal fogginess of grief and sorrow. The worst part was that I knew it was entirely my fault. He was done with my fickle bullshit; how could I blame him?

He'd taken everything that was his in the apartment, even the T-shirts I would wear. It was like he'd never existed. I would look for him on the street and through store windows. I went to the Montosh, where Bradley, the other bartender, told me he'd quit in typical Will fashion.

"Yeah, the place was packed the night he left. He stood up on the bar and said, 'I love every single one of you.' He was pointing and yelling 'I love you and you and you and you' and then he pulled out a sheet of paper from his pocket and read a prayer he wrote. I don't remember it word for word, but I remember the last line was 'Save your souls and stay away from love or you'll be a madman like me,' and then he said, 'That's it, I'm done, I'm outta here! Gonna go sleep and drink!' Maybe not in that order, but at least he seemed happy, in a crazed kind of way."

The words stung. I knew Will wasn't happy—he was never neurotic like that when he was happy; it was just his coping mechanism.

I walked out feeling like the world was folding in on me. I gasped for a breath, but the weight of my mistake was crushing. I thought Will must have been completely insane to quit his job; it wasn't like him to be that irresponsible. I imagined him in some storage closet somewhere, drinking himself to death.

I begged Sheil to try to find him through the mutual friends they had, but she told me no, that I needed to learn my lesson. She's a tough cookie. Martha was a little more sympathetic; she gave me a copy of *The Prophet* by Kahlil Gibran, complete with her own highlighted notes. I sat in the back of the café, scanning the book for some answers, advice, anything I could use; I was grasping at straws. Most of what I got out of it was just a reminder that I'd fucked everything up.

I ran my fingers over the quote: "Ever has it been that love knows not its own depth until the hour of separation." I squeezed my eyes shut, cursed myself, then threw the book down and screamed.

Martha came over and put her arm around me. "You need to eat—you're disappearing on me and you're scaring the customers."

"I deserve it."

"You're wrong. Will is a deeply sensitive young man and he knows what you've gone through this year and he's been patient with you. I don't think you deserve any more heartache, but this is your own doing and you know it. You're not being punished; you're punishing yourself. You can't fault a man for loving you, Mia."

"That has nothing to do with it."

"Are you sure about that?" She sniffed me. "Child, you need a shower. Go home. I'll close up."

I went home and decided to skip the shower. Instead I found an old Sinead O'Connor cassette, covered the top hole with tape, stuck it in my father's ancient stereo, got a microphone, and put it next to the piano where I composed, then recorded, the saddest piece of music I've ever heard. I timed the song "Nothing Compares 2 U," and recorded my wretched song right over it. I thought *Sorry, Sinead, my sorrow knows no depth; my song is so much more pitiful than yours. My song is so pathetic; there is only one suitable title for it: Hell.*

Having spent almost every day at Kell's for an entire year, I started declaring Sunday as my official day off. Although my hope was that I would use my free days for some form of self-improvement, either exercise or composing more pieces, I did neither one of those things. Instead, I slept away nearly every moment I wasn't at the café. I lost weight and felt exhausted all the time. There was a growing distance between Jenny and me. While she worked on starting a family and enjoying her marital bliss, I was focused on surviving a monumental heartbreak. Because Will stayed away and avoided me, I felt robbed of the opportunity to right my mistakes, which made me grow angry toward him. The memories of him were so heartbreaking, I couldn't bear idle time in my apartment, so I would just sleep or sit at the park and watch the children play. I envied the simplicity of childhood and let my mind wander to memories with my father in that same park.

That was my only solace as the anniversary of his death passed along with my twenty-sixth birthday and Will's thirtieth, all events that I essentially ignored. I got a few "Happy Birthdays" from people at the café. Martha made me a casserole, insisting that I eat half of it in front of her. Jenny made me a cake and Tyler did a comedic birthday slam for me on poetry night. On Will's birthday, Jenny asked for the night off but didn't tell me why, not that it wasn't obvious.

When I did make an attempt to write music, the notes would inevitably turn dismal and monotonous, so I gave up playing the piano and writing music. I put all the other instruments away in closets and bought myself a nice flat-screen TV and would watch hours of meaningless, shit programing in the middle of the night when I couldn't sleep.

I woke up one Sunday morning months after that fateful night in LA. It was spring and the new warmth in the city came flooding through my windows, providing me with a modicum of energy, just enough to get out of bed before noon. I finally addressed the mountain of mail piling up on my countertop. Sipping coffee while I perused one of the many *New Yorker* magazines in the pile, I got lost in a modern fiction excerpt, particularly a few paragraphs from the novel by author Lauren Fuser-Biel.

> *Isabelle watched the majestic creature pensively as he paced behind the ironclad fortress. His captivating beauty drew her closer, her eyes locked on his. She began mimicking his movements with acute precision, back and forth, forging a new path in the unmarred earth on her side of the bars. They studied each other with determined stares; her mouth fell agape. Faint whispers escaped in haunting tribute as she fixated on the beast. "Wolf, you are beautiful, admired because you are flawless, adored because you are predictable, envied because you are cherished . . . empty because you are caged." The beast stilled. Isabelle, like a dammed river, slowed with a lingering motion as she appraised her counterpart. The trepidation in his sharply angled eyes, blue as the glacial depths, bore deep into her mind. She discovered a weakness in the magnificent and mercurial vision in front her, simultaneously revealing her own.*
>
> *Protecting the flesh that was her only possession, she recoiled into herself to examine the surroundings. Where would she go for escape within the confines of her cage? As if the answers were predetermined, she stood and began pacing once again, for the worn path had become a familiar and safe refuge, the bars her warm blanket, the ferocious animal her protector.*
>
> *Tormenting whispers echoed with the beast's penetrating gaze. "Back and forth, beautiful creature. Back and forth, Wife."*

I pondered the meaning and wondered if the author was speaking of herself in it. Was it a warning about marriage or life in general, or was it simply a statement about the traps we make for ourselves, the walls we build, the prisons we are comfortable within? Was I guilty of choosing safety over happiness and freedom, like the character in the book? I wondered if anything mattered at that point. It was all in the past; I was left with nothing but regret now, and no power to change things.

Flipping through the stack, I came across a birthday card. The front was van Gogh's *Irises*; when I opened the inside I sucked in a breath at the sight of Will's handwriting.

> HAPPY BIRTHDAY
> HOPE YOU'RE WELL
>   LOVE, WILL

Was he kidding? He basically fell off the face of the earth with no explanation except for a few words scribbled on a dirty napkin. I had resorted to scanning the faces of homeless men, thinking I would find him drenched in drunken sorrows at the street corner. I thought I was solely responsible for destroying a great musical talent, not to mention the love of my life, and here was his writing, perfectly legible, hoping that I'm well, signing off with love. It was just enough to break my heart all over again. I scoured the envelope for a return address, but there was nothing. Clenching my jaw, my fists balling in anger, I decided I needed to do something I hadn't done since Jackson died. I threw on a pair of sweats and tennis shoes and started running. I ran until I couldn't run anymore and then I collapsed on the bench overlooking the playground at Tompkins Square Park.

A familiar face caught my attention but I struggled to place it. I stared at her long dark hair, dark eyes, and alabaster skin, similar to mine. It wasn't until I saw her reach down to hand a young boy a water bottle that I realized it was the woman I had helped at the airport over a year ago, just after my father's death. It was the day I met Will and the memory was still vivid. I walked into the playground area and took a seat next to her on the bench. She glanced over and smiled, but there was no sign of recognition on her face. I was feeling bold and intrigued that I had run into this woman again.

I turned toward her and stuck my hand out. "Hi, I'm Mia. I don't know if you remember me, but I helped you in the security line at Detroit Metro last year?"

She smiled, then pointed at me and nodded. "Yes, I do remember." I could see in her face that she did recognize me and there was something else, she recognized herself the same way I had. "I'm Lauren."

"I remember—hi. Wow, your boys have grown so much in just a year." She nodded and smiled. "How old are they?"

"They're four and five—fifteen months apart and very busy, I might add," she said, laughing. "Which one is yours?"

"I don't have kids, I just love this park. I used to come here with my father. So, you must be very busy with two little active boys?"

"Yes, fortunately I work from home so I get to spend lots of time with them."

"What do you do?" I asked.

"I'm a writer."

"Really? That's so cool. What do you write?" I realized I was being really nosy, but she didn't seem to mind. I looked down at my appearance and wondered briefly if she thought I was a homeless person or an asylum escapee. I must have been quite a departure from the put-together Mia of last year.

"I write fiction. I wrote a book called *Bountiful Lies* that was just recently published."

"You're kidding me?" I looked at her like she had three heads.

"Oh no, you didn't like it?" I could tell she was bracing herself for criticism.

I sat there, stunned at the coincidence. "I literally just read an excerpt in *The New Yorker* this morning."

"Well?"

"It was great. I'm gonna buy it for sure."

"Thank you. I appreciate that, Mia."

"Is Isabelle you?"

"Oh, good lord, no, it's purely fiction. But I suppose all the characters have a little piece of me."

She was kind and seemed a bit lonely, like me, which gave me the urge to tell her my entire life story. I ended with my heartbreak over Will and how he had thrown away a promising future, which led to our breakup. I told her how I missed everything about him, but mostly our friendship, the music, and the way he took care of me. She listened attentively while I tried to explain how my life had been turned upside down. I said I felt like I was drowning in a huge chasm created by some obsession I have with getting things right. She seemed unusually interested in what I was saying, and I wondered if I was providing her with some fodder for the next book. *Oh no. That's not good. My story would certainly be a cautionary tale.* I turned the conversation back to her.

She told me how her husband was a writer as well, Pulitzer Prize winning, in fact. She believed that the passion they shared was the ultimate catalyst in the relationship. She didn't believe opposites attracted. She said, "My husband is my soul twin, and I wouldn't have it any other way."

"Was he a writer when you met him?"

"Aspiring. We met in Atlanta at a small art house theater,

where he collected tickets. At the time he was still living with his parents and working on his first book. He picked me up for our first date in the most beat-up Chevy truck I had ever seen. It was the middle of summer and ridiculously humid. His truck didn't have air-conditioning and the window handle was broken, so he reached over me and rolled my window down with a pair of vise grips. Pretty impressive, huh?"

The story was clearly for my benefit. She wanted me to hear something deeper in the words; it was an anecdote. She understood my dilemma, which gave me the sense I was going through some painful rite of passage she had already experienced.

"How did you know your husband would be successful?"

"I didn't. I knew I loved him, and that meant I trusted him. I was never obsessed with material possessions, but I had the same concerns as you. I eventually realized as my love grew that, more than anything, I believed in him because of his passion and determination. It boils down to one word: faith."

"Oh no, not that word."

"Yes, committing yourself to someone requires a leap of faith—that's why it's so hard for some. There is no crystal ball, but if you love someone enough and you share a similar dream, then your faith in that person becomes faith in yourself, and that's the best part of sharing your life . . . you're better for it. Isabelle in the book is trapped by her own fear and nothing else . . . no one else. It's a cautionary tale," she said, watching my reaction.

I almost choked on my tongue. I pondered her words in silence as I looked on at the exuberant children. When it was time to go, I hugged her and gave her my phone number. I felt like she was sort of a big sister; it was a connection I'd longed for my entire life. I ran home with my newfound determination and called Jenny.

"Jenny, you have to tell me where he is."

She paused for a long beat. She had been avoiding me and any conversation related to Will; I only saw her at the café, where she was all business. I knew her and Tyler were taking Will's side in the whole thing, which made me feel even more alone. "I don't know where he is," she said.

"Why won't you talk to me about this?"

"About what?"

"Stop being like that, Jenny. About Will—where is he? I need to talk to him."

"He doesn't want to talk to you and I have nothing to say."

"I need you. I messed up and I'm sorry."

"Yeah, I'd say."

I started crying. "Please, I'm having a hard time."

"Okay," she said quietly. There was a long pause. "I'll be over later. We'll go out, get some dinner or something."

"Thank you. I know I've been a mess and I've made mistakes. I can't make things right with Will, but I want to with you and Tyler."

"Okay, Mia, I'll see you in a little bit."

I couldn't understand why Jenny was so mad; it really had nothing to do with her. I was nervous to find out. With my newfound energy I took a little extra time getting ready. I hadn't had plans in ages and it was nice to look in the mirror and feel somewhat put together. I wore skinny black capris, plain black heels, and a dark blue, low-cut tunic top.

"Why are you so dressed up? We're just going to Sam's."

"I haven't been out in a long time; I thought maybe we could try that sushi place in SoHo?"

At first Jenny's look was disapproving, but it immediately turned to pity when she saw the hope in my face. "Okay, let's do it," she said, reaching out to hug me. It felt so good to be hugged by her. I missed my friend.

Over dinner, I asked her about life and Tyler. Things were going well for them. I told her about Lauren and the book. The restaurant was small and packed, so we sat at the sushi bar and shared quite a spread along with a bottle of sake and a giant beer. Our conversation was interrupted when I recognized familiar words being piped through the speakers. It was Sonja singing Will's song. I could hear his sexy voice backing her up in certain sections, which created a huge lump in my throat. The song was much more juvenile than the way Will had originally written it, but it suited Sonja. "Wow, it's on the radio?"

Jenny looked at me, scrunching her eyebrows. "Yeah, it's number one on the billboard chart. You didn't know that?"

"No, I guess I've been a little out of it. Well, good for her, then."

"And Will, too."

"Yes, good for him." I was glad she brought him up first. "How's he doing, by the way?"

She took a deep breath through her nose. "He's hanging in there."

"Why won't he talk to me?"

She paused for far too long. "Well, Mia, the guy told you he wanted you to be his wife and the mother of his children and you basically said he was a loser. I believe his exact words were, 'She ripped my soul out, poured gasoline on it, and watched it burn.'"

I briefly wondered what our souls would look like if we could see them. What kind of shape would mine have? I decided Will's would be the ever-changing clouds in the sky: heavenly, serene, but sometimes dark, brooding, and filled with electricity. Then I thought about what his soul would look like on fire. I cringed.

Instead of pleading and begging or calling Will dramatic, I just calmly said, "I made a huge mistake that I have regretted every single day. I've changed. I know what I want, but it's too late and I'll never get that. I just want him to know that I'm sorry and that I did love him, I do love him, and I just want to see him."

Her expression changed from tolerance to sympathy. She had my best interests at heart and I didn't always like what she had to say, but usually she was right. Sometimes things were as black and white as she saw them, and even though she wanted to help me she knew when to step back—she knew when she couldn't help. "I'm sorry, too, Mia. I believe this has been a very tough year and a half for you, and I feel really bad, but Will said he doesn't want to talk to you or see you under any circumstances."

I tried to mask my frustration by drinking more and changing the subject. "Do you want to go to the club around the corner and dance?"

Clubbing wasn't really our scene, but I think Jenny knew I needed to burn off some steam.

"Sure."

Once outside I started heading toward the end of the block. Jenny stopped dead in her tracks. "Let's go this way."

"It's twice as far that way—it's right around this corner."

She huffed and then caught up to me. She talked fast the entire way, trying to distract me, but it didn't work. When I got to the end of the block, I heard the glorious sound of Will's music in the bar across the street. The haunting drum-

beat and a long bluesy guitar riff were floating through the
air with Will's smooth, soulful voice. My heart was pounding
in my chest. The sign outside said WILL RYAN EVERY SUN-
DAY NIGHT. I shot a scorching look at Jenny and then darted
across the street as she yelled at me to wait. When I got to the
bouncer, he said the bar was full. I stood outside and peered
through the crack in the doorway while Jenny stood behind
me. I watched Will onstage along with three band members
I had never seen. He was so composed behind his guitar—he
wasn't the type to run around or even interact much with the
crowd. He just focused on singing well and playing perfectly.
It was always just about the music for him. He told me once
that he loved playing live to small crowds that didn't know
him because he liked to change the songs up. "Songs are always evolving, Mia, like us. That's what it's all about. That's
why we play so well together . . . because playing and singing
is more about listening and feeling than anything else." Funny
how he wouldn't listen to me now.

There were a handful of girls vying for his attention at
the front of the stage, but he remained centered in the song.
Until it ended, anyway, and then I watched him take his guitar
off, walk up to a girl in the front row, bend down and kiss the
back of her hand; all the groupies went crazy. He was wearing
black jeans and a bright pink T-shirt that said "I'm A Virgin"
in big bold letters, and underneath in small writing, "but this
is an old shirt." Rolling my eyes, I turned around and took off
toward the club without saying a word to Jenny.

She stood next to me at the bar as I ordered us both two
shots of tequila.

"So he still plays?" I yelled over the loud, thumping house
beat. She nodded impassively and remained silent.

When the bartender pushed four shots toward us, Jenny

narrowed her eyes. "Just one for me tonight. I had too much sake!" she yelled, but I knew it wasn't true because I'd downed pretty much the whole bottle.

"Suit yourself!" I smiled as I threw back one shot after another. We danced for at least an hour; I had a couple more drinks and my mind was severely clouded. Jenny stepped out to call Tyler, so I took the opportunity to get one more shot.

A blond, blue-eyed musclehead in a tight shirt approached me. "I've been watching you," he said with a slimy grin.

"Oh yeah? And?" He looked exactly like Dolph Lundgren, except this guy had a Jersey accent.

"You can drink." He grinned like he was impressed. Really, he was mistaken because my brain had become nothing but a tequila whirlpool at that point. "You wanna dance?"

"Sure!" I yelled, pulling him onto the dance floor.

Once on the floor, he started groping me and trying to get me to grind on him—yuck. I tried pushing him away but he persisted. Finally I stopped moving and pushed him back. "Quit it!" I yelled, but it fueled his attempts more. His giant arms reached around and grabbed my ass, pulling me into him. I squirmed, trying to get out of his grip.

Just as I was ready to sock him, I heard a familiar, smooth voice behind me. "I think this dance is over, buddy!" I turned around to see Will, who had a beyond-calm look on his face. He never met my gaze, but just the sight of him did weird things to my heart. In my drunkenness, I moaned from the memory of what he could do to me. I stared, transfixed, my mouth gaping. Thankfully, the unintentional moan was drowned out by the pounding music.

Dolph Two yelled back, "Get your own piece of ass, dawg!" Will shrugged like he was conceding. He turned on his heel to walk away and then a split second later he turned back and clocked Dolph Two right in the temple, laying him out cold on the floor. He grabbed my hand and began pulling me off the dance floor.

"Whoa, Rocky, what was that?" He ignored me and continued yanking on my arm until we were outside of the club. I shimmied my hand out of his grip. "I didn't ask for your help," I spat. "Where's Jenny?"

His voice was low and husky. "She's inside with Tyler. You're wasted, Mia. Let me get you home."

My eyes began to well up as I studied the handsome man in front of me. My vision blurred, but he was still perfectly sexy, his hair a little longer, a light stubble growing along his defined jawline. The pink T-shirt was covered up by a black hoodie that came up over his head and shadowed his eyes. Taking a cautious step toward me, he moved into the light of the street lamp. His eyes were sullen and distant, but his hands were outstretched to me, palms up like Jesus Christ himself.

"Please, let me help you get home?" He moved toward me.

"What do you think, you can just disappear for months and then show up here to save me? What? You think I need you?" I could hear belligerent words leaving my mouth, but I couldn't stop. He shook his head slightly, eyes narrowed and pained.

Suddenly my world was spinning. I walked two feet and began heaving into a planter box. I felt his hands on me, holding my hair and rubbing my back. I did need him. Collapsing into his side, I wiped my mouth with the back of my hand and tilted my head back to look into his eyes. He was searching my face. "Baby, are you okay?"

That's when I lost it. Tears poured from my eyes, I sobbed loudly. "Don't call me baby!"

"Settle down," he said in all seriousness and then in one swift move, he reached down and scooped me up. That was the last thing I remembered until I woke the next morning with my head in his lap, and not in the way either one of us would have liked. We were on my bathroom floor, his back was propped against the wall, his legs stretched out in front of him and crossed at the feet. He was sound asleep, sitting almost perfectly upright. I surveyed the room and myself. My head was throbbing, my shirt was stained and smelled awful, but I didn't want to move because I didn't know how long I had with him. I had clearly been throwing up, probably all night, and Will must have stayed to watch over me. I put my head back down in his lap and dozed off again.

I woke later that morning to the sound of his muffled voice in the kitchen. I was lying on top of my bed where he must have put me. I was always amazed at how gentle he was; moving a grown woman without waking her was a gift. I scurried down the hall, hoping I would catch him preparing breakfast in a way that would say everything was back to normal, but he wasn't. He was dressed with his backpack on and a glass of water in hand as he finished up a quiet phone call.

"I've gotta go. I'll see you in a bit," he whispered into the phone and then reached out to hand me the glass of water. He put his phone in his back pocket, looked over at me, expressionless, and said, "Take care of yourself," before turning to leave.

"Wait, Will. Can I talk to you?"

"I have nothing to say." He continued walking away.

When his hand reached the knob, I protested. "Wait, please! I have something for you."

He paused and turned, leaning his back against the door. I went to my room, grabbed the Sinead O'Connor tape and ran back toward him. As I handed it to him, I gazed into his eyes. He looked away, like my stare caused him pain.

"I'm sorry."

When he glanced at the tape, I caught a tiny smile playing on his lips, but it was fleeting. "Me, too." He spoke so quietly that his words didn't seem meant for me.

"Listen to it, please—it's not what you think."

"Okay."

"Do you still love me, Will?"

He looked right into my eyes and whispered, "More than you know." Then he was out the door and down the stairs before I could find my voice to beg him to stay.

I went into the café and muscled through a hundred lattes even though I thought my head was going to explode. By the end of that day, I was back to my wallowing, pitiful self. I closed up Kell's at nine, went home, took a shower, and then walked to the corner market in a pair of pink flannel pajamas covered by my light-blue terry robe. I had really lost all self-respect at that point. I spread my groceries out on the counter. Benton reviewed my choices. There was a pack of cigarettes, a bottle of peppermint schnapps, hot cocoa mix, vodka, a box of tissues, and one of those rolled-up horoscopes.

"I didn't know you smoked, Miss Mia?"

"I'm starting today," I said.

Benton looked up at me with sympathy. "How about some food? I buy you a sandwich?"

I shrugged. He motioned to the guy working behind the deli counter, pointed to the top of my head, and yelled with his thick accent, "Make her something to eat, she starving."

Later that night after smoking ten cigarettes in the comfort of my living room, I still couldn't understand the act; it's disgusting and it causes cancer, but I'm not one to judge. My horoscope said that I was in an optimistic phase of my life, I handled pressure well, and I gravitated toward social situations that would help me achieve my goals. *What a crock of shit.* There was also some other mumbo jumbo in it about relationships; that was when I decided to burn it in the sink. I went back to my concave spot on the couch to stare at the TV while I drank a combination of vodka, peppermint schnapps, and hot cocoa. Around eleven p.m. the buzzer rang—it was Jenny. I pressed the button, opened the door, plopped back down on the couch, and lit a cigarette.

When she walked in, her mouth fell open at the sight of me. She looked around the smoke-filled room. *Chasing Amy* was playing on the TV, there was an ashtray full of butts, a half-eaten sandwich on the coffee table where I'd haphazardly set it after spilling little slices of lettuce all over the floor, and a coffee mug shaped like a Rubik's Cube holding my concoction.

She picked up the mug and sniffed it. "Good god, Mia, it's like the fucking nineties in here. What's going on with you, Winona Ryder?"

"I think I'm gonna be a lesbian now," I said.

"Okay." She walked over and sat next to me on the couch, observing me from the corner of her eye.

Gazing at the TV, I blew a puff of smoke out and mumbled, "Why the long face, Ben?"

Jenny started cracking up. "At least you still have a sense of humor." She joined me in a mixture of laughing and crying throughout that night. She told me funny stories and tried to get my mind off Will as she continually plucked cigarettes out of my hand. When I asked her why he was still playing at bars around town, she said that's what he liked to do and left it at that. She told me he was living alone in Brooklyn and getting on with his life. The pain of losing someone is always worse when you know you could have prevented it.

The next morning I woke up to Sheil, Martha, Tyler, and Jenny all hovering over me on the couch. Before I opened my eyes, I decided to listen for a few minutes to the hushed conversation.

Sheil whispered to Martha. "She looks like a sick little baby."

Tyler's voice sounded unusually concerned. "I can see her hip bone through her sweats."

Jenny said, "She's fine. She'll snap out of it, but I think we should still stage the intervention."

That's when I shot my eyes open at the three of them inspecting me. "Come on, you guys—an intervention? I'm fine. Everybody scram, I have to get ready for work."

Martha blocked me from moving past her. She motioned to the piano. "I'm having that thing moved to the café. Someone should get some use out of it."

"You can't do that; that's my piano."

"Well, you don't play it, and I'm sure your father is turning over in his grave right now with you going about like this," she said, motioning with her hand up and down my body.

"Going about like what?"

"All mopey and glued to the television." I looked past Martha to Sheil, who raised her eyebrows in agreement. I glanced at Jenny, who just shrugged and turned toward Tyler, who was staring at the ceiling.

"Fine, move it. I don't care," I said, and I really didn't.

TRACK 20: The Sound of Her Soul

Martha stuck to her word and had my piano moved to the café where practically all the customers pounded a key as they walked by, reminding me why the damn thing was there in the first place. I forced myself to resume some semblance of a normal life, and after a while I actually started to feel *normal*. I thought about Will every day, but I stopped beating myself up over what had happened. More than anything, I was just curious, but no one would utter a word to me about him.

At some point the old piano called to me again and I began playing it in the evenings, drawing a little crowd to the café, which was good for business. Every night I would play the same long piece of music I wrote. It included the movements I shared with Will on both the CD and the Sinead O'Connor tape earlier that year. I added and changed parts as the healing took place inside of me. I mourned my father and Jackson and my relationship through that piece of music. It eventually evolved into a familiar score that the regular customers recognized. It was the soundtrack from the year and a half I had spent in New York figuring out who I was and who I didn't want to be. It was pure catharsis until I realized I had a fairly decent finished product. Jenny and Tyler encouraged me to pursue writing music, and for the first time I felt like I had a real purpose. I had a piece of the puzzle and it was something that resembled faith in myself.

One warm spring day I made the decision that it was time for closure. Jackson's ashes were housed in a small redwood box that I'd had engraved with the words "Jackson: My Friend. The Best." I took the box along with a small garden shovel to Tompkins Square Park, where I discreetly buried it under his favorite tree overlooking the children's playground. I fell asleep under that tree, thinking back to the way Will had treated Jackson, so loving and affectionate, the same way he'd been toward me. I had so carelessly rejected that warmth and love and I was learning the hard way what happens when you take the people who love you for granted.

After my nap, I was ready for the next step. I went to Kell's and asked Martha if she could cover the café for the next couple of days.

"I'm taking Pops to Memphis," I said, struggling to hold it together.

"He'll love that." When she began to cry, I wrapped my arms around her.

"I know. Thank you for helping me do this," I whispered.

"Helping you do what?" she said, dumbfounded.

"Thank you for helping me mourn . . . live . . . find myself, and thank you for loving me."

"Oh, sweetie, like your father, you're easy to love." I smiled at the idea of being like him.

"Thank you. I love you."

Back at my apartment, I opened my father's metal urn, relieved to find his ashes packed nicely in a velvet bag. It was going to make flying with Pops a lot easier. I packed light, bringing only a few necessities inside the hemp backpack Martha had given me.

I arrived in Memphis in the late afternoon. It started getting dark, so I took a cab straight to Beale Street. I walked to the end and stared out at the Mississippi until the sky darkened and I could no longer see the ripples in the water. It became a black void. The only light came from a tugboat slowly disappearing in the distance. I wondered what sort of magic that dark river had swallowed in its day.

Okay, Pops, time to find the music.

I turned and followed the poignant sound of a Southern blues guitar floating through the thick, spring air. The music lured me to a dive bar right off Beale. The poster read:

TONIGHT: THE LEGENDARY TOMMY RAY BOOKER

When I got inside I looked up to the stage to find a man dressed in a bright red suit, complete with a red fedora and red harmony guitar. He was playing fast blues; everyone in the place was moving to the beat. When he lifted the guitar to his mouth and began plucking the strings with his teeth, the bar went crazy with applause. The saxist got on his knees, belting out the riffs while Tommy Ray continued shredding his vintage guitar. I felt alive, letting the pulse of the town, the patrons of that bar, and Tommy Ray Booker course through my veins.

My father would love it. Will would love it.

"We're gonna take a little break. Be back in five," Tommy said to the crowd.

I slowly made my way toward the stage. When it looked like the musicians were getting ready to go back on, I approached the drummer. He was a John Goodman–looking character, an overweight and disheveled middle-aged man wearing faded jeans and a Hawaiian shirt.

"Excuse me." I caught his attention right as he was about to climb the first step up to the stage.

"What can I do you for, Poppet?"

I giggled at the nickname and then pointed to a very old upright piano sitting to one side of the drum kit. "Is she tuned?"

He appraised me for a long beat. Tommy came into my view at the top of the stairs. Without taking his eyes off me, the drummer said, "Hey Tommy, I think Poppet here wants to play."

I looked up at Tommy. He smiled and then adjusted the feather in his bright red fedora before speaking. "You got the blues, baby?"

"Just the good kind," I yelled up to him.

"Well. let's hear it, little girl."

I climbed the steps and then looked out at the eager crowd. It was the first time I'd stood on a stage without feeling even slightly nervous. I had Pops with me and I didn't know a single soul in that bar; it was freeing. That was what Will had talked about so much, playing music for the sake of the music. I turned the piano bench perpendicular and then set my backpack on the space behind me. Tommy started right away with a typical one, four, five blues chord progression; the rest of the musicians joined in, so I followed suit. I kept the tune going while Tommy and the sax player soloed. On the next round I looked back at the drummer and he winked; that was my cue. I played my heart out, fingers swirling and fluttering. I even played with my elbows. When I kicked my foot up on the high keys and played like Will had at the wedding, the bassist yelled out, "Get it, girl!" I knew it wasn't the most ladylike thing to do, but man, the audience loved it.

When the song ended, Tommy went to the microphone.

He stretched his arm out in my direction. "That's our little girl, Poppet, over there on the ivories. Everybody give her a hand." The crowd clapped and cheered and I smiled from ear to ear. I bowed and then grabbed my backpack and headed offstage. As I passed Tommy, I quietly said, "Thank you."

He gave me a one-armed hug around the shoulders and said, "Anytime. You did great."

The neon lights from Beale Street glowed in my dark hotel room that night as I dozed off, feeling fulfilled for the first time in a long time.

The next day I found a street fair and browsed the artisan craft stands. I came across a young, homeless man. He had a hiking pack and sleep roll propped against a small folding table with several pieces of silver jewelry laid out. When I got closer, I realized the bracelets and rings were all made from bent antique spoon stems.

"Where do you get all the spoons?" I sorted through the bracelets.

"Thrift stores, estate sales, stuff like that," he said, smiling. He wasn't bad looking, but he was very dirty, which made his eyes seem like the brightest green color imaginable. I pulled my hotel key from my pocket and handed it to him. "I have to take off, but I have this room until one p.m. if you want to use it."

"Really?" he said, eyebrows arched. I nodded. "Wow, thank you so much."

"Sure." My eyes were instantly drawn to a bracelet that had the same silver-plate pattern as the spoons from Kell's. I picked it up. "This is beautiful. How much?"

He reached over and closed my hand around the bracelet.

"It's yours. I want you to have it." Then he held up the hotel key. "Thank you again for this. I'm dying for a shower."

I put the bracelet on and then looked up and said, "Thank you."

After the street fair I took Pops by Sun Studios, where it had all started for Johnny Cash and Elvis. I had a passerby take a picture of me sitting on the bench outside, right in front of the big neon sign. I texted the picture to Jenny with the words "Me and Pops at Sun."

She texted me back, "Love you both. I'm proud of you, Mia."

My last stop was the Memphis Zoo. I spent hours roaming from exhibit to exhibit until it started sprinkling. I saw people hurriedly rushing toward the exit. Looking around at the almost-empty zoo, I said aloud, "To the butterflies!" Inside the enclosure I followed one white butterfly around for several minutes until I noticed a chrysalis. With my hand over my heart, I thought back to my father's words: *"It's the change that happens in here that matters."* I cried thoroughly until I allowed myself to accept the finality of death and realize that my father's love was his legacy and it was living on in me. I knew I was changing and that I was finally feeling like the person I wanted to be.

When I landed in New York, I went straight to Central Park and decided to release some of my father's ashes in Turtle Pond. Staring across to the opposite shoreline, I whispered, "Rest in peace, Pops . . . and thank you." A cool breeze caressed the still water, forming faint ripples along the surface. I had closure.

I was grateful to my father for the invaluable gift he had given me with the café, my new friends, the music, and ultimately the freedom to be whoever I wanted to be. Kell's was a remarkable place in that it allowed people to come together and just be, without judgment. I finally saw the value in that, so I decided I wanted the café to remain what my father had made it.

We continued holding poetry nights there; my piano playing became the usual opening act. I always hoped that Will would show up and treat us to one of his sweet prayers or amazing songs, but he never did. One Thursday night, after I played some familiar tunes, I decided that it was time to share some of my own words with the crowd.

Everyone cheered when I cleared my throat and hesitantly removed a piece of paper from my pocket. I looked around and absorbed the faces of my eclectic little crew of friends that I had come to know as family. Martha was smiling with peace and reverence like she was channeling my father. Jenny and Tyler looked a little shocked at my newfound courage, but eventually they, too, smiled, rooting me on.

Sheil wore a look that said she believed in me and it reminded me of how Will and I had looked at each other when we played music together. It's what faith looks like, and I was glad at that moment to finally be able to recognize it. Some of the other members of the poetry group looked on with encouraging smiles. Many of them were essentially strangers, but they were willing to stand up and bare their souls for one visceral moment every Thursday night in the corner of our little café, and for that I owed them.

"Hi, everyone. First of all, I want to say thank you for coming here each week and giving a little piece of yourself through poetry. This is a really beautiful tradition my father started and I want it to continue for a long, long time. Taking the lead from an amazing person I know, I've written a little prayer for all of us—it's actually more like my promise to you and the café. It's my first crack at this poetry thing, so take it easy on me . . .

Share Your Coffee

Share your words
Share your music
Share your love, your passion, your fears
Your hopes, and your dreams

Share your precious heart
Share your wild mind
Share your special soul with me
And I promise to
Give you all of mine.

Everyone clapped. I smiled shyly and high-fived a few people on my way back to the counter. Jenny looked like she was about to cry as she wrapped her arms around me. "Ahh, Mia, you're coming along, aren't you?" she whispered. I folded up the paper and handed it to Tyler.

"Shot in the dark, but would you pass that on to Will for me?" He had sympathy in his eyes and I wondered if he thought it was a futile gesture. It didn't matter to me how Will reacted to the poem. I was sure he had moved on, but I still wanted to give him those words.

Martha stayed with me to close up Kell's that night. I took my time washing the old mugs my parents had made with love all those years ago. I ran my fingers over their engraved initials as I thought about the mystical alchemy they must have shared, however brief. Martha came over and hugged me around the shoulders. "Full circle, Mia Pia."

I looked up and gave her a warm smile. "Love you, Martha."

"Love you, too."

"Thank you for everything. You can go, I got this."

"Okay, see you tomorrow." She stared at me for a minute before turning and leaving.

After she left, my mind wandered aimlessly as I scrubbed away at the dishes. I felt a sense of peace and satisfaction. I was finally able to own the mistakes I made and although I missed Will like crazy, I was happy at the idea of him being happy, playing his music in a dive somewhere, listening to the sound of his soul. I hummed a mindless tune while I thought about the next piece of music I would write. What would become the next song in the soundtrack of my life was starting to take shape when the jingling of the café door startled me. I thought Martha would have locked up, but apparently she knew something I didn't.

"We're closed!" I yelled from the back as I quickly dried my hands on a towel. When I turned the corner I saw him, leaning against the inside of the doorway. He was wearing dark jeans, Converse, and a plain white T-shirt. He looked healthy and put together—he could have been wearing a paper bag for all I cared—but I was happy to see him looking so well. His head was down, his hands shoved deep in his pockets as he waited. I stood there silently, burning his image into my mind. When he finally looked up, he took a long cleansing breath while he slowly ran his hand through his hair. When he saw me smile, he grinned from ear to ear with that listening-to-God look. His eyes kissed mine; I sucked in a sharp breath at how his gaze made me feel. God, how I missed his handsome face, those soulful, deep eyes that could say everything with just a glance. He mesmerized me, the way he stared at me, the way his face changed when he saw that I was happy.

"Hey," he said, his voice low but playful.

"Hey," I breathed. Our eyes remained locked on each other as he walked toward me. I took a step back but opened my arms and leaned against the counter. He buried his face in my neck and pulled me into a hug. I threw my arms around him and whispered, "Never let me go."

He tightened his grip as his mouth moved to my ear. "Never."

"Where have you been?"

"Waiting for you."

"I've been here. Why did you go away?"

"You needed to figure things out on your own. I was just waiting for you to come around."

"God, I've missed you," I said, my voice cracked and pained.

He leaned back, narrowed his eyes, and studied my face as he ran his thumb across my bottom lip. "Baby . . . I've missed you . . . I've missed these lips." He kissed me sweetly without hesitation.

I literally went weak in the knees, but it didn't matter because he was practically holding me off the ground. I tried to deepen the kiss; leaning back, I hitched my leg up, pulling him toward me. His mouth stopped; he lifted me onto the counter and rested his hands on my thighs. Looking down, he took a long, deep breath and then looked up with a cocky grin. "Whoa, kitten, slow down." I looked at him with mock disappointment. He chuckled. "I have plans for you, little Mia."

"What are you gonna do to me, Wilbur?" I whispered, touching my index finger to his lips. He wrapped his hand around my wrist and pulled it away.

"One-track mind you have," he said, laughing.

"You started it."

There was a long pause and his expression turned serious. "I have to know that you're all in."

"I am," I said instantly.

"It's just me, nothing else, no fame, no record deal. Maybe I'll be a bartender forever; maybe I'll rent a room from you for four hundred dollars."

"Just you and your guitar?"

"Yep."

"I don't care, that's all I want. I love you."

"What did you say?" He smirked and cupped his hand behind his ear.

"I love you."

"One more ti—"

"I love you," I said and then socked him in the chest. "Can we go home now?"

"I'll walk you home. I have somewhere to be."

I scrunched my eyebrows. "Where?"

"I can't tell you. You just have to trust me," he said as he motioned toward the door.

"I trust you."

"Good, let's go."

When we got to my apartment, he stood on the landing. I motioned for him to come in, but he just shook his head and smiled.

"Come on, Will. Come to bed?" I said, wiggling my eyebrows suggestively.

"You have no idea how bad I want to."

"Then why won't you?"

He smiled. "I told you, I have somewhere to be. If I get into bed with you now, I'll never get out."

"I'm okay with that."

He leaned in and kissed me but pulled away too soon. "I'll come and get you tomorrow morning." He pecked my lips again and then kissed my nose. "Dream about me, okay, sweet thing?" he said as he turned and headed down the stairs.

"Always," I whispered, too low for him to hear.

Lying in my bed that night, I wondered if Will was an apparition. He was just too good to be true: too forgiving, too sweet, too beautiful. I remembered someone saying crazy people don't know they're crazy. Surely I had imagined Will that night. I was truly losing my mind—there was just no way that man would want me back after what I had done. I didn't deserve him. My own fear of not being worthy started to cloud my mind again, but I stopped it. I remembered what I learned from Gibran on love: *to return home at eventide with gratitude; And then to sleep with a prayer for the beloved in your heart and a song of praise upon your lips.* So that's what I decided to do as I dozed off, perfectly tranquil, thinking about how grateful I was to have Will in my life again. I also made a tiny request to the universe regarding the subject of my impending dream . . .

I woke up the next morning to the sound of my own voice as I squirmed under the glorious sensation of my dream. After thanking the universe, I opened my eyes and smiled at the sunshine coming through the window. In the shower I took my time shaving my legs and afterward I patiently dried my hair and clipped one side back. I put on a blue-and-white striped sundress and a brass cuff bracelet and some lip gloss. I stood at the counter and flipped through a magazine, paying little attention to what I was actually looking at. Instead my mind was on the kiss Will and I had shared in the café and in the doorway the night before. I touched my fingers to my lips and closed my eyes. What if it were all part of the dream? I went to the door and replayed what had happened. I looked at the space where I'd stood while we'd kissed and wondered when reality stopped and the dream started.

I jumped, startled by the sound of the buzzer. "Hello?"

"Hey, kitten, come down. I have a cab waiting."

Yes! He was real!

When I reached the bottom of the stairs, Will swung the door open and pulled me into his arms, kissing me passionately. "I've been thinking about that kiss for hours. You look beautiful, as always."

"Thank you."

He was clean-shaven, wearing the black pinstriped suit pants, his usual belt and wallet chain, and a black T-shirt; he looked and smelled like heaven. I looked him up and down, letting my eyes pause where his pants hung so perfectly. When I got back to his eyes, I smiled sheepishly.

"What?" he said with a brazen smirk.

"Nothing . . . I just . . . I love you in black."

"I know, I can tell." He grabbed my hand and pulled me toward the cab.

He gave the cabbie an address in Brooklyn. "Are we going to your place?"

He just nodded and squeezed my hand. When we got across the Manhattan Bridge into Brooklyn, he turned to face me.

"Okay, I want you to do something for me."

"Anything."

"Close your eyes and just trust me for a while. I know that's hard for you, but you're just gonna have to have faith, okay?" he said, chuckling.

"I can do that now." I closed my eyes. He took my hand and placed the digital four-track recorder in it.

"Hold this for a while and don't open your eyes."

"Okay."

When the car stopped, he took my hand and told me where to step. I felt us enter a building. "No peeking."

I heard him exchange hellos with a few people before we went through another door, and then we were in a room that had a familiar plastic smell of electronics. He told me to stand still; the room was so quiet you could hear a pin drop. He stood behind me and touched my hand that held the digital recorder. "This has four tracks," he whispered, then he took my other hand and placed it on something with dials and knobs. "This is limitless. Open your eyes."

I looked around, quickly absorbing my surroundings. I stood in the middle of a sizable, state-of-the-art recording studio with high-tech buttons and dials everywhere. Beyond the glass I saw instruments and microphones galore along with an isolated vocal booth. The only thing I didn't see was another soul in sight.

"Did you rent this out for us?" I asked tentatively. He just shook his head and then pulled me toward another door that had a rectangular window in it. I peered through the window into the adjacent room, which could easily accommodate a full symphony orchestra. I spotted two Steinway grand pianos, timpani drums, and a xylophone in the corner along with dozens of chairs and music stands. He appraised me, waiting for a response, but I just stood there dumbfounded. That's when I glanced over at a desk with a pad of paper that was embossed with the name "Alchemy Sound Studios." My eyes shot open at the realization.

"This is yours? How?"

"Well, it was many nights in the storage closet, cheap rent—thanks to you—slinging a whole lotta cocktails at the

Montosh, writing and producing credit on a number-one song, and some great referrals from Frank." He paused for me to say something, but I couldn't speak. "We're booked for six months solid. We have some big names that Live Wire is sending our way."

"Our way?"

He pointed to the larger room. "For you to score, for film."

I just stood there, mouth gaping. He gestured around the room. "This is my passion, to be part of the process for others in a place like this. I'll still make my own music because I love doing it, but this   this is my dream, Mia . . . and my hope is that it's your dream, too."

I reached out to him, my hands shaking, legs trembling. He smiled and laughed lightly as he pulled me into his arms.

"You okay, baby?"

"Yeah, more than okay." I thought about all the mystery throughout the last year. Will spending days away from the apartment, working on websites with Tyler, the master plan Frank referred to. It was all part of the dream, and I was included in that and it was all coming true.

"So will you do this with me, Mia?" he said, looking hopeful.

"Yes," I breathed.

"And will you play music with me every day?"

"Yes."

He got down on one knee, popped open a ring box and said, "For the rest of your life?"

I sucked in a breath and stared at the gorgeous antique ring, the oval-shaped pink diamond glimmering in the overhead light. I knelt down to his level, cupped his face and said, "Yes. Yes. Yes," between kisses. I had never been so sure of anything in my life.

We stayed there kissing for a long time until he finally broke the embrace and slipped the ring on my finger.

"Thank you. It's beautiful."

"You're beautiful."

I kissed him until we were breathless. "Take me to bed."

He held my face and then leaned back to look into my eyes. "You're in luck, it's right upstairs. I bought the loft above this place." And then he wiggled his eyebrows.

"I guess we're Brooklynites now?"

His look went from surprise to pure elation. "So you'll live with me here?"

"Of course. I want to be wherever you are. I want to do this with you. It *is* my dream—all of it."

"Baby, that means more to me than you will ever know," he said and then proceeded to trail kisses up my neck.

"So, are you gonna show me your place or what?"

"Our place."

"Show me our place."

He led me through the sound studio to the lobby where I met Maryse and Bret. Maryse was the spunky office manager and blogger extraordinaire. Will said she was responsible for getting quite a few of the bookings. Bret was the percussion virtuoso who had been playing with Will at the bars and would certainly become a key player at the studio. Will said that Tyler and Jenny were going to run the website and Sheil and Martha would both be part of the artistic team from time to time when they weren't busy at Kell's.

We practically jogged up the stairs to the loft. "There's one more girl you need to meet. She's actually a partner, or more like a silent partner." He opened the door and there sat the sweetest, tiniest yellow Lab puppy. Her head cocked to one side as I knelt down in front of her.

Will crouched beside me. "Mia, meet June." My eyes darted to his, both of us smiled serenely and simultaneously said, "After June Carter Cash."

I picked her up. "Ahh, I love her."

"I love you."

I put June down and cupped Will's face. "I love you, too," I said between laying kisses on his lips, nose, and cheeks. "Wilbur, I want to have like a million of your babies."

He looked happier than I had ever seen him. "Really? Should we start now?"

"Definitely."

And then he led me to our room where we stayed for hours, maybe days, just tangled in each other.

Something So Sweet

By Mia Kelly

Been looking for a way to get home,
it seems there's no directions left for me.
I'll follow the trail on my own,
and hope that something sets me free.
The darkness falls fast without warning,
just left with my soul to captain me.
But there's someone waiting for me in the morning,
pulling me into the light so I can see.
He knows my face in the darkness,
he knows my hopes, my reverie.
But he's waiting for me to find him,
so that I can set him free.
So I let go and let him in.
Everything dissipates into feeling,
we allow our souls to meet.
We're the static in the chaos,
the one thing . . . the something so sweet.

Epilogue

Lauren

It was a perfect day in the city. I went to breakfast with my husband and two beautiful boys and then I spent the afternoon browsing the streets of SoHo. I was sitting on a little wooden bench outside the Earth Room when I saw them. He was animatedly telling her a story, his hands flailing about as she gazed at him with boundless love in her eyes. They walked hand in hand up the opposite side of the street. He was wearing a black hoodie and jeans, his wallet chain jingling. She wore a gray babydoll dress and a purple scarf. As they got closer, I noticed one of her hands was resting on top of a very swollen belly. The vision of the two of them together like that filled me with an unreasonable amount of joy.

They stopped to look into a store window. He stood behind her, wrapping his arms around her plump belly as he nestled his face in her neck. She was a far cry from the feeble, frail girl in the park last spring. She looked healthy, blissful, almost seraphic. He appeared to have the neurotic charm of a person whose feelings got the same clout as his thoughts, which is exactly how I knew it was him.

As they crossed the street toward me, I spotted the look of recognition on her face. She turned and asked him to wait before running up to me, arms open with a huge smile on her face.

"Hey, Lauren, how are you?"

"Great, it's good to see you. Congratulations," I said, pulling out of the hug and running my hand across her belly.

"Thank you. We're so excited. We're having a boy."

"That's wonderful, Mia."

"Oh, hey, I read your new book. I loved it . . . absolutely beautiful story."

"Thank you so much. So you two figured everything out, I see?" I said, glancing at her belly and then in Will's direction.

She nodded and smiled serenely. "But what about you? Did you figure everything out?"

I paused for a long second. "Yes."

"Good." She leaned in, kissed me on the cheek, and then whispered, "So what's next?"

I glanced over at Will, who was looking at me like he knew my face but couldn't place it.

"Well, I can tell you that things may get all muddled up again, especially after that little guy comes along," I said, pointing to her belly. "Just remember, you can always hear the answers in the music, just the same way I hear them in the writing. Sometimes we have to remind ourselves to listen."

"Right," she said, nodding. "The sound of our souls."

"Yep."

We hugged and then she walked over to Will, who was holding a cab door open for her. She whispered something in his ear; he glanced back and studied me as he got into the car. When he closed the door, he smiled really big, blew me a kiss, and mouthed the words *Good-bye, Lauren*. I thought I caught "sweet thing" as he left my view.

Acknowledgments

I owe a supreme thanks and credit to the following people for their hard work and professionalism on *Sweet Thing*.

To those who worked on the original e-book edition: Jennifer Pooley for developmental editing; Anne Victory at Victory Editing for copyediting; Guido Henkel for digital formatting; Carla Toson Photography for the original cover; Sarah Hansen at Okay Creations for the revised cover; and Angela Fones, Heather Floyd, and Rachel Ryan for final proofing.

To all of the musical muses: there are no words to express the appreciation I feel for your art, and the art born from it.

Seth Fischer and the WWLA gang: Aisling, Aja, Christina, Geoff, and Rose. I'm thankful for your passion and assistance.

Gushing gratitude for the friends and relatives who have supported me through this process, and extra love to my parents, mother-in-law, brother and sister and their families, and Dad—thank you especially for your mad Internet researching skills.

Tracey Garvis Graves, I was inspired by you and your writing and I'm so grateful for the time you took to answer my e-mails just to help a fellow writer and relative stranger. I could not have ventured into the self-publishing world without your help.

To Maryse and Paula, two girls who are unrelated but so similar. A blogger and reader who are both in love with reading and talking about books. They are the same in that they didn't know me from Adam but championed *Sweet Thing* everywhere they could. Thank you so much for rooting for my book and me throughout this journey.

Tanner J. Jupin—not just because I said I would, but also because I'm grateful for your kind words and encouragement.

Thank you to authors Carey Heywood and Penelope Reid for carting my ass all over Orlando and for just generally being awesome people.

Katy Evans, Kim Karr, Patricia Mann, Kylie Scott, Corie Skolnick, Bridget Sampson, and Joanna Wylde: authors who have been the greatest sounding board, support system, and sometimes virtual wake-up call when I needed it. Thank you, girls!

To all of the enthusiastic readers and bloggers who have shown *Sweet Thing* the love and helped me spread the word: YOU ARE AMAZING! Every positive message, comment, and review truly made me smile from ear to ear. Thank you from the bottom of my heart.

To my editor, Jhanteigh Kupihea, thank you so much for investing yourself in me and this story and giving it your fine attention to detail. I can't wait to do the next one with you.

Thank you to the Jane Rotrosen Agency and Christina Hogrebe—you're my Jerry: professional all the time, but warm when I need you to be, fun when I want to let loose, and calming when I'm freaking out. Thank you for that, but more than anything, thank you for working so hard and believing in me.

Rachel, thanks for listening to the meandering, late-night rants and for helping me put Mia and Will through the wringer.

There were so many great lessons I learned on this journey. None more than the importance of taking it seriously while laughing to the point of tears and being brave and embracing vulnerability, taught to me by Terry Littlefield, a great beta reader, friend, and Yogi.

To Heather, who was able to find even the most elusive of errors—you have hawk eyes, lady. I will never forget our conversation the night you finished the book. Thank you for your words and friendship all these years, and thanks for everything you did for me on the road, especially the deodorant right before Book Bash.

My dear friend, Carla, I could not have finished it without your time and energy. Thank you for treating this with a seriousness that gave me the courage to continue.

I know *Sweet Thing* would have been a nameless, twenty-five-page purge of silliness forever entombed in my computer had it not been for Angie, the ultimate first reader, cheerleader, BFF, and hopeless romantic—thank you every step of the way for basically saying, "Write more, send more, and I still love you."

To Sam and Tony: my beautiful, brilliant, and patient boys, thank you for inspiring me to do better. I love you above and beyond the world around and the spirit within.

And finally, to Anthony, who for the record pointed out Will should not say, "Please, woman" to Mia because he thought is sounded misogynistic. You are the coolest, most hardworking, and honest guy I know. Thank you for encouraging me, believing in me, and loving me wholeheartedly . . . and thank you for all the raw material . . . wink.

For Jackson, the best damn dog in the world.
RIP, buddy.

Read on for two bonus chapters from

Will's perspective . . .

TRACK X: Learning to Fly

Three shots of tequila, please." I leaned my bag and guitar case against the bar stool and looked around before hopping up. Airport bars are weird. It's not like a regular bar where you go to meet people and socialize. It's where people who are stuck in a terminal and scared to fly go to get fucked up. Everyone in the place was zoned out and staring at the massive TVs above the bar.

The bartender looked like the most interesting man in the world. I wondered for a second if I should order a Dos Equis.

"Hey boss, I'll take a Dos Equis, too."

"You got it."

Pour faster. I need a drink. I hate flying.

I felt a tugging at my pant leg. I looked down into a pair of terrified blue eyes. I hopped off the stool and bent over until I was face-to-face with this tiny kid. He was shaking.

"What's up, guy? Aren't you a little young to be in a place like this?"

"I wost my mom." His lip started quivering and then his eyes started watering and then—*oh, shit*—his face contorted just before he burst into full-blown tears.

"Calm down. Calm down, buddy. I'll help you find her." I waited as he tried to control the sobs; he took two big gulps and then started hiccupping. This kid was cute, all watery blue eyes and blond, shaggy hair in his face. "Okay, man, what does she look like?"

"Ummmm . . . She wooks wike my mom."

"Yeah . . . I'm gonna need a bit more than that." I smiled really big; he hiccupped and then giggled a little.

"Ummmm . . . She has fancy haiw."

Shit, this kid's screwed. He can't say his Rs or his Ls.

"What else?"

"She's a cute giww."

"She's a cute girl, huh?" I grinned when he nodded his head. "I bet."

Right at that moment, I looked up to find a hot mess of a woman breathing frantically, clutching her shirt just over her heart, and looking down at the kid and me.

"You weren't lying, bro. She's cute."

He giggled again.

Mom let out a long breath and then whispered, "Thank God."

"No need to thank me," I said as I stood up. Her serious face immediately turned into a giddy smile.

"Funny," she said.

I grinned and then winked at her. An instantaneous blush spread across her face. "You're adorable, you know that?"

Oh man, that made her so nervous.

I spotted a second kid hiding behind her legs. I also spotted the glimmer of a wedding band. She started fumbling her words, "Are . . . are you hitting on me?"

I arched my eyebrows and she began laughing hysterically.

"I'm a little ol—"

"Baby, love doesn't discriminate. Anyway, I see you're taken . . . The good ones always are."

Over the speaker I heard last call boarding at my gate. *Shit.*

"Okay, I gotta run," I said to her and then directed my attention to the boys. "You turkeys stick close to your mom so you can look out for her, okay?" They both nodded. I reached out to shake her hand. "I'm Will. It's nice to meet you . . . ?"

"Lauren, and same to you."

Glancing back at the bar, I could see that my drinks were no longer there. I said a final good-bye and then took off toward my gate, totally sober with my guitar banging against my back.

I fucking hate flying.

I go back to Detroit to visit my family a few times a year and every time I vow that I will never fly again. Three years ago I started going to this shrink, Dr. Payne. Seriously, that was his fucking name. Why anyone would go to a doctor with the last name Payne still baffles me, but I did. Worse than that, his first name was Richard. His goddamn name was Dick Payne. Anyway, Dick Payne wanted me to do this special kind of therapy called In Vivo to get over my fear of flying. I had to imagine and then write down all these horrible scenarios. It started with the normal flying bullshit: turbulence, strange noises, crying babies, disgruntled passengers. Then we moved on, week by week, until I was making up stories about plummeting to earth in a fiery ball, people's bodies being sucked out of windows, appendages, carnage, you name it. Dick recorded these horrible stories as I read them aloud and then he would replay them over and over while I cringed and tossed and turned and practically wept like a baby on his weird shrink couch.

Evidently the thought was that I would eventually become desensitized to the idea of crashing after replaying the worst possible scenarios over and over. It did nothing for me; it was painful. Dick Payne. I should have known—Dick fucking

Payne. The last time we met, he gave me a prescription for Xanax and basically said In Vivo had a pretty low success rate. His parting words were "Here, Will. Here's a prescription if you feel you need it. Try not to think about dying, and a couple of shots of tequila wouldn't hurt either."

Rushing onto the plane, I looked down the aisle and spotted my seat right away. And then I saw her. I saw her . . .

She appeared to be sleeping; she had earbuds in and a travel pillow around her neck. Right before I approached, she glanced up at me and that's when I blurted out, "Hey!" I paused, searching for words as I stared directly into her eyes, her really gorgeous eyes, the kind you just want to dive into and swim around in. "Do you want the window seat? It's all yours if you do."

She scowled. "Huh? Uh, no thanks."

I think I pissed her off. Man, this girl was cute, pretty, no . . . beautiful. She had a bunch of silky, dark hair wrapped in a bun on top of her head. I never get nervous around women, but in that moment I was more nervous than I had been in my entire life.

"I'm a terrible flier," I told her. "Please, I need to be in the aisle. I'm sorry, do you mind? I'm Will, by the way . . . "

She stood abruptly and grabbed her things. Without making eye contact, she stuck her hand up and mumbled, "Yeah, fine, you can sit there. I'm Mia."

Rearranging the overhead compartment, I startled her when I threw her bag on my seat. She looked up at me. *Man, those eyes.*

"Sorry, baby, I've got to make room for her." She shrugged and pretended to ignore me, but seconds later I caught her staring at me out of the corner of her eye. I was totally getting to her.

I plopped down in my seat, looked over at her, and smiled. My eyes were immediately drawn to her blushing mouth with its naturally pink, pudgy little bottom lip. I wanted to suck on that lip.

"Why didn't you request an aisle seat?"

"Well, you see, sweetheart, I like to be right behind the emergency exit. I'll hop over this seat, jump out the door, and be down that super slide in a split second."

"Then why not request the exit aisle?"

"I am not the person for that job, trust me."

"Damn, chivalry *is* dead. It doesn't matter anyway; our lives are in the hands of these hopefully sober pilots and this nine-hundred-thousand-pound hunk of metal, so . . . "

"Can we stop talking about this? I don't think you un-derstand." I didn't want to shut her down, the banter was re-freshing. Plus, I love girls with brains and a backbone, but my nerves were getting to me. I took out the rosary I'd bought in the gift shop and started to peel the price tag off. She con-tinued needling me with her melodic little voice. It was hard to concentrate on what she was saying because I was mesmer-ized by her, completely enchanted by the way she smelled, her eyes, and man, those lips.

After chuckling at another one of her digs, I finally turned toward her and whispered, "Hey, little firecracker, you like taunting me, don't you?"

"Sorry," she mumbled. I winked at her and watched her reaction. She sucked in a breath, making the tiniest sound, and then swallowed and looked away, but not before her eyes trailed down my entire body and back up.

While I was memorizing the safety procedures, the pilot scared the shit out of me when he came on the speaker to an-nounce that we were cleared for takeoff.

"Jesus Christ! Did he sound drunk to you?"

With a look of sympathy, Mia turned toward me and in the calmest voice said, "Not at all. Relax, buddy, everything will be fine and you should probably tone down the Jesus Christs, at least while you're still wearing that thing."

I asked her to open the screen so I could see us get off the ground and then I leaned over and inhaled deeply. She smelled so clean.

"You smell good," I told her. "Like rain." She blushed again and then asked me about my guitar. She knew something about guitars, I could tell. When the plane started to take off, I gripped the armrest. She put her hand over mine and just held it there while we continued our conversation. The warmth of her hand was calming. When I would tighten my grip, she would tighten hers. I think it was subconscious. I'm sure she didn't notice she was doing it, but she comforted me.

When she mentioned that her father had just passed away, her eyes started to well up. I took my other hand and put it on top of hers. I think that was first moment she realized where her hand had been because she yanked it away and wiped her eyes. I immediately apologized for her loss.

"It's okay, but I'd rather not talk about it right now. Let's talk about guitars." She had this really sweet, genuine, but totally pained look on her face. It was like she was trying to be strong and hide the hurt, but her expressive eyes and face made that impossible.

We talked the whole length of the flight. I just kept thinking that I had to know this girl. I needed to be in her life, but I could tell she was going through something, so I tried to keep it light.

As we started to descend, I panicked at the thought that

we could walk off this plane and never see each other again.

"Mia, we're going down. I need to know everything about you right now! How old are you, what's your last name, what street do you live on? If we make it out of this, I think we should jam together, you know, musically or whatever."

"My last name is Kelly, I'll be at my father's café most days—Kell's on Avenue A. Come and have a coffee with me sometime and we'll talk music. Oh, and I'm twenty-five."

It seemed like we had so much in common. I couldn't believe my luck getting to sit next to her. She was beautiful, but in the humble way, not insecure, humble. She was smart and funny and sarcastic and witty and she loved music, but on top of that she was gentle. She wanted to comfort me, even if she didn't realize she wanted to, and that's what she'd done. Maybe it was fate that I sat next to her that day, or serendipity, divine intervention, who knows? However you look at it, I got seated next to the first girl to ever really steal my heart. I was in love from that moment on. I knew Mia, with all her grief, sensitivity, and depth would be a challenge, but that made me want her even more.

I lowered my voice. "We both have double first names. I'm Will Ryan, twenty-nine. I live at 22 Mott Street in the storage closet. I work at the Montosh. I'm O negative, you know, the universal one, and I play in a band called The Ivans. Oh, and I love coffee. It was nice to meet you, Mia."

"It was nice to meet you, too," she said.

"We made it," I told her. "You know, they say people who have stared death in the face together are bonded for life?"

She giggled. "Your antics are cute, Will."

"I was going for irresistible," I said and then I watched her stumble and nervously grab her things. I walked behind her, up the aisle toward the exit. Some dickwad practically knocked her over when he tried to cut into the line. "Hey! Watch it, buddy!" When Mia turned and shot me the cutest smile, I said, "See, baby, chivalry isn't dead."

I followed her all the way out to the curb. She didn't turn around once as she waited for a cab. I lit a cigarette, looked up to the sky, and prayed. Right as her taxi began to pull away from the curb, she glanced over at me. I waved really big and mouthed, *Good-bye, Mia, you sweet thing.*

At that moment I wanted so badly to call Dick Payne and tell him about the flight. I wanted to tell him I hadn't thought about dying once . . . All I had thought about was living.

TRACK Y: A Prayer for Us

Looking around at the remaining guests, the little white lights everywhere and the glistening pond, I thought Jenny and Tyler's wedding couldn't have been any better; it was complete magic. Playing music with Mia made an already perfect night spectacular. I wanted to grab a bottle of champagne and stroll around the little pond with Audrey, but I couldn't find her anywhere.

I made my way up to the cottage and entered the front door. Right away I could hear movement. The moment I turned the corner to head down the short hallway, I saw Mia in sneaky mode, quietly closing one of the bedroom doors. When she turned, she ran right into my chest.

"Have you seen Audrey?" I said. She just stared at me, blank-faced. "What, Mia?" She remained expressionless and then dick-stick Dustin walked out of the room and stood behind her. "Oh no. Really? Really, Mia? You and him?" *Holy shit, she was fucking him in there. Oh my god, she's gonna need disinfecting.* And then Audrey walked out and stood next to Dustin. "What?" I started laughing uncontrollably. *Why wasn't I invited to this party?* "The three of you? What the fuck?" I searched Mia's face. She looked sad. I couldn't believe it. I turned and headed down the hallway, thinking what a travesty this was—my best friend and my girlfriend together with Dustin, the filthiest, STD-ridden dirtbag in the universe.

I went straight for the bar, grabbed a bottle of whiskey,

and then headed toward the pond. I could hear Mia yelling behind me. I kept my head down, got into the little white boat, and rowed away from the dock. I just kept thinking, *How could Mia do that, did she have no dignity?* and, *How could Dustin use her that way when he knows how precious she is to me?* How could he, when he knew that I would have given anything to be with her, to be with Mia?

She yelled at me to come back and talk to her.

"I'm not. Talking. To. You. *Ever!*" I screamed. I saw Dustin with his arm around Audrey, standing behind Mia. I stood up in the boat, barely able to keep my balance, and flipped them off with both hands. "Fuck all of you!" I almost fell over, so I sat down and rowed farther into the darkness before yelling a final, "Don't look for me!"

I could still see them under the lights, but I knew they couldn't see me. When I got to the other side, I pulled the boat up onto the shore and started on the whiskey. First I heard her and then I saw her coming toward me from the footpath.

"Will?"

"Don't fucking come near me, Mia. I swear to God I will row myself into the middle of that goddamn pond and stay there till next year."

She stayed where she was and in the calmest, sweetest voice, said, "I walked into the room and thought you and Audrey were having sex. I couldn't see who it was behind the screen. I tried to sneak back out, and that's when I ran into you. I was confused."

I believed her, but I couldn't face her in that moment. Audrey and Dustin had humiliated me and I knew Mia felt sorry for me.

"Go away, Mia."

I spent the next hour in that little boat, thinking about

everything, thinking about my life, thinking about the time Mia had asked me what my hopes and dreams were. I knew without a doubt they included her, but I also knew I had to be patient with her. The fact that Audrey and Dustin, that pencil-dick, were probably screwing around right in front of my face, didn't even bother me. I just thought about how relieved I was that it wasn't Mia.

I headed back to the cottage and found her sleeping, absolutely peaceful and beautiful. Her long, dark hair was braided and resting over her shoulder. She was on her side; the quilt was shrugged half down, exposing her almost completely in her T-shirt and underwear. Honestly, by that point I had gotten over wanting to fuck Mia. When I thought about being with her, I only thought about making love to her, sweetly. That night I wanted so badly just to have slow, soft, sleepy sex with her. I lay beside her on top of the quilt and watched her sleep. I thought back to earlier that day at the wedding, when she'd walked down the aisle, how badly I wanted to see her in white, but still how stunning she looked. I thought about her reaction when she'd seen Jenny and the way she'd lovingly but enviously stared at Jenny on her dad's arm. I knew Mia was thinking about her own father and that the grief and pain were still weighing heavily on her. I thought about how she was always alone, even when she dated that dipshit, Bob. Mia just seemed like this lost little soul and I knew it would be a while before she came around. I passed out thinking about what it would be like to hold her and praying that she would let me, and praying for us.

A few hours later I woke up to the feel of her gentle hand pulling my belt open. I noticed she had removed my shoes and tie. I looked down at her through foggy, squinted eyes. She smiled lovingly at me. There was just a hint of pity in her expression, but her face was warm and kind.

"I got it," I said. "Come back to bed."

She slid back into bed while I stripped down to my boxers. She turned away from me and onto her side. I curled up behind her and hitched my leg over hers. I reached my hand up under her shirt to her warm, soft skin. I was holding her, and she didn't stop me. It felt so good. That moment was tender, raw, and sacred, and I would take a fleeting moment like that any day over an eternity of mediocrity.

"Are you okay?" she whispered.

"I am now." I kissed her hair and inhaled deeply. "It hurt more when I thought it was you," I said and then I dozed off again. I woke up practically lying on top of her. My hands were on her sides and my head rested on her stomach. I think I was crushing her, but she didn't seem to mind. She was running her hands through my hair. She smelled like Mia always smelled, clean and cozy and like home. I stayed there as still as I could; I wanted it to last forever. And then I thought, *Oh screw it. I'm going for it.*

I anchored my fingers and tried slowly to pull her panties down. She pressed herself against me like she liked it and then I think she felt me hard beneath her and jerked away to sit up. I watched her blushing face. She bit down on that pouty bottom lip.

I whispered, "Sorry, baby."

Her lips curled into a tiny smile, and she leaned over, kissed my shoulder, and breathed, "Get some sleep," just barely loud enough for me to hear.

When she left the room, I looked down at myself and laughed. *Patience, my friend, patience.*